"This luscious tale will enthrall you. Enjoy!"
            —*New York Times* bestselling author Sabrina Jeffries

"Sinfully sexy . . . Wickedly witty, sublimely sensual . . .
Renee Bernard dazzles readers . . . Clever, sensual, and
superb."   —*Booklist*

"Scorcher! Bernard debuts with an erotic romance that
delivers not only a high degree of sensuality, but a strong
plotline and a cast of memorable characters. She's sure
to find a place alongside Robin Schone, Pam Rosenthal,
and Thea Divine."   —**Romantic Times*

"Very hot romance. Readers who enjoy an excellent,
sizzling Victorian story are going to thoroughly enjoy
this one."   —*Romance Reviews Today*

"*Madame's Deception* is shiverlicious! A captivating
plot, charismatic characters, and sexy, tingle-worthy
romance . . . Fantastic!"   —*Joyfully Reviewed*

"Crowd-pleasing."   —*Publishers Weekly*

"Steamy historical romance is a great debut for this new
author . . . Filled with steamy and erotic scenes . . . The
plot is solid and the ending holds many surprises . . .
Tantalizing."   —*Fresh Fiction*

Berkley Sensation Titles by Renee Bernard

REVENGE WEARS RUBIES
SEDUCTION WEARS SAPPHIRES

Seduction Wears Sapphires

RENEE BERNARD

BERKLEY SENSATION, NEW YORK

THE BERKLEY PUBLISHING GROUP
Published by the Penguin Group
Penguin Group (USA) Inc.
375 Hudson Street, New York, New York 10014, USA
Penguin Group (Canada), 90 Eglinton Avenue East, Suite 700, Toronto, Ontario M4P 2Y3, Canada
(a division of Pearson Penguin Canada Inc.)
Penguin Books Ltd., 80 Strand, London WC2R 0RL, England
Penguin Group Ireland, 25 St. Stephen's Green, Dublin 2, Ireland (a division of Penguin Books Ltd.)
Penguin Group (Australia), 250 Camberwell Road, Camberwell, Victoria 3124, Australia
(a division of Pearson Australia Group Pty. Ltd.)
Penguin Books India Pvt. Ltd., 11 Community Centre, Panchsheel Park, New Delhi—110 017, India
Penguin Group (NZ), 67 Apollo Drive, Rosedale, North Shore 0632, New Zealand
(a division of Pearson New Zealand Ltd.)
Penguin Books (South Africa) (Pty.) Ltd., 24 Sturdee Avenue, Rosebank, Johannesburg 2196,
South Africa

Penguin Books Ltd., Registered Offices: 80 Strand, London WC2R 0RL, England

This is a work of fiction. Names, characters, places, and incidents either are the product of the
author's imagination or are used fictitiously, and any resemblance to actual persons, living or dead,
business establishments, events, or locales is entirely coincidental. The publisher does not have
any control over and does not assume any responsibility for author or third-party websites or their
content.

SEDUCTION WEARS SAPPHIRES

A Berkley Sensation Book / published by arrangement with the author

PRINTING HISTORY
Berkley Sensation mass-market edition / August 2010

Copyright © 2010 by Renee Bernard.
Excerpt from *Revenge Wears Rubies* by Renee Bernard copyright © by Renee Bernard.
Cover art by Alan Ayers.
Cover design by George Long.
Interior text design by Laura K. Corless.

ISBN: 978-0-425-23596-6

BERKLEY® SENSATION
Berkley Sensation Books are published by The Berkley Publishing Group,
a division of Penguin Group (USA) Inc.,
375 Hudson Street, New York, New York 10014.
BERKLEY® SENSATION and the "B" design are trademarks of Penguin Group (USA) Inc.

PRINTED IN THE UNITED STATES OF AMERICA

10 9 8 7 6 5 4 3 2 1

To Geoffrey, because you are the man I want in my lifeboat even when it's leaking. Because you not only give me beautiful babies, you smile every time you hold them, even when they're crying. Because you can't find anything in the house without me, and that gives me the illusion that I know what I'm doing. And because no matter what happens next, you're still the One for me.

Acknowledgments

This was a tough one and I can't deny it. There were hard lessons learned recently about how fragile life is, and why they don't hand out sedatives to mothers in the emergency room is beyond me! (The girls are now fine, and my local hospital staffers at Marshall are all getting Christmas cards next year.) On the other side of the country, my grandmother passed away, and it's been a series of difficult weeks reconciling loss and trying to count blessings.

But I *am* blessed. I'm blessed with a great editor in Kate Seaver and I want to thank her for her support. Neurotic authors may be the cliché but I never wanted to be one! I don't think therapy should be in the list of services provided by one's publisher, but Kate kept me sane and that is truly saying something!

I'm blessed with family. And not the brace-yourself-for-holidays kind of family, but the kind of family that really loves you when your socks don't match or you lose track of the days from a lack of sleep (and they still pretend you're in charge). My father still won't read my books, but I think he's rented a billboard in his local town, he's so proud of his youngest. And my mother still reads everything I write, listens to every radio show, and holds the power to make me blush whenever she says nice things about me to her friends. I'm blessed to be loved by family near and far who make it all worthwhile and will admit to being related despite everything (see above sock issues).

I'm blessed with phenomenal friends. Sheila Clover English and COS Productions forced me to laugh at myself at least once a week on our Internet radio show, "Canned Laughter and Coffee." Sheila is one of those incredible people that doesn't really know that she's incredible (so she still takes my calls). I love the program we've created and the opportunity to talk to so many people, but I'm more grateful for her friendship.

I want to thank all the wonderful authors that kept me afloat and shared horror stories with me so that I wouldn't feel so alone. Thank you, ladies. (I'm not listing you all because it just looks like name dropping, which reminds me again of how lucky I am to know you!) And thanks, of course, to RT and their staff and volunteers for giving me the boost of confidence and the chance to reconnect and recharge every year at the conventions. I'd have a pile of moldering manuscripts in a drawer if it weren't for you!

Thanks also to Carol and Lisa for all the "hands-on" help. The wheels would have come off the train a long time ago if not for your presence and friendship to Tom and Gini. And to the Shire, I can't imagine how colorless things would be without you in our lives.

But most of all, I have to thank the readers. Every single note and e-mail has been so important to me and I'm thrilled and humbled every single time I get one. You've kept me going, and as the smoke clears, I'm inspired to do better and to try to make sure I've earned even a fraction of the nice things you've said.

And yes, I will write faster. I promise.

The way of love is not a subtle argument.

—RUMI

Prologue

1859

The clipper ship's deck pitched hard, and Caroline's grip on the railing tightened until she couldn't feel her hands. She had always aspired to be a woman of modern sensibilities, but sadly, there was one thing she hadn't anticipated.

Seasickness. God, what would Aunt Emilia say now?

As miserable as she was, the thought of Aunt Emilia's last lecture was enough to make her smile. Her aunt had screeched about inappropriate travel for young ladies and the disastrous consequences that were sure to follow such a headstrong course until Caroline was convinced that the woman would be mute for weeks afterward. Her elderly aunt would have forbidden the journey outright, but the vague notion of someone else taking Caroline off her hands for a time had proven too irresistible. Even so, complaining was her aunt's favorite pastime, so she'd still screeched her dire warnings as if to sway Caroline from her decision to leave Boston and America and voyage to London.

Caroline didn't think anything short of her own demise

would have stopped her from seizing this chance and escaping Aunt Emilia's "generous care." The letter and proposal she had received from her grandfather's old business partner had been unique to say the least. And the challenge presented had proven too powerful a lure to set aside. If she succeeded, then all her dreams of independence would be within her reach.

If Aunt Emilia knew the truth behind my social visit to my grandfather's friend, she would have locked me in the basement and thrown away the key!

The ship rolled and pitched and Caroline shut her eyes tightly, wishing she could divert her internal landscape away from every thought of an early watery grave. *I am not a sailor.*

Built for speed, the clipper ship was a narrow and sleek vessel, cutting across the ocean at full sails. Caroline knew that every captain felt compelled to approach each voyage on the newly designed ships like a race, as if to prove the success of their innovations and seamanship. The cargo they carried on this run was premium tobaccos and cotton, along with a few special boxes of personal effects of the ship's owner. Passenger berths were extremely limited, and she'd felt lucky to secure her accommodations aboard the *Maryland.*

She'd approached her journey to London with the planning precision of a general contemplating a long siege. She'd had illustrious visions of holding her own as an intrepid traveler with her well-organized trunks, books, and a serviceable umbrella. She'd been sure she was ready for anything.

"You'll want to stand at the leeward side, miss," a shy and gruff voice came at her elbow.

"Pardon?" She tried to straighten as if she'd been doing nothing more than enjoying the view. Mr. Gilbert was the first mate and the very image of an old salt, but he'd been extremely conscientious toward her.

"If you're not feeling too well." His cheeks grew ruddier

as he talked, awkwardly offering his advice. "The wind's so strong . . . if your stomach turns . . . you'll want to be at the leeward so as not to ruin your skirts."

He looked as miserable as she felt discussing an indelicate matter, and Caroline had to smile. *I am most definitely not a sailor.* Her last illusion of romantic courage dashed, she meekly allowed Mr. Gilbert to escort her to the opposite railing.

"Are you off to visit family in England, miss?" he asked.

She shook her head. "Not to visit family, but friends of my family whom I've never met. This is my first journey to England so I can only hope to hold my own."

"You'll shame them with your lovely manners! Can't tell you how many hoity-toity slicks we've hauled across the Atlantic so they can rub elbows at some titled fool's big doings!" His color deepened. "Not that I was likening you to . . . I mean, you've been nothin' but politeness, Miss Townsend—a true lady. Not like some others I could tell you about. They think they're too good for their own skins, much less up to wasting a single breath with a kind word to a deckhand."

A true lady—I wonder if my host will agree. I've heard that the English are very discerning, and if they find out the truth of my situation in Boston . . .

Caroline could only imagine what a few elite passengers would make of an old salt like Mr. Gilbert, and she wasn't unfamiliar with the disdain of her so-called betters. Her grandfather had made a vast fortune in business and done all that he could to improve his family's social standing, but even in a young country like America, pedigree was everything. Her parents had preferred to live a quiet life of scholarly pursuits over the flash and fashion of the cities. "You've been so courteous and forgiving with me, Mr. Gilbert. I was afraid I'd caused more trouble than most of your passengers with all my questions and efforts to enjoy the air."

"What's to forgive? You've a keen mind and that's no trouble to an old man, miss. It's nice to think you'd bother with staysails and stunsails."

Her hands gripped the rail again as the ship swayed and dropped with another wave and her courage once again faltered. "I only wish I were a better . . . traveler."

"Ah, you're doing well enough. I'll leave you to enjoy the air, as you say. Just mind you keep your feet firmly beneath you. Captain Coffin would have my hide if we arrived in London short one Boston miss." He tipped his misshapen wool cap and retreated to his duties, no doubt to provide her a small measure of dignity should she lose the battle to hold on to her breakfast.

She turned her gaze back to the majestic view of ocean and sky and thought again of her Aunt Emilia. She was as far away from the dreary quiet of her aunt's drawing room as she could imagine.

Caroline took comfort in the notion. *No matter how my stomach protests, at least I'm not on the brink of madness trapped in ladylike quiet broken only by her wretched little dog's snores.*

No, this was to be the adventure of a lifetime! Hers was a unique quest, and she tried to summon her grandfather's spirit and courage, sure that he alone would have understood and supported her desire to take this chance to make more of her life than a charitable case for her relatives.

The ship pitched again, and she squeaked in fright, mortified to think that the men on deck would have heard her.

If only I can arrive with my life, since I've already forfeited my dignity.

Chapter

1

"Don't you take anything to heart, Ashe?"

Ashe Blackwell shrugged before returning his focus to the target at the far end of the archery practice courtyard. The sports club was one of his healthier escapes, and Ashe wasn't about to let his friend's attempt at distracting conversation put him off his game.

"Josiah, you are not a man in any position to lecture." Ashe paused, drawing the string taut and squaring his shoulders. "Which makes me wonder if you're just trying to make sure you win this wager."

He released his arrow on a slow exhale and watched with calm pleasure as it sailed toward the center of the target, striking with a solid *thuck* and then jutting out proudly as an unmistakably perfect shot.

"What a show off!" Josiah Hastings stepped forward to the line, shaking his head. "And no, I can defeat you without relying on misdirection, old man." Josiah's stance was equally flawless, but his shot struck the outermost ring of the wooden boards.

Ashe tried to hide his genuine surprise. Josiah had always been the better shot, and the wager between them had been more of an excuse to honorably give Ashe a reason for refilling his friend's pockets. Josiah's pride made any open offer of a loan impossible for the struggling artist, but Ashe wasn't about to accept victory at a humiliating cost to Hastings. *He hasn't a farthing and I'll be damned if I'll be the one to force him to admit it. Though where his fortune went from our misadventures would be a mystery I'd give my teeth to solve . . .*

Ashe set his bow aside. "You did that on purpose! You're trying to coddle me, Hastings!"

"Coddle you?" Josiah asked quietly, his disappointment in the afternoon's outcome all too evident. "Were you in need of a good coddle, Ashe?" Josiah's wry wit was contagious.

"Clearly you think so." Ashe calmly stripped off his wrist brace. "All this talk about hearts and my wretched existence, and now *this*! Something must have set it off, Josiah, so let's have it."

The confusion in his friend's eyes cleared. "Even you have to admit that there's been a bit more of a mercenary edge to your pleasurable pursuits lately."

"I'll admit nothing. A man is entitled to his interests."

"Your perfumed and pouting little pretty 'interests' aren't unusual, but even for you, I'm beginning to wonder . . ."

"Oh, for God's sake! I can't believe I'm hearing this! From you! You have almost as wild a reputation. Don't artists have their fill of lovely models to choose from? I don't recall any protests before now when I invited you out for an evening or two of adventure."

"You're going to run out of trollops and whores at the rate you're going, Ashe. London is vast, I grant you, but ever since Galen fell from the ranks of bachelorhood, it's as if you've been trying to make up for the fact that there is one less man on the field."

"Galen was hardly in the game at all, the wretched sour-puss, before he got tangled up and lost his head. So I don't think there were many women left weeping in their pillows for him—but it's a grand notion." He sighed theatrically. "I suppose if anyone were to heroically try to make up for my peer's shortcomings with the ladies . . ."

"I wasn't trying to encourage you to increase your pace."

"Well, I should if I now have to make up for your lagging as well. You disappear for weeks, and when the Jaded catch you in company, you seem . . . different. Come, Josiah, have you found religion or what's going on that you're trying to rein in a prize stallion?"

"A prize stallion?" Josiah gave him a skeptical look. "Are you actually likening yourself to an elite breeding animal?"

"A poor metaphor, but you're trying to avert the question!"

"I heard no question." Josiah leaned his bow expertly to the inside of his leg, then pushed it back against his thigh, unstringing it in a single motion. "Only some endless nagging about how we should all be keeping up with your ridiculous amorous campaigns, when all the while I'm wondering why you're so determined to waste yourself."

"I'm not wasting myself."

Josiah set the last of his equipment aside. "Then what *are* you doing?"

"I'm living life to its obvious limits and enjoying what I can." Ashe pressed a small purse with the amount of the wager inside of it into Josiah's palm. "And I'm honorably settling my debts and praying we can mercifully put this conversation behind us."

"You didn't lose the wager, Ashe."

"A technicality. I would have, so take it." Ashe rebuttoned his waistcoat, casually ignoring his friend as they moved back toward the club's entrance onto the green park square.

"I don't need it, Ashe!" Josiah held the purse back out to him solemnly. "Hell, I've probably got more than you in my accounts since I don't bother with—"

"Nonsense! This isn't about needing anything! And I'll refrain from mentioning that you look like a man three steps from debtor's prison from the condition of your coat. You'd have defeated me easily if you weren't deliberately tossing the game, so the money is rightfully yours. And there's an end to this discussion, about the wager *and* my personal business, Mr. Hastings."

Josiah opened his mouth to protest, but a small boy clutching a note interrupted their conversation.

"Urgent message fer ye, Mr. Blackwell, sirs," the young lad said breathlessly.

"Urgent?" Ashe took the sealed note and fished out a generous coin for the smudged-face child. "We'll see, won't we?"

"Thank ye, sir! Thank ye!" he yodeled and was gone in the blink of an eye.

Ashe scanned the lines, a pang of anxiety and irritation changing the tenor of his afternoon. *The roads are going to be a sloshy slice of hell, but it can't be helped. Damn it!*

"Bad news?" Josiah inquired carefully.

Ashe folded the paper and slid it into his coat pocket. "Hard to say, but it seems my plans have changed."

A carriage pulled up, and both men's eyes were drawn to the brightly costumed inhabitant leaning forward to give an inviting wink and wave with one pink gloved hand.

Damn! I forgot about Margot!

Ashe shook his head. "And so apparently have yours, old friend. I'm afraid it falls to you to extend my regrets and make up to the lady for a promised rendezvous I'll be forced to miss."

"What? I'm not—"

"Come, now! Margot is a shameless flirt and I think even you can charm her into an unforgettable demonstration of her unique talents." Ashe clapped Josiah on the arm. "Take my place and do your best not to look so sour, friend. You're starting to remind me of Michael."

"Now, there's a compliment!"

"You're an artist. Tell her you're looking for your next muse," he suggested, then turned with a quick wave to Margot and headed down the lane to find a hackney for hire, leaving Josiah to sort it all out with the lively and delicious bird pouting in her carriage.

Though she'll part him from his money, I'd say he'll make a fair trade of it. Whereas I, on the other hand, am starting to get the sinking feeling that Fate may have put my own pleasures out of reach in the meantime.

His grandfather's summons was not a thing to ignore, and Ashe only hoped the old man wasn't truly unwell. With messages hinting at the worst, he'd been called home to his family's estates at Bellewood only to endure a grueling lecture or an ambush of distant relatives and dry conversation.

But Ashe was far too loyal to hesitate. If his grandfather needed him, then he would go. Duty reigned over all things in his life, despite appearances, and Ashe Blackwell wasn't a man to shirk his responsibilities.

Though he did take one soulful look backward at Margot's carriage and wished the day had gone differently.

* * *

The quiet of the country ate at his nerves and Ashe had to force himself not to pace. Bellewood, his family's home, was less than a day's ride from Town, but it felt to Ashe like it sat on the farthest edges of civilization. His grandfather's library had always been his least favorite room as a child, with its gloomy colors and dusty shelves. It was

here he'd been brought if there was a punishment to be determined or a stern reprimand to be given. Gordon Walker
Blackwell was not a man Ashe had ever wanted to face
after he'd been caught at one childhood misadventure or
another.

*Damn! How is it a man can live for more than three
decades and then suddenly feel like an eight-year-old in
short pants? Hell, it's not like I've recently been around to
break vases or get caught snogging the—*

"Is that the style in London these days or did you not
change your clothes after arriving?" His grandfather's
voice was edged in familiar icy authority, but the years had
robbed the older gentleman of the power of volume, and
Ashe winced to hear it. It saddened him to see the dear
monster losing his teeth. "Your coat is rumpled, Ashe, like
a man who takes no care of himself."

Ashe managed a half bow and tamped down on his ha-
bitual sarcasm out of an old love for the codger. "I only just
arrived and meant to change after a muddy ride, but your
butler brought me here and indicated that your business
could not wait."

"Nor can it! I've no time to waste as you seem to have."

"I make the most of every day, Grandfather," Ashe
countered gently.

"How dare you, sir! You make the most of your nights
and I suspect you haven't seen much of a morning ever
since you returned to England! You are a disgrace, Ashe. I
hear report after report of your carousing in London and I
marvel that you can stand before me without hanging your
head in shame."

Ashe's spine stiffened, not enjoying the lecture. "I'm
flattered that you would follow my pursuits so closely. But
the gossips may exaggerate my—"

"Do they?" His grandfather stepped closer, cutting him
off. "Is it all wrong? Am I misinformed? Are you a moral
example of what a gentleman should be, my boy?"

Ashe hesitated at the strange new tone in the older man's voice. *Was that desperation?* But a lie wasn't possible. "No, Grandfather, you are not misinformed."

Silence strung out between them and Ashe's chest ached at the look of raw disappointment in the old man's eyes.

"Which brings me to the reason that I summoned you out of Town."

Here it comes. Lecture finished and now we'll get to whatever is troubling him.

"I'm dying."

Shock froze Ashe in place at the unvarnished announcement. His grandfather was older, yes, and looking a little slighter, but on the verge of passing? Finally, he managed to reply, "Is this Dr. McAllister's opinion as well? Are you . . . ill?"

An impatient gesture cut off the awkward sympathetic line of Ashe's questions. "I hate doctors and, of course, I'm not ill! Don't be daft! Do I look desperately ill to you?"

"You just said you were dying. I'd say that was a logical inquiry."

"We are all mortal, and don't give me that knowing look. I'm sharper than a man a fraction my age and I've not gone soft in the skull."

"A relief to hear." Ashe struggled not to smile.

"Mind that wit of yours!" He straightened his shoulders and Ashe caught a glimpse of the formidable younger man again. "I'm closer to the end of life than I care to contemplate! And who do I have before me to carry out even the saddest parody of a legacy?"

Damn. The lecture hadn't even gotten started.

Ashe's smile faded. "No one could match your legacy, sir."

"You could at least try!" The old man turned away, moving to the great marble fireplace over which his own great-grandfather's portrait looked down on them both. "When I lost your father—when your parents were killed, I took you on and never thought that all the promise and potential you held would be squandered before my eyes."

"I'm not an opium addict, Grandfather, and I'm certainly not squandering—"

"You had your moments of mischief before, but I was never alarmed. But ever since your return from India . . . I'm not even begging you to marry. Although, God knows, it's not a ridiculous thing to ask you to make a good match and provide this family with a healthy heir or two." A sigh rattled through his slender frame, and he leaned against the carved Italian marble mantel. "Give me some hint that you're not completely lost, my boy."

"I am not lost."

His grandfather turned back, the same odd intense light in his eyes that had made Ashe wary at the start of their conversation. "You are so far into the dark woods, I don't think you remember who you are. It's whatever that India business was, but it's no matter. I have the solution, Ashe."

"Do you?"

"I could threaten to cut you off, naturally. I could tell my solicitors that your name is to be struck from the will. I could do it, Ashe."

"It is your right to do so. And since I've disappointed you, not even I would dare argue against that decision, Grandfather." Ashe spoke as honestly as he could. "I would rather forfeit ten fortunes than earn your disdain. And I'm sorry for it."

"Ah, hell!" His grandfather drew closer. "Enough! I know that even if I removed every farthing from the will, it won't leave you destitute, since you clearly made some sort of fortune on your misadventures—but there is more to an inheritance than money, my boy."

"True."

"So . . ." He circled Ashe, as if assessing a new race-horse. "I understand you are a gambling man."

Ashe nodded slowly. "I've been known to take a risk or two."

"Then hear my proposal." His grandfather gestured toward two waiting chairs by a small side table, and the men settled in. "I want some reassurance that if you truly wanted to, you could rein yourself in."

"Rein myself in?"

Gordon Blackwell growled in displeasure. "You used to be a living example of gentlemanly restraint, Ashe. Even in the fever of youth, you had a cool and temperate head, but ever since your return from India, it's as if you've pointed your toes down a path of self-indulgence and destruction that defies belief. And since you have refused to share any details of your adventures there . . ."

"I am the same man," Ashe answered stoically.

"My greatest fear is that you're now beyond the call of discipline, my boy, and while I love you beyond measure, I will not leave our family's fortunes, land, and holdings in the hands of a jackass who can't keep his pants buttoned."

Ashe leaned back in his chair. "Some reassurance? Are you asking me to reform in a religious flash of fervor? Join a monastery? Or did you just want some kind of vow that I could, as you put it, rein myself in, if and when I wished to?"

A black look answered his questions. "I'll take a simple demonstration."

"What kind of demonstration?"

"Reform yourself! Between now and the end of the winter Season can you exist and not cause a solitary scandalous ripple in the wide and murky pond that is London?" The older man leaned forward. "It's not much, Ashe, in the greater scheme of things, but I'd be hard-pressed to think you'd admit that you don't have the spine to behave for the briefest span of a few months. Or have you grown so weak that you're sitting over there wondering how you might possibly survive such an ordeal?"

"Not at all. I was wondering why you'd set the bar so low."

"Oh, it may not be as easy as it looks. After all, with a reputation like yours, a single unremarkable Season may not truly be possible. And I'm not going to allow you to hide in the country and wait it out, either. You'll be in Town with all your demons. But"—he sat back, shifting as if to feign indifference—"if you managed it, then all threats of cutting you out would forever be gone. I'll face my final years knowing that when the crisis comes, you still have the potential to live up to your lineage."

"And if I fail?" Ashe asked, aware that no dare was without consequences.

"Not only will I cut you out, but I will hand all things over to your second cousin, Mr. Yardley, who, by the way, has been less than subtle in expressing his desires to improve the house and make a better show of it."

Yardley? Winston Yardley is a sniveling excuse for a human! The memory of the ferret-faced man who'd often been a childhood companion and occasional acquaintance made his skin crawl. Of all the people to stand in the wings, Yardley was the last person on earth that Ashe wanted to see benefiting from a great man's passing. "Like hell he would!"

His grandfather's smile held no hint of mirth. "But that's not the last of it. For you see, Ashe, I would then see your name published with infamy and make it publicly known on both sides of the Atlantic that you are a scoundrel and irredeemable in your family's eyes."

My God, he's serious.

He went on before Ashe could respond. "I'll take an article out in every paper of note on this globe warning every woman of quality to shun you and every man of name to reconsider his friendships." The threat was quiet, but Ashe didn't think a gunshot would have resounded any harder.

"So, let me understand your meaning. I take this challenge, or . . ."

"Or the worst unfolds, just as I've described it."

Ashe hated feeling cornered, but it was difficult to think of a soothing argument that would divert his grandfather now. Once the old man was set on an idea, he was notoriously stubborn.

But this? What trap is this?

"A few weeks of impeccable behavior and all is forgiven?" Ashe asked. *I'm missing a step here, but if it means keeping Yardley's clammy hands off my grandfather's silverware . . .* "And it didn't occur to you to just ask without all this posturing?"

"I'm fairly certain I've already attempted simple requests—to no avail, Ashe." He shook his head. "I can't face seeing you drag our name through the mud, and while you may think your activities have gone unnoticed, I can assure you, they have not."

Ashe clenched his jaw, feeling defensive and impatient. "Have no fear, Grandfather. I'll be the consummate gentleman."

"You've agreed then?"

"Yes, but not because of the inheritance."

"No, of course not, but I am pleased to know that some small part of you cares enough about your reputation and the future of our family to give me the demonstration I need." His grandfather stood, and Ashe reflexively did the same. "Take my hand, Ashe, and swear to me that you won't so much as twitch off the respectable path of invitations and activities I've laid out for you. No gambling and no whores, my boy, or I'll prove that one of us, at least, is a man of his word, and I'll make good my threats."

Invitations and activities he's laid out for me? I think a part of me is twitching already, but there's no out now.

"I swear it." Even as he spoke and shook his grandfather's cool, dry hand, Ashe felt the weight of his words for the first time. He was vowing to genuinely behave for a winter Season, which would have been challenging enough, but this Season had promised to be particularly wild and exciting—and the temptations that abounded in London would be hard to resist. *Well, at least Josiah and the others will get a chuckle out of this ironic twist of Fate.*

"Good." The elder Blackwell moved over to a sideboard to pour himself a small measure of port. "Oh, I forgot one small caveat."

Ah! Here's that missing piece. "And what was that?"

"You'll understand if I cannot simply take your word for this good behavior. Not that I don't trust you"—he lifted his glass in a token salute—"but I don't trust you, Ashe."

"Will you be accompanying me to London then?" Ashe asked, praying the answer would be no.

"Hardly! I'm too old for Town and, frankly, too old to try to keep some sort of watch on your person at every hour!" He scoffed then downed his port to set the small glass aside.

Thank God. Not that I'm off to cheat this wager, but—

"No," he continued smoothly. "I've arranged for a chaperone."

Ashe blinked twice. "A what? You arranged for a . . ." He couldn't say it. It was too unbelievable.

"A chaperone." His grandfather's smile was far more genuine now, as he openly enjoyed his grandson's discomfort. "I have arranged for someone who will be at your elbow and accompany you at every event to guarantee that you don't forget what's at stake."

"You're serious! I'll be damned if I'm walking about like some virginal debutante with a dragon in tow!"

"Nonsense! Look on it as my way of showing support for your new moral effort. By providing a chaperone, you'll be less likely to stumble. And no one need know of the position you're in! Your chaperone won't declare their role openly or the nature of our arrangement."

"Well, there's one thing we agree on. I'm not about to announce to my peers the reason I'm playing choirboy and tooling about with a chaperone!"

"Mind your manners!" his grandfather said, his stern looks returning. "All this protesting makes me think you had every intention of botching this wager from the start! Well, if you want out, and your word means nothing, then say so now. Because if you meant your oath honestly, then it shouldn't matter if I hire a legion of chaperones and spies, should it?"

Well, there's a point of logic I should have anticipated. . . . Oh, well. I'm already in up to my eyebrows, so why complain about the temperature of the water?

Ashe let out a long, slow breath. "You're right and I have no intention of backing out. I just—I have never heard of a man with a chaperone, so you'll have to give me a moment to accept the notion."

His grandfather nodded and moved over to the bellpull by the fireplace to give it a firm tug. Within seconds, the butler materialized in the doorway.

"Yes, sir," Mr. Frasier said with a curt nod.

"Bring in Townsend, Frasier." He walked back to Ashe, his hands behind his back. "Try to be polite when you meet your chaperone, my boy."

Ashe felt a twinge of confusion. *Why wouldn't I be polite to the chap? Hell, if he thinks we're the best of friends, I may actually get to take a deep breath without a dispatch flying back here and setting off cries of alarm.* "I am always polite to your friends."

His grandfather said nothing but gave him an arched look full of skepticism. Within seconds, the library doors opened again, and Ashe turned to see what flavor of windbag his chaperone would be.

A petite woman in a pale gray gabardine dress that was several seasons out of fashion came toward them, and Ashe's first impression was that his grandfather's new housekeeper was a good bit younger than he'd have expected. But as she drew closer, a new and more startling idea occurred to him.

He wouldn't! She cannot possibly be—

"Allow me to introduce you to your chaperone and companion for the next two months. This is Miss Caroline Townsend. A relation to my very best friend and American business partner, Mr. Matthew Townsend, now sadly passed away. I have invited her here to attend this very serious and delicate matter, and after a week in her company, I am convinced that she is entirely suited to the task at hand."

"This is preposterous!" Ashe turned to his grandfather, rudely ignoring her and cutting her out of the exchange. "I might have managed to accept this if you'd sailed in some granite-faced old dowager, but you cannot possibly think that a—how in God's name were you thinking that this might work?"

"It will work because a young woman gives you the perfect excuse! It will work because you will present her as a family friend and you will take the role of guardian! It will work because, with her at your side, you may actually get admittance into respectable houses and decent company! It will work because no one would suspect the truth!" The years dropped off his face as he spoke, and Ashe had to remind himself not to take a step backward as the old intimidation began to work its magic. "It will work because I'm telling you to make it work!"

For long seconds, they faced each other, until at last, Ashe was forced to blink. He reluctantly stepped back and barely spared a quick glance back at the woman before closing his eyes in frustration. *A plain, drab little pony of a thing, but the old man's probably guessed correctly. If I'm to have a dreary winter social Season, she'll provide the perfect dreary excuse. Damn!*

"My grandson will apologize for his rudeness," the elder

Blackwell said, his voice full of warning. "And I, too, Miss Townsend, for not preparing him and raising him properly to mind his manners in the presence of a lady."

"Not at all," she spoke, and the strong silk of her voice and strange flat American accent caught Ashe's attention immediately. "Your grandson is a grown man and old enough to do and say what he pleases. And if it pleases him to be rude and boorish, then that's no reflection on you, Mr. Blackwell. You've been nothing but kind, sir."

Rude and boorish? Ashe clenched his jaw in frustration but managed to growl out his words. "I apologize, Miss Townsend. But as you've pointed out, I'm a grown man, and hardly in need of a chaperone, despite what my grandfather believes."

She tilted her head to one side, a small bird openly unafraid. "What you're in need of, sir, is not for me to say for fear of seeming equally rude, but I've promised your grandfather I'd do what I could to assist you, so we'll just have to make the best of it, won't we?"

Ashe forced himself not to sputter in astonishment at the woman's cheekiness. She'd openly insulted him and then stood there as calmly as if they were discussing the weather. He looked at her more closely, his first impression of a gray dove giving way only slightly. Her brown eyes were large and framed with impossibly long lashes that gave her an inquisitive countenance but not an owlish one. Her gaze was far too direct for an English woman of breeding, but the intelligence there made it difficult to look away. Her features were balanced and pleasing, but her color was far too high for the current fashion. Ladies were encouraged to look as porcelainlike as possible, hinting at a lofty station that allowed them to shun the sun and all excesses that might put a permanent stain on their faces. Instead of dainty curls and a lace headdress, her dark blonde hair was pulled back with a simple fall of waves down her back without a single ornament.

She was plain but for those mesmerizing eyes. . . . But the Ton will tear her to pieces—an American! With the manners of a rough and tumble Colonial, no doubt, to match that saucy tongue of hers!

His grandfather laughed, and the surprising sound of it arrested the dark vein of his thoughts. "I'll leave you to get acquainted for a few moments."

"I hardly think that's necess—" Ashe started to protest.

"Nonsense! You'll talk and make amends to the lady." He turned to take Miss Townsend's hand. "I will see you both for a cordial dinner and then you may both take your leave in the morning in my carriage. Ashe will take you into Town and see you settled at his home."

"Thank you, Mr. Blackwell."

He left without another glance at his grandson, and Ashe let out a long sigh before attempting another start with his "chaperone." "I am genuinely sorry, Miss Townsend, for my behavior. But I am also sorry that you seem to have been thrown to the wolves without your knowledge. I'm having trouble understanding why my grandfather thought to put you in such an untenable position, but as you seem to grasp, I have little say in the matter."

"Are you the wolf in question?"

He shook his head. "Not this time."

"Then I fail to see the difficulty, Mr. Blackwell."

His brow furrowed, unsure of how realistic a portrait to paint for her. After all, if she refused to proceed with the plan, he could hardly be blamed. But if she went into it without any idea of the obstacles ahead, he wasn't sure he'd be able to live with himself. "Are you well versed in the etiquette of London society, Miss Townsend?"

Ashe watched a flash of fiery temper alight in her eyes and knew the answer before she supplied it.

"Good manners are common sense, Mr. Blackwell, and I'm sure I'll pick up on things quickly enough. We are not entirely without the social niceties in Boston."

"No, I didn't imagine you all in mud-covered huts, Miss Townsend."

"Yet you seem to look at me as if I'm wearing animal hides, Mr. Blackwell."

"Now there's a wicked picture," he said, unable to keep from smiling at the thought of the little terrier of a woman in front of him wearing nothing but a few furs. He went over to the side table. "Port, Miss Townsend?"

"No, thank you."

Why am I not surprised? He smiled and turned back to lift his glass in a mock toast. "What kind of woman agrees to chaperone a rogue such as myself? What in the world would appeal to you to come so far for such a ridiculous task?"

Caroline Townsend fought the urge to throw something at his smug face and did her best to compose a reasonable answer. He was a rogue, without question, and while he was far more handsome and imposing than she'd expected, he was also more annoying and ill-mannered. *So much for the superiority of an English gentleman!*

She stepped forward, tipping her head back to look up into his face with what she hoped was her sternest and most unforgiving expression. It had previously brought more than one pupil to tears, and while she didn't expect the pompous wall of a man to crumble, Caroline was determined not to give any ground. "I see nothing ridiculous in helping my grandfather's dearest friend."

"Your grandfather's dearest friend may not have considered all the risks when he asked you for this favor."

"You repeatedly speak of risk and I can't help but think you're trying to frighten me away, Mr. Blackwell." Her chin lifted a defiant inch, and Ashe had a small glimpse of just how immovable Miss Caroline Townsend could be when pressed. "And since you are a self-confessed rogue, I don't believe I need to defend or explain anything to you. Your grandfather said you couldn't be trusted not to disgrace him, and while I can only imagine what you've done to earn his censure, I don't care. My life and reasons for being here are my own."

It galled him a little that his grandfather would have said such a thing to an outsider, but then his chaperone would undoubtedly have to know the worst to understand her strange employment.

"As are mine! I have agreed to my grandfather's request, but know this, Miss Townsend—I won't waste any more time warning you away from your noble quest to play my moral guardian. And you can trust me when I tell you this: Since you're so determined to have your way, I'll not interfere. I don't need you to keep me from disgrace. Rogue or no, I'm capable of holding my own without some drab little tight-lipped American nipping at my heels. Frankly, I would rather haul a tiger around on a bridle than cart you through a Season."

Hands fisted at her hips, she faced him squarely. "I'm glad we have an understanding then, Mr. Blackwell. Especially since I am the one with the unhappy task of holding *your* bridle, which from here makes you look less and less like a tiger and more and more like an ass!"

She turned on her heels, her spine ramrod straight, and crisply left the room. The sound of the library door shutting in a most unladylike manner behind her made his jaw drop open in astonishment.

Women blushed and fluttered at the sight of him and generally yielded to his every whim, he reminded himself. *Hell, and that's the ones I don't pay! Damned if my grandfather hasn't found the one woman on this planet I believe I can genuinely confess to loathing at first sight—and who apparently shares the sentiment when it comes to me!*

Ashe's eyes narrowed as he considered his petite opponent in the upcoming game. The stakes were too high to underestimate her. Whatever his grandfather had promised her, the sooner he could find it out and match the offer, the better. Not to break his word, but to eliminate at least one miserable element from the Season ahead.

Though he had a sinking feeling the petite terrier was not going to be amenable to a bribe. His grandfather's business ventures had been very successful, and he'd heard him mention Townsend's phenomenal success across the Atlantic. The little chit had no doubt inherited enough to make her impervious to any offer he might make.

If she's incorruptible, then I'm trapped unless I can find another way. But no matter what, I'm not going to be outdone by an upstart American and forfeit my pride and abandon my family's honor into Yardley's sweaty hands. If I have to cart the chit around, I will—but I'll be damned if she doesn't regret every minute that she thought to hold the whip hand with me.

He lifted his glass in a quiet salute to the closed library door. "You'll wish you'd stayed home, Miss Townsend, for this is one favor you're going to beg me to release you from before the month is out."

* * *

"Well! I cannot remember a more delightful dinner!" The elder Blackwell leaned back against his elaborately carved chair's high back. "My compliments to Cook, Frasier."

Ashe smiled at the gesture, aware that it was yet another sign of a new, softer temperament from the old monster. Despite all his grumblings, it was clear he was determined to amend his world on all fronts before too long—even with the cook, Mrs. Edgars, whom he'd been infamously battling for years and accusing of trying to make him fat. But Ashe's amusement faded as he wondered what had inspired the change, hoping his grandfather hadn't lied about his health.

You cannot die just yet, beloved monster. You're all I have left.

Conversation had been meager at the meal as Ashe

struggled to understand how he'd managed to land himself in such a nightmare. It was one thing to be lectured, but another to be tied to a dowdy and mirthless piece of American baggage. Even so . . . it was even harder to see an honorable way out now that he'd given his word.

"You barely touched your plates, Miss Townsend. Have my grandson's manners set you off your appetite?"

Caroline shook her head. "Not at all, Mr. Blackwell."

His grandfather beamed. "You must call me Grandfather Walker."

Ashe started to choke on his dessert and had to take a quick drink to recover. *Grandfather Walker? What the—*

"You're too kind, Mr. Blackwell . . . I mean, Grandfather Walker." Miss Townsend looked shy at the honor, and Ashe had to bite the inside of his mouth to keep from protesting. The craggy old man had never allowed such familiarities outside the family and was deliberately trying to provoke a comment.

"Don't mind my grandson," the patriarch interjected, giving Ashe a dark look. "He's worried that we have such a strong alliance, you and I, and that neither one of us seems too impressed with his charms."

"It's the least of my worries, Grandfather." Ashe set down his glass. "And since Miss Townsend is now 'family,' I'm sure it would be inappropriate to consider charming her into doing anything."

"You'd have more luck trying to make Frasier blush," his grandfather growled. "But see that you don't set out to prove me wrong."

"I believe"—Caroline pushed away from the table— "it's customary to leave you to smoke after dinner, and quite frankly, I would like to finish packing for the journey tomorrow. So, if you gentlemen will excuse me."

They both stood as she did, and his grandfather was quick to offer his blessing. "Enjoy a good night's sleep, then, and thank you again for your service to me."

"Good night . . . to you both." She nodded, her cheeks flushing as she left the room.

As the door closed behind her, the men reseated themselves, and Ashe let out a long sigh. "I don't suppose you'd reconsider, even out of mercy for the poor girl?"

"Why? Are you going to do away with her between here and London?"

"London will do away with her, cruelly enough, and you know it. She didn't even change out of that ghastly dress for dinner, and her manners . . ."

"Her manners are suitable enough for *my* house," his grandfather countered. "London does not hold the high ground for anything but foolishness from what I can see."

Ashe did his best not to pull a face. His grandfather's opinions of the Ton and London society grew less approving with each passing year. He had a countryman's sense of superiority over Town dwellers and made no secret of it. "Foolish or not, they may not—"

"She has no interest in social climbing, and from all that I know of her, Caroline Townsend can hold her own."

"She'll have to. I'm not holding her hand while she—"

"She is in your keeping, Ashe, and you'll keep her out of harm's way! I like her," the elder Blackwell stated with finality that ended debate. "She speaks her mind without hesitation, and speaks well at that! She's fearless and doesn't seem to have a propensity for female flights of fancy or silly games. Since her arrival, she's inquired to the gardener directly about the proper names of every plant in my garden and has made more use of my library than any soul I can recollect. She remembers the names of every servant in the house and cannot sing." He smiled at the last as if pronouncing a great discovery. "A woman who cannot embroider or play the pianoforte but can quote Dante and Socrates—imagine that!"

"All of London will swoon at her feet," he intoned sarcastically.

"Mind your manners!" He stood up, and Ashe dutifully rose as well. "I could tell from those eternal silences at dinner that you'd defied me and made no apologies to Miss Townsend. In fact, I would better surmise you somehow made things worse."

"As you pointed out, my charms seem to have no effect on Miss Townsend, Grandfather."

"Good! It's just as I anticipated, and if you're foolish enough to exacerbate things with the woman who holds your future in her hands . . . well, then this should be exactly the experience I was hoping you'd have!" He turned, and without looking back said, "Good night, Ashe. I won't see you off in the morning, so I'll wish you a pleasant journey. Good luck."

The door was closed behind him and Ashe was completely alone before he could respond that he wouldn't be the one who would need luck. *Miss Caroline Townsend will!*

*   *   *

Caroline made her way to her room with even steps, hating the whip of humiliation that cracked through her with each footfall. She'd expected to meet an oversized spoiled brat, even from the veiled polite descriptions she'd received from Mr. Blackwell, but this?

Drab little tight-lipped American? She'd let her temper get the best of her, but Ashe Blackwell's words had struck back with equal force.

Except it shouldn't have stung like that. . . .

It wasn't as if she expected men to look at her twice, or ever invited them to, so being dismissed by him should have come as no surprise. She'd never thought of herself as anything but plain. But despite what the elder Mr. Blackwell had said about her immunity to Ashe's formidable charms—Caroline knew that it wasn't entirely true. Instead of a caricature of a pasty-faced English dandy with soft sausage hands and mincing steps, the younger Blackwell was a tall, broad-shouldered brute with golden brown curls and piercing blue eyes. Ruggedly handsome, there was nothing soft about the man to hint at the life of a wastrel. When his grandfather had indicated that his indolent heir required a watchful eye, she'd secretly wondered before meeting him if the older man weren't exaggerating the situation from a simple misunderstanding or misperception.

After all, her own great-uncle had been convinced that her father was some sort of artistic radical because he'd preferred to pursue architecture and philosophy over banking and politics.

But seconds in Ashe's presence had erased her doubts and only reinforced how potent and impossible he could be. This was no errant schoolboy. This was a dangerous predator, self-assured and genuinely skilled in the hunt, and she'd agreed to try to hold his tail!

All her pride in being an example of feminine sensibility, independence, and scholarly achievement had evaporated in a flush of appreciation of male beauty, and in the next breath, pride alone had allowed her to hold her ground as if his disdain meant nothing.

Months ago, she'd readily accepted his grandfather's invitation to come to his family's aid and enjoy a visit to London. But she had never told another living soul the true reason for her agreement. In exchange for her discretion, Mr. Blackwell had offered a generous reward of twenty thousand British pounds. It was a staggering amount that had banished every argument she could construct against the unorthodox arrangement. Not that she'd confessed anything at all to her Aunt Emilia! As far as her aunt knew, she was merely away visiting her grandfather's business partner who had offered her a tour of London society.

For years, she'd relied on the charity of her family, charity they'd begrudgingly given after her parents' deaths. Her dear grandfather would never have believed that his own brother would have been so cruel, but after he'd passed, her great-uncle's disapproval of her father had been a weapon that had banished them from good society until it was too late. And when her great-uncle had finally died, it was his eldest daughter, Emilia, who had taken her in. But Aunt Emilia's charity did not extend so far as depriving her own children of a single penny of their inheritance by undoing her father's wrongs. Instead, Caroline's education had been provided for only because it was understood that she would have to make her own way in the world, without benefit of fortune or husband.

Her education had proved to be her salvation, and Caroline had no regrets. Instead, she'd marveled at the freedom it had afforded her and had grown more and more convinced that other young women could benefit by a similar chance. She'd been frustrated at the limitations on higher education because of her sex, and inspired to change things if she could.

The compensation that Mr. Blackwell had promised was more than enough to found the school of her dreams and create a foundation for everything she'd hoped to achieve. She'd come to England absorbed with visions of a small college where young women could achieve an equal education to their male counterparts and begin to defy the conventions that held them back.

She'd never even thought of her charge, somehow imagining him in terms of a troublesome adolescent or just a lackluster man in need of a woman's advice and subtle guidance. His grandfather had said in his letters and repeatedly after she'd arrived that all his grandson needed was the presence of a steadier character to improve himself. And when she'd questioned why a man wouldn't serve better in the capacity, the elder Mr. Blackwell's answer had flattered her into agreement. "Men are too easily corrupted, and if not corruptible, then it would simply become a manly competition that Ashe's pride would never let him lose. He would misbehave on purpose to put the other gentleman in his place. But a woman evokes more courtesy and respect, and I am convinced that he will demonstrate the discipline he needs."

Twenty thousand pounds if I succeed in chaperoning a grown man through a winter social Season without scandal, but what cost if I fail? This will be like a blind woman herding a mouse through a cheese factory!

Caroline reached her room and closed the door firmly behind her. It was a temporary sanctuary at best. In the morning, the carriage would be waiting to take them to London, and there would be no going back.

She caught a glimpse of herself in the dressing table mirror across the room, and the storm of her thought slowed for a moment. *Drab . . . how can one word from his lips rob me of so much? I'd managed twenty-four years of my life without a care when it came to appearances. I took pride in my indifference to fashion and nonsense and now . . .*

She shook her head and approached the mirror, as if studying her reflection for the first time. Her parents had always encouraged her independence and supported her desire to make more of herself than a pretty ornament for someone's home. Losing them as a child had only strengthened her resolve to follow her own path, and her chosen profession of teaching hardly encouraged more than a practical nod to a mirror now and then.

What difference does it make? Peacock or pigeon, I'm nothing to him, nor do I wish to be anything to a man like that! Let him throw out his petty insults and growl like the sulking overgrown child he's become!

She turned away from the table, dismissing the silly game. Caroline wanted to think only of the college of her dreams and not the handsome obstacle in her path, and she began to pace the floor.

"What am I going to do?" she asked the empty air.

A knock at the door made her jump guiltily. "Yes, come in."

One of the maids came shyly through the door carrying her freshly pressed traveling dress. "Mr. Frasier wanted to make sure you had all the assistance you needed. I took the liberty of freshening your dress for the journey and can lay it out for you."

"You're too kind, Molly. I should have thought of it myself," Caroline apologized. "But apparently, I've been . . . distracted."

"He is a distracting man, so handsome! It makes it hard to keep a thought in one's head." The young girl nodded knowingly, setting the dress out across a small settee in the corner. "You should hear the housekeeper fuss whenever Mr. Ashe arrives."

"Oh! I'm not—" Caroline's cheeks blazed with heat at the insinuation, horrified that such a thing would be so obvious. "I meant by the thought of London!"

"Beg your pardon, miss." Molly curtsied, her smile sincere. "Of course you did! I should have known better, I mean, you being so . . ."

"My being so . . . ?"

"Serious," Molly finally supplied.

Caroline tried to smile. It might even have seemed a compliment on any other day, but today she'd met Ashe Blackwell and the word sounded hollow in her ears. *But if I weren't so serious, I wouldn't be in this position.* "Thank you, Molly. That will be all for tonight."

"Yes, miss." Molly curtsied and withdrew.

Caroline walked over to finger the sleeve of her favorite traveling dress, the light wool so soft to the touch. She traced the lines of black silk braid piping and tried to savor a little pleasure in the trim outfit that modestly flattered her figure. Her bags were packed but for a few items, and she felt like a woman standing on the edge of a cliff considering her fate. *I'm between the devil and the deep sea.*

She could still beg off and return home. She still had a position teaching at a small, prestigious boys' academy waiting for her in the spring, but her heart ached at the idea. It was stifling to think of the defeat, relinquishing her dreams to dreary subservience teaching in an environment without inspiration or freedom.

Or she could ignore every instinct that was telling her to get as far away from Ashe Blackwell as she possibly could, and climb in that carriage tomorrow morning.

Home.

London.

She wondered if Ashe Blackwell knew how tenacious a woman could be when she'd run out of choices. His grandfather had been too kind to her already for her to abandon her promises so quickly. And he reminded her too much of her own dear grandfather for his pleas of family honor not to capture her loyalty.

The monetary reward had been the initial lure to solidify her commitment, but it was Ashe who had sealed her fate. If he'd been less hostile . . .

I might have begged off. But now, you are my only thought, Ashe. And if you think to frighten me away or break Grandfather Walker's heart, you will need to think again, Rogue.

Chapter
2

❦

Ashe climbed down from the carriage, doing his best to ignore the screaming agony of a knot in his lower back and the popping of his knees. His height had never leant itself to the amenities of a carriage and he'd always hated the confinement. But despite his preference for horseback, defying his grandfather at the very start of their agreement hadn't seemed like a wise choice. Even so, the physical discomfort of the journey back had only been slightly less painful than the icy silence between him and his traveling companion.

He'd deliberately tried to ignore her existence, determined to let her stew a bit in her own anxiety about the weeks to come. Despite her show of defiance, he was sure he'd given her pause.

Although, not enough of a pause to keep her from climbing down Bellewood's front steps that morning in the most horrifying straw bonnet and brown traveling dress and matching wool coat he'd ever seen. She'd sailed past him and accepted a footman's hand to aid her up into the carriage with a grace all her own.

He'd expected her to grow impatient and make some ploy to initiate a conversation during the long hours of their journey, but the terrier had proven more stubborn than he'd expected. He'd never known a woman who could refrain from chatter, but Miss Townsend had defied his every preconception. She'd snapped open a book of some rusting dissertation on the human condition and effectively dismissed his very existence.

Impossible woman!

He reached back to hold out his hand, half expecting her to refuse it, but her slim gloved fingers grasped his and he helped her down to alight on the steps. "Welcome to my humble home."

She shook her head, smiling at his jest, since the elegant brownstone didn't radiate humility with its rose-colored stones and elaborate wrought iron. "It isn't a mud hut, Mr. Blackwell, but I'm sure it will suffice."

Impossible woman who apparently never forgets a single word uttered in her presence!

He relinquished her hand as the front door opened. "Ah, Mr. Godwin! We made good time."

"You did indeed, sir." Not that Mr. Godwin had been informed of any schedule, but as usual, he was far too unflappable to show even a twitch of surprise at either his employer's unannounced return or the presence of a young lady at his side.

Ashe escorted his unlikely chaperone up the stairs and inside the foyer as the butler signaled the footmen to bring in their bags. "Godwin, this is Miss Caroline Townsend. She will be staying with us for a while to enjoy the social Season. Please ask Mrs. Clark to make sure she has everything she needs."

"Very good, sir." He gave Caroline a polite nod and held out a hand for her coat and bonnet. "Welcome, Miss

Townsend. May I offer you any refreshments after your journey?"

"You are too kind, Mr. Godwin. Yes, please." She smiled at the man as if he were her dearest uncle, and Ashe watched in amazement as his icy Godwin seemed to melt a bit.

He withdrew to see to a tray for her, and Ashe gestured for her to follow him upstairs into the drawing room on the first floor. "Godwin will find us here, and I thought we could catch our breath before Mrs. Clark whisks you off to get you settled in."

"Catch our breath?" she asked, her caramel brown eyes alit with questions as she took in her new surroundings.

"And establish a few rules," he asserted, pleased to see that the drawing room was well lit and comfortable. *Godwin's clairvoyant, I swear it, but one of these days, I wonder if I can catch him off guard.*

"Ah, rules!" she echoed softly. Caroline's expression was instantly more serious. "Are you dictating the rules, Mr. Blackwell? Or was this to be a consultation?"

He decided to ignore her. "Since you'll be playing the role of my ward, I'll ask my housekeeper, Mrs. Clark, to find you a ladies' maid and see that all proprieties are observed. My grandfather's strange humors aside, we are not related by blood and I'd like to avoid the obvious scandal that will undo all his efforts to keep things trouble free this Season should anyone ask too direct a question about our connections."

"How thoughtful of you!" she exclaimed with a light dusting of sarcasm.

"If anyone does ask, I'll tell them you're a distant relation and a favorite of my grandfather. I think the less information we provide, the better." He walked over to pour himself a measure of brandy. "I'd hire a chaperone for you, but truthfully, I don't think I can manage more than one of you. So we'll occasionally rely on the wives of friends of mine to give an illusion of propriety."

She gasped in fury behind him, and Ashe had to struggle not to grin before he turned back around to face her. *Go on, little terrier. Storm off and leave a man in peace.* "The pace of a social Season can be grueling, Miss Townsend, but you look hale and hearty enough for the challenge. I will say it's refreshing to see a woman not prone to fainting spells and hysterics."

"Do all the women in your acquaintance suffer from such maladies?"

"Only the ones with good breeding, Miss Townsend. And those, I avoid whenever I can."

"Do you? Or do women of good breeding avoid you, Mr. Blackwell?" she countered, apparently unruffled as she took a seat on the divan as if settling in for a good argument.

He shook his head. "Hardly. Women do not, by their nature, avoid me, Miss Townsend. I have the good fortune of being able to select those with whom I would spend my time."

"Until now," she corrected him with a sweet smile that grated on his nerves.

"Until now," he repeated begrudgingly. *But not for long.*

"And what women exactly do you prefer in your selections?"

The unexpected question nearly made him drop his brandy glass. "Are you asking for introductions?"

"No, just a general description of the qualities that intrigue you—if not good breeding and a penchant for fainting couches." Those large brown eyes of hers looked at him as coolly as if they were discussing the weather, and Ashe wasn't in the mood to play shy. He tried to think of the most abrupt and repulsive reply he could give her.

"I prefer women who are never serious, loathe conversation when there are other entertainments to be had, are compliant and eager for my company, and who never, ever argue with me." He raised his glass to her in a mock salute. "And trust me, Miss Townsend, they are worth every penny."

"So long as you have pennies enough, Mr. Blackwell, I imagine they are."

A wave of suspicion washed through him at the change in her tone. *Was that pity?* "In any case, we were discussing the rules for your stay in my house, Miss Townsend."

"Were we?" she asked, all innocence. "By all means, continue."

"You'll not leave the house alone, unless you have your maid with you. Otherwise, I'll attend you at whatever engagements I think suitable for this ridiculous charade and we'll make the best of it."

"And you?"

"And I, what?"

"Will you be leaving the house unattended? Will you be attending only the engagements deemed suitable?"

"I'll come and go as I please, Miss Townsend. The agreement with my grandfather is to avoid any public scandals, and I'm certainly capable of that without becoming a prisoner in my own home!"

"The agreement was for you to demonstrate impeccable behavior at all times."

Ashe crossed his arms. "And I intend to be every bit the gentleman that my grandfather would wish—whether I have you nipping at my heels or not."

"I am pleased to hear it, Mr. Blackwell, for you'll make my job so much easier if that is truly your intent. But let me make *my* intentions equally clear. I am not going to be cowed into forgetting my purpose, and you may spout your rules until you turn blue, but you are not in charge of me!"

"You, Miss Townsend, are an impossible—" He stopped himself, refusing to lose all in some childish exchange that he had foolishly started. "Very well, my dear chaperone. You, and you alone, are in charge." He took a slow, deep breath before laying out her first challenge. "Will you be seeing me to bed each night, or should I ask Godwin to report when I retire?"

The sharp intake of her breath and the blush on her cheeks was sweet revenge and Ashe savored her reaction. The color made her look almost pretty, her pert features softened in her dismay.

A knock on the open door frame spared her from being forced to respond, and Ashe looked up to see Godwin, just as expected, with a light supper tray for Caroline. "Shall I set this up for you here, Miss Townsend?"

Ashe answered before she could. "I'm afraid the journey was far more taxing than anticipated. Can you show her directly to her room for a private meal and see to her comfort there, Godwin? I'll eat dinner alone in my rooms tonight as well."

"As you wish, sir." Godwin stepped back with the tray to allow her to follow him out into the hall. "Right this way, miss. Mrs. Clark has already seen to the room to make sure that it's ready, if you'll follow me."

For a moment, Ashe was sure she would refuse, but then she squared her shoulders, back stiffening, and walked out with Godwin. Ashe watched her go, her diminutive frame radiating fury, and he had a fleeting sense of regret. Angering her may not have been the wisest course of action, just as his grandfather had suggested. But the woman provoked him past reason, and Ashe knew he could fulfill his oath far easier without her underfoot. And if it were Caroline Townsend who quit her position in a snit, he was sure he could convince his grandfather to see reason.

* * *

Mrs. Clark was a bustling woman who never slowed to take a breath. But she was a welcome distraction. "What a tiny thing you are! Mr. Godwin said nothing of it when he told me that the master had a guest—and an American! Men never think to mention the interesting bits, do they?"

"Is it interesting to be an American?" Caroline watched as her items quickly and efficiently disappeared from her trunks to be hung in a beautiful mahogany wardrobe in the corner.

"Naturally! A novelty for the house, at least, and . . ." She unfolded the first of Caroline's day dresses from the box. "Well, here's a practical thing! I'd always heard Americans were . . . self-reliant and . . ." She pulled out the next two, and it was clear that for once in her life, Mrs. Clark was having trouble coming up with something to say. "Durable."

Caroline abandoned her tray, tired of pushing the food around, and retrieved her dresses, lending Mrs. Clark a hand. "I wanted to bring clothes that would suit any weather, and I wasn't sure what to expect. The shopkeeper assured me that these were just the thing! And the materials wouldn't show any wear or stains."

It was her pride that made her defend the dreadful clothes. Her budget hadn't allowed for anything frivolous and, with Aunt Emilia's supervision, only the dingiest choices were approved. Her grim aunt had refused to even look at anything "unsuitable" for her—which meant anything with a hint of flattering color that might draw attention. The sabotage had not been subtle, but at the time, Caroline had been grateful for any new clothes for her journey. She was aware that her wardrobe tended to be dreary, but the new day dresses had been tailored just for her hourglass figure, and Caroline hoped that the hangers might not be showing them to their best advantage.

"Was there another trunk?" Mrs. Clark asked as she hung up the last of the dresses, this one a light blue silk that Caroline considered her best.

"There's a smaller leather case with my books, but . . ."

The look on Mrs. Clark's face stopped her. Clearly, she'd missed a critical point in the conversation. "No, no other trunks."

"Have you no evening dresses, ball gowns, and the like, miss? Did I misunderstand? Mr. Godwin said that the master had informed him that you were here to enjoy the Season, and from the pile of invitations and notes in the study, I'm sure you've a dozen outings in the next week alone!" Mrs. Clark peered back into the trunk she'd just emptied, as if hoping to discover a miraculous hidden compartment. "I only counted two bonnets and two pairs of gloves."

"Yes." Caroline nodded. "One for everyday and one for special occasions."

"Oh, my!" Mrs. Clark shook her head, her eyes full of kind sympathy. "Well, I'm sure the master has things well in hand! I'm to find you a ladies' maid, and if I may make a suggestion, there's a sweet girl upstairs I think might suit. She has a good head on her shoulders and has never given me a moment's worry. Mr. Godwin said something about placing an ad for a proper French maid, but . . ." Her look wandered back to the empty trunk. "I think Daisy will be a happier match."

Caroline knew that one of a ladies' maid's compensations was her mistress's cast-offs, and it was obvious that there was little in her trunk to currently excite a new hire. She only hoped Daisy's disappointment wouldn't be as obvious as Mrs. Clark's reaction foretold. "Yes, thank you, Mrs. Clark, though I confess I have never had a personal maid, so please ask Daisy to be understanding."

"Aren't you a dear!" Mrs. Clark beamed. "I'll let her know in the morning. For now, I can help you into your nightclothes and see to your personals. There's a water closet on the other side of your dressing room, just through there, and I'll arrange for a bath tomorrow morning. We have hot water pipes on the ground floor for the kitchens, but the rest of the house hasn't been improved yet. Mr.

Blackwell has great plans for it, but these things take time, I always say!"

"I can imagine." She smiled as the woman continued to busy herself, now with the bed linens. "Have you been with your employer long?"

Mrs. Clark nodded. "For many years, since first he set up a house of his own, I'm proud to say. My aunt has long been at Bellewood and I was happy for the reference when it came. Mr. Ashe has always been the best of employers, never too cross or demanding. Not like some I've heard others speak of. Not that I'd waste time gossiping with other households!" Her face colored a little at the slip. "Terrible thing, idle chatter."

Caroline looked away, unsure of what to say since Mrs. Clark's beloved employer apparently provided his neighbors with more than enough gossip on his own—even if all his servants never said a word. "You seem to me a woman far too loyal to be distracted by idle chatter, Mrs. Clark."

"Aren't you a dear!" The woman puffed up at the compliment. "I keep my own counsel when I can."

"You are very wise." Caroline walked over to the vanity and idly rearranged the one luxury she'd kept throughout the years. The silver hairbrush, comb, and ornate mirror had been her mother's, a legacy from another life of ease and wealth that Caroline couldn't even remember now. She'd been too young to appreciate the blessings of her grandfather's generosity, and instead, innocently believed that everyone must live as they did. It was only later after her grandfather's passing and the loss of her parents that she'd learned a painful lesson about the precariousness of the world.

"Shall I help you to bed, miss?" Mrs. Clark offered behind her.

"Yes, thank you." She accepted shyly, more to try to appease the housekeeper's expectations than out of need.

She'd been seeing to herself for so long it felt indulgent to have the attention. But her time at Bellewood had already taught her to appreciate the benefits of another pair of hands, and Caroline knew it would be something she would miss when her adventure was over.

Her white cotton nightgown was retrieved from a drawer, and within moments, she was free of her traveling clothes and seated at the dressing table for Mrs. Clark to brush out her long hair.

"Oh, my!" Mrs. Clark remarked. "All these lovely curls! I'll have to ask Daisy to see if she can help you show them off a bit more."

Caroline blushed, sure that the woman exaggerated to be kind. But she stole a glance at the mirror and allowed that her hair looked prettier this evening than usual. The sensation of the long, gentle strokes of the brush was soothing and brought the slight waves of her hair to life in the lamplight.

"Shall I braid it for you, miss?"

Caroline shook her head. "I'd prefer not." She'd always disliked the strange jolt of waking up with a rope of hair around her neck and faulted that she must toss and turn a great deal in her sleep.

"Well, there you are then! Just as pretty as a picture!" Mrs. Clark set the brush down and stepped back to begin making sure the bed was ready. "It's lovely to have a guest in the house and I'm sure I'm not the first to wish you a lovely visit!"

"Thank you, Mrs. Clark. You have been so sweet and I am grateful for that welcome. I hope to be as little trouble as possible and not burden the staff." She waited until the woman had left the room before climbing up onto the soft mattress and nestling under the bedding. The carriage had been well sprung, but it was always a little bruising to travel, and of course, her travel companion had added to the day's tensions. He'd deliberately tried to make it an

eternal ride from Bellewood, although she'd anticipated
him and brought a book along.

Even so, they'd managed yet another argument, their
second in as many days. . . .

*I wonder if it's possible to chaperone a man without
actually speaking to him! He's deliberately provoking me,
and what's worse, I seem to be incapable of not rising to
the bait. Dratted man!*

Exhaustion began to overtake her, and Caroline fell
asleep thinking of poor Mrs. Clark's face when she'd held
up the dark green woven poplin dress. . . . *Oh, well. I'm
not here to compete with the lovely ladies of England's
peerage or play the coquette, nor would it be appropriate
to try. I'm here as a chaperone. And tomorrow, I will strive
to do better. No matter what the man says, I will hold my
temper and my tongue!*

As deep sleep claimed her, her last thought was of a
strange image of Ashe, in all his tawny glory, like a stallion
fighting against the leather straps that held him back—and
in her hands were reins.

* * *

Ashe glanced again in disbelief at the pile of vellum folded
notes and engraved invitations that graced the silver platter
on the writing desk in his bedroom. Godwin had brought
it up along with his dinner tray, giving his employer a
glimpse of the days and weeks ahead.

*Grandfather hadn't been speaking figuratively when he
said he'd made arrangements for my respectable Season
in Town. Hell, there are at least six notes telling me how
thrilled they are to receive my acceptance and how they're
looking forward to meeting my ward, Miss Townsend! An
afternoon party? He can't be serious!*

He lifted an invitation, marveling at the turns of his life.
He'd never made plans, deliberately keeping himself away

from the ebb and flow of mainstream society, ever since their return from India.

"You are so far into the dark woods, I don't think you remember who you are. It's whatever that India business was, but it's no matter." His grandfather's words came back to him, an odd echo in the quiet of the room. "That India business" had more to it than anyone had yet guessed. Ashe knew that each of the Jaded would carry more than a few private scars of that time to their grave. The Jaded were known in London as some kind of secret club, named for their handsome members' notoriety and wealth. The group deliberately protected their privacy and allowed the rumors about their disdain for society to keep casual inquiries at bay. The men shared a bond unlike any other, but each man's wounds were different, and most of Ashe's had come just before he'd met the others.

He'd been broken before his capture, sitting drunk in the shadows, waiting for the worst. He'd put up almost no resistance to the thugs storming his house. He'd expected to be murdered, and it was only later in the pitch dark of an ancient prison that the bitter gall of disappointment at finding himself alive had insulated him from his heartbreak.

No fortune would have been vast enough to act as a healing salve, but the accidental wealth from their shared misadventure in a raja's dungeons had gone a long way to ensuring the Jaded's independence from their peers after their return to England.

They'd been strangers before they were captured by a mad raja who thought to use them for political or financial gain. Truthfully, the man had never explained his purpose while he held them in dark and filth. They'd learned almost nothing except how to suffer and survive.

But secrets had been exchanged and lives altered forever.

Escape had come through miraculous providence, but

Ashe wasn't sure that any of them would ever really leave "that India business" behind. *Especially me—for ghosts are rarely that merciful. And I still cannot even speak her name.* . . .

Even now, thoughts of India evoked an ache sharp enough to force him to swallow a moan—and on its heels, the urge to push it all away through some mindless release provided by a woman's soft skin and the unquestionable welcome of her body to his. He'd lost his heart in India and vowed after walking out of that prison to never again risk that kind of love. Instead he would drown himself in all that life had to offer—and hold back the pain. *Hell of a time to become a celibate, eh?*

The invitation in his hands recaptured his attention. None of his friends would believe the mess he'd landed in. But he intended to compose a few notes to warn them that he would be unfortunately occupied for most of the Season and not to ask too many questions. If all went as he expected, it would be a temporary misery, and if they cared for his company or companionship, they would avert their gaze and busy themselves elsewhere until it was over.

The clock on the mantel struck one, and Ashe stretched out his legs and pushed away from his desk. Fatigue made his head ache, and it had been a long day. Rather than ring for his valet, he began to undress himself, preferring his solitude. He shrugged out of his shirt and carelessly dropped it on the back of a low settee before starting on the buttons of his breeches.

The sound of the door's latch captured his attention in the space of a single breath. No servant in his employment would dare to come into his private rooms without summons, and Ashe's muscles tensed, adrenaline dictating an immediate, instinctive response.

In bare feet, he silently sprang into motion, crossing the room to put himself against the wall. The door itself would shield him from the intruder's view and give Ashe a fleeting advantage. Fists clenched, a dark calm flooded his frame as the latch moved again.

I'm unarmed, but with the element of surprise, I can still emerge victorious if I—

The door opened slowly to admit the most unlikely villain Ashe could imagine.

Miss Caroline Townsend glided into the room, her blonde hair cascading down her back to her waist in a surprising silk waterfall of curls. She wore nothing more than a simple white cotton nightgown, a frayed ivory ribbon tied loosely at the neckline revealing an astonishing glimpse of a bare collarbone and shoulder as she walked calmly past him. The candlelight flattered the pale honey of her skin and set the unassuming gold in her hair off in a shimmering show of hidden riches.

Even more breathtaking for Ashe was the glimpse of a silhouette of his chaperone's smooth curves and firm backside through the thin fabric of her nightgown as she stood before the lamplight on his desk. Her breasts were ripe and set high, without the aid of a corset, the tiny pink nipples tilted up to invite a man's kisses and endless attentions. Her hips were just wide enough to make Ashe's mouth pull into a smile, and her bottom was almost impossibly attractive. His hands itched to trace each round curve and pull her up against him.

His cock was ignoring the illogical turn of events and had naturally turned blistering hard against his half undone breech buttons. The familiar weight of it goaded him into ending the encounter as quickly as possible.

If she means to sabotage me . . . Can that be part of some plan she has?

The thought helped him to rein in the blaze of raw lust and address the problem at hand—why in God's name was Caroline Townsend in his bedroom?

"Miss Townsend?" He stepped forward, deliberately making no effort to race for a dressing jacket or make some show of false modesty. *It would serve the little terrier right to get a taste of her own medicine.* "If you meant to call me on my jest about helping me to bed . . ."

She turned to face him, and he knew immediately that something was off. The crisp intelligence that generally shone from her eyes was muted behind a dreamy glow. She smiled as if they were the oldest and dearest of friends, and Ashe had to swallow at the strange power of this softer, gentler Caroline. "Can you believe it? I never thought to make such a good sailor, but the seas are so calm."

"Are they?" Ashe smiled and shook his head at the amazing revelation that his prim and impossible little chaperone suffered from a most delightful malady.

The lady sleepwalked.

Chapter
3

◈

"And where are you voyaging, miss?"

"To England and then . . . perhaps I'll see more of the world I've read about." She reached up to push her hair back off of her face, unwittingly accenting her curves again as she arched her back, making Ashe almost groan. "I find that I like to explore."

"The world may never be the same, Miss Townsend." He shook his head again, trying to clear the heat from his veins and reconcile the relaxed and sensual creature in front of him to the woman he'd spent almost two days actively disliking.

She laughed, and the sound of it captivated him like nothing he could recall. Unlike the practiced melodic giggles that generally made him want to run from all civilized company, this was like warm water tumbling over smooth stones—a natural sound of purest joy that enchanted without inhibitions. He couldn't remember hearing a woman laugh like that. But there she stood, an unlikely sprite, with her unfettered blonde hair and sparkling brown eyes, innocently unaware of the havoc she was wreaking on his nerves.

He was trapped with her in a dreamlike exchange, unsure of how to guide her back to bed without waking her up. Not that it didn't occur to him for one fleeting moment how entertaining it would be to see how the terrier would react to finding herself nearly naked and less than six paces from his bed—the risk would almost be worth the reward.

But Ashe knew better. One scream and he'd forfeit all in a mortifying avalanche of consequences and regret. *Hell if my grandfather would understand this particular wrinkle!*

"Miss Townsend," he tried again. "Perhaps we should see about disembarking and getting you to . . . bed."

She shook her head, sweetly demurring his suggestion. "You can hardly just step off a ship, sir, while she's at sea."

She's talking to me in that kind tone one uses with the village idiot.

"Yes, of course, what was I thinking? But, the tide was with us and isn't that our first view of the port there?" He pointed toward the fireplace and dared to hope.

"Oh!" She followed his gaze and stepped forward, the strange, dreamlike haze in her eyes taking on a new, excited shine. "Oh, isn't it lovely?"

Ashe nodded solemnly, praying the humor of it all didn't undo his efforts to maintain his self-control. "We should be there within moments, and then you can disembark."

She clapped her hands in childlike merriment. "I can hardly wait! Just think of it!" Caroline reached out to touch his bare arm, the silk of her fingertips sliding up to his elbow. "A few weeks ago, there was nothing to look forward to. But now, everything seems possible."

Ashe had to look away from her, and he diverted his attention back to the fireplace. "Does it? I have never known London to inspire such change."

She slipped her hand around his arm, as if he were escorting her about the deck in her dreams. "You have never been in my Aunt Emilia's downstairs parlor for one of her teas and wished for the blessed release of a house fire."

Ashe smiled. "Ah, the perspective of an old woman's tea—it's a wonder we haven't all run away."

"I'm not running away."

Her solemn tone caught his attention, and Ashe looked down at her, inadvertently treating himself to a delightful view of her cleavage. "Not even from Aunt Emilia?"

"I'm going to change the course of my life."

His breath caught in his throat. She was so hopeful—so impossibly sweet. "And where was it heading before, Miss Townsend?"

"Oblivion," she answered solemnly.

There's a destination I know well enough.

"But now you're here." *It's all nonsense and dreams talking and I'm a fool if I take any of this conversation to heart and think for a minute that the terrier is an object of sympathy. She's a grown woman who's decided for whatever reason to place herself in my path and assist my grandfather in providing for a humiliating Season.* "And let's see about getting you ashore, shall we?"

She put her head on his shoulder and sighed. "Yes."

Ashe ignored the bolt of heat the simple contact initiated back down his spine and across his skin. Instead he retrieved his shirt from behind her off the arm of the settee and shrugged into it before holding out his arm to attempt to direct her from his rooms. They'd be a sight for the staff if anyone spotted them, but Ashe was determined to return her to her own room as quickly as possible and end the surreal encounter before she awoke and the dream turned into a nightmare.

"Here we are, Miss Townsend." He deliberately walked her with the care of a man approaching a gangplank, guiding her through the door and back down the unlit hallway.

"London is dark," she remarked, her voice tinged with a fear and awe. "I don't think I expected it to be this gloomy."

"It's the fog, Miss Townsend." He smiled in the shadows. "It's one of the charms of the great city."

"Oh!" Her grip on his arm relaxed slightly. "It does add a touch of mystery, doesn't it?"

Ah! Miss Townsend harbors a bit of the romantic! "A woman's point of view, and one of your charms, Miss Townsend."

"That I'm a woman? Or that I have a point of view?" she asked, as sweetly as if inquiring after the weather.

Ashe laughed softly, unable to stop himself. "With you, I suspect the two are irrevocably intertwined."

She laughed again, and the magic of it wasn't lessened in its new familiarity. Ashe liked this lighter and merrier version of the terrier. *This* Miss Townsend was all feminine sweetness and corruptible curves, without the glowering looks and prim little sniffs of disapproval. *This* Miss Townsend had an appeal that transcended his opinions about pushy American women and chaperones in general.

But *this* Miss Townsend was just as forbidden to him as any other woman, and Ashe bit the inside of his cheek hard enough to sting and remind him that, while she had the luxury of dreams, his feet needed to stay firmly planted in the waking world.

"Here we are." He stopped at her door, opening the latch for her and glancing inside to note the lack of light. "Let me see if we can't light a candle and get you settled," he said, guiding her just inside the doorway.

She put her head on his shoulder and he could feel her nod in acquiescence. She was clinging to him innocently enough, but the sensation of her pert breasts pressing against his arm and side through the thin silk of his shirt was pure torment. He tried to recall the room's arrangement by memory, but he'd never bothered much with the guest rooms.

Ashe instinctively acted to protect the terrier's shins and avert a bad ending to their adventure. "Wait here, miss, and I'll make sure everything is as it should be." He gently guided her hand to the door frame, anchoring her safely so that he could make his explorations.

"You're so kind to me." She sighed.

Kind. I'm the devil in the dark, and she thinks I'm kind.

He strode toward what he thought was a best guess of the direction for her bed and side table and instead was rewarded with a bruising blow across his shins from one of her traveling trunks. Ashe bit down hard to swallow a string of curses from the throbbing pain before trying another direction and finding success. With a hand on the bed curtains, he traced the edge of the mattress and found what he was looking for.

The glow from the single taper was more than enough to illuminate the waiting figure in the doorway, and Ashe forgot about his bruised shins at the vision she presented. Once again, her thin cotton gown did nothing more than accent everything her dowdy fashions struggled to hide from view.

The heat in his blood reignited and Ashe smiled, wondering if his grandfather had any idea of the hellfire he'd poured on his grandson's head. Sacred oaths and familial duties aside, his chaperone was proving to be an unexpected problem.

"Must I go to bed now?" she asked, and Ashe's cock instantly became painfully hard, its swollen head pressing against the waist of his pants. When he risked a glance downward, he could see it, one pearl of moisture beading from its tip.

He closed his eyes and tried to banish the demon that snaked through his body, its power emanating from the raw hunger between his thighs. "Yes," he managed to grind out, roughly pulling the covers aside. "In, Miss Townsend."

"Won't you be showing me more of London?" She

walked toward him, her voice giving no hint of an intimate double meaning to her words, no trace of an illicit invitation—but her nightgown had fallen even farther down her shoulder, revealing the top of a creamy orb, an invitation in itself.

Oh, the things I could show you, Miss Townsend.

"Not tonight." He tugged at the covers again, his hands itching to see just how much of a pull it would take on the ribbon of her gown to allow it to fall to the floor. He forced himself to look away from the frayed strip of narrow satin so tantalizing within his reach. "Time to rest and tomorrow . . . we'll see about you beginning your adventures in London."

She sighed, lifting the hem of her nightgown with the innocence of a child to allow her to climb unencumbered up into the bed and giving Ashe a delicious peek at her legs in the process. "I've never had an adventure before!"

It was all he could do not to grab one of her ankles and drag her over to the side of the bed and ravish her without apologies. Instead, he stiffly threw the covers over her and took a firm step back. "Stay. In. Bed."

"As you wish." She smiled sweetly, pressing back into the pillows, her blonde curls fanning out to frame her face. Her eyes looked at him without seeing him, and Ashe finally accepted that retreat was his only option.

He took the taper with him, hoping to avoid another stumble on his way out. He'd nearly made it to the door when she called out softly, "I can hardly wait until tomorrow."

He shut the door behind him and blew out the candle.

God, give me strength.

* * *

Caroline arranged the last of her books on the small desk in the corner, comforted by the familiar titles, each volume's heft and touch something she would have known blindfolded. The morning light gave her room a more cheerful atmosphere, and she was pleased to be setting out her own things. It made the room feel more like a place of her own.

"Was there anything you needed, miss? I waited for you to ring, but Mrs. Clark said it was better to just come up and ask."

Caroline turned, startled by a young maid in a freshly starched bob cap she realized was probably the promised Daisy. "That was very thoughtful of you, Daisy."

The girl's eyes widened with happy surprise. "You know my name!"

"Why, yes! Mrs. Clark said she thought you were the very best young lady to assist me, and I couldn't imagine her sending up anyone else at this hour."

"She said you were nice, for bein' an American, and all." Daisy curtsied awkwardly, then headed straight toward the bed to remake it.

Caroline blushed to think her efforts to straighten her own bedding weren't up to the house's standards. *So much for my show of independence!*

"Just so you know," Daisy went on cheerfully, "I'm determined to be the best ladies' maid you ever saw. I'm a quick learner and Mrs. Clark said she'll keep an eye out so I don't make a muck of things! There, that's better! Now, I'll just . . ." Daisy hesitated, eyeing the nightstand unhappily. "Where's the candlestick? Usually I'm to change it if the taper's burned too low, but it's not here. Did you move it?"

"No," Caroline said, glancing around the room to make sure she hadn't inadvertently rearranged the item when she'd unpacked her things. "I remembered it there last night."

"Well." The maid shook her head but then regained her good spirits. "It's bound to turn up! I'll tell Mrs. Clark all the same, to be safe."

Caroline certainly hoped it turned up quickly, as she couldn't imagine anything more awkward than being accused of pilfering her host's housewares. When she was sixteen, her cousin Mary Louise had misplaced her favorite earrings and Caroline had never forgotten the blame or the bruising beating that had followed. Even when the earrings had been discovered later in one of Mary Louise's reticules, there had been no apologies from her Aunt Emilia.

She wasn't sure how Ashe would react to any signs of theft in his household, but she wasn't in any rush to find out. He might seize on the excuse to rid himself of an unwanted and cumbersome chaperone—an excuse that even the elder Blackwell couldn't dispute.

"It was here on the dresser when I went to sleep. I can't imagine—"

"Don't fret, miss!" Daisy put a hand on her arm to give it a comforting pat. "One of the housemaids may have thought to change it while you were in the dressing room and forgot to put it back. It's no trouble. You mustn't look so concerned."

"Thank you, Daisy. You're right, of course."

"Now, then, you're already dressed but you must promise to ring for me if you need to change. And I'll ask Cook to send you up a breakfast tray. After all, it's the least a ladies' maid can do, yes? See to her lady's comforts?"

"Yes, though I'm not hungry, Daisy, but I can see I'm in the best of hands." Daisy had curtsied and left before Caroline could ask her a bit more about herself or the routine of the household—or even if Mr. Blackwell had already eaten or where she could find him. But she was used to being on her own and preferred it.

Caroline left her room, glancing down the hallway to decide which direction to take. Either one looked promising, with its dark wood archways and hanging artwork.

She turned to the right, beginning a casual exploration

to savor the quiet of the house before the next storm. *Despite my vow to behave better, I think only a fool would expect a miraculous turn in both of our temperaments overnight.*

Every house was thought to reflect its owner in some way—his tastes, his interests or lack of them, even his personality. So Caroline had to wonder what Ashe's home would say about him. But the portraits from ages past and the artwork didn't seem to reflect anything at all—they were all unfamiliar faces and fashionable choices that betrayed little of Ashe's soul.

She didn't venture into any of the closed rooms, but instead headed down to the first floor to retrace her steps back to the drawing room where Ashe had instructed her about the "rules." On the way, she spied an open doorway and a room awash in powder blue and soft light.

It was a music room with a piano and a harp near the windows, and it made her wonder if anyone played them or if it was all for show. Or did he invite those nonargumentative, nonconversation-loving ladies over for private concerts for his own entertainment?

A pointless flash of jealousy struck her at the thought. Not that it made any difference to her if every nymph in London wished to perform concerts for his amusement. Caroline suspected it was her own lack of talent in music that fueled her feelings. She trailed her fingers lightly over the keys without depressing them to give away her presence.

Mr. Godwin interrupted her reverie from the doorway. "Miss Townsend. Do you play?"

"I'm afraid not." Caroline turned around, hoping she didn't look as guilty as she felt for snooping about. "Do you often have music in the house? Would it be too forward to ask if Mr. Blackwell is a musician?"

"His mother was the musician and a fine one at that. A voice like a nightingale, my uncle used to say. He was the butler here many years ago and shared wonderful stories of the family." Mr. Godwin shook his head. "No one has played them in years since her death."

Caroline felt a new flood of guilt that she'd been so quick to imagine the worst. "What a shame!"

"Mr. Blackwell instructed me to make sure that you knew of an afternoon party today that he wishes to attend. I'll advise Daisy so that she can help you prepare."

"It sounds as if I'm going into battle," she said, laughing.

Mr. Godwin smiled. "I would not expect casualties, Miss Townsend, but I imagine the principles of war often apply to London's social Seasons."

"The Chinese general Sun Tzu said that all warfare was based on deception."

It was Mr. Godwin's turn to chuckle. "He sounds like a very wise man who may have attended more than one party in his day."

"I'm not sure I'm a good enough liar to win the field, but I'll do my best not to embarrass my host." Caroline decided to forge ahead on the question at the head of all her thoughts. "Where is Mr. Blackwell this morning?"

"He's at his sporting club, miss. He and Mr. Rutherford have a standing appointment for fencing and exercise, but he'll return shortly to make his own preparations for the battle—or rather Lady Fitzgerald's party."

"I see." She took a deep breath. "Then perhaps you could direct me to Mr. Blackwell's library, if he has one."

"Yes, of course, right this way." Mr. Godwin led the way, and Caroline followed, trying to gain control of her emotions. The butler had given her more information than required about his employer's whereabouts, and she was grateful to the man. Her first thought had been to accuse the dratted Ashe Blackwell of running off into mischief to spite her after their dreadful argument, but even so, her limitations as a chaperone chafed.

Mr. Godwin stopped outside a carved heavy door. "Here it is, Miss Townsend."

"Mr. Godwin? May I ask . . . that is, this may seem a bit strange, but . . ." She hesitated, unwilling to offend the butler but determined not to fail without a fight.

"I'll naturally do my best to accommodate any request you care to make, Miss Townsend," he offered diplomatically.

"If I knew beforehand when Mr. Ashe intended to leave the house, it would be . . . extremely helpful."

He shook his head. "I'm afraid I will have to disappoint you." He pushed open the door and stepped back to allow her to pass him. "Perhaps you'd have better luck with your ladies' maid regarding this matter."

Daisy? Why in the world would Daisy be familiar with Ashe's comings and goings?

Before she could make sure she'd understood him, Mr. Godwin bowed politely and made his way back down the hallway.

Caroline bit her lower lip, accepting that her choices were very limited. Asking Daisy seemed unlikely to lead to success, but doing nothing would guarantee her failure to meet her obligations to the elder Mr. Blackwell.

Ashe truly couldn't be a prisoner in his own home—and she'd set her mind on finding a way to make sure he was holding to his oath. But asking his staff to betray him . . . Caroline worried that she might be going too far.

God, give me strength.

Chapter
4

Ashe waited in the downstairs salon for Caroline to appear. This was to be their first public outing and he wasn't sure what to expect. He'd deliberately seen nothing of her since their strange nocturnal encounter the evening before, nervously wondering if she'd recall any of it.

Not that she'd openly confess to such a thing, but let's hope she doesn't. It would undoubtedly be a blessing if the entire affair was beyond her. God, what an odd wrinkle to this impossible drama!

He glanced at the clock on the table, wondering if he should waste the energy it took to wish the girl would beg off with a headache or some other invisible female malady to allow him to escape the torture of an afternoon party. It was a bit too late to throw himself on her mercy and beg off himself.

"I'm sorry if I'm late." She spoke from the doorway, and Ashe had to instantly put on his best gambler's face. There was no trace of the sensual minx that had unnerved him so much last night. In a sensible, modest dark blue day dress of indestructible cotton with her hair pulled back in a firm chignon, it was hard to even imagine that this was the same woman who had deprived him of sleep. *Is that gray or blue? Hell, it's not a funeral! Does this woman own a single thing that didn't qualify as drab and unflattering?*

"Most women seem to spend more time at their dressing tables worrying about the tint of their cheeks rather than the time. You're actually more prompt than I'd expected." Ashe put his hands behind his back, briefly wondering if he'd padded the time enough to allow her to run upstairs and change. But the wickedest part of him shook off the idea. She'd scoffed at all his warnings, so perhaps it was best that Miss Townsend got a small taste of the cruel tongues of the Ton. *Poor girl! She's making it all too easy for them!* Their hostess, Lady Fitzgerald, was a notorious dragon of a woman, and he was willing to bet his finest horse that after one look at Caroline in her ridiculous garb, she'd be dismissed as a servant and given the attention of a houseplant.

"You, Mr. Blackwell, have wretchedly low expectations when it comes to women." She pulled on her gloves and gave her redingote a small tug. "A small tragedy, in my opinion."

It was clear that his chaperone remembered nothing of her visit to his bedroom as she bundled herself up for the carriage ride. "I hope the staff has made you feel comfortable, Miss Townsend, and that you've enjoyed your first night here."

"Very much so," she assured him. "They seem to go out of their way to be kind."

Unlike their employer. Ashe held out his arm to escort her out and down to the carriage. After today, despite all his posturing, there would be no retreat. He had always been a man of his word, but he had never felt so tested. As impossible as the girl was, throwing her in the path of

Lady Fitzgerald's ire was stinging his conscience. He was submitting to his grandfather's wishes, but he wasn't showing any mercy to Miss Townsend in doing so.

A true gentleman of impeccable behavior would find a way to keep his word and protect the lady. But I'm still too wicked a man not to wish her gone—and not one to waste an opportunity to let someone else take the blame for her departure.

He hesitated at the open carriage door. "Lady Fitzgerald isn't known for being kind, Miss Townsend. If you'd prefer, we can choose another venue for your debut."

She gave him a questioning look, then she lifted her chin defiantly. "I'd prefer that we weren't late, Mr. Blackwell."

So much for a show of mercy.

* * *

The party was an intimate affair, with about thirty guests. Lady Fitzgerald had touted the occasion as a chance to show off her newly acquired paintings, but Caroline could see little innovation in the simple landscapes and an oddly out-of-place drawing of a Grecian-style temple with a fountain at its center. She didn't recognize the stone goddess having water perpetually dribbled on her marble head, but she imagined it was an ignoble fate to fall from Mount Olympus and end up as a damp perch for pigeons, immortalized on canvas.

"Lady Fitzgerald." Ashe drew Caroline forward toward a thin older woman swallowed up by the fashionable over-abundance of flounces and ribbons of her elegant dress. "May I present my ward, Miss Caroline Townsend of Boston? She's just arrived in England and yours is the first introduction I had hoped to make for her since I knew you'd be the most gracious."

"What flattery!" Lady Fitzgerald said with a dismissive laugh, but her cheeks turned as pink as any schoolgirl's. "Naturally, I'm"—her eyes lit onto Caroline and it was

clear that some of the lady's graciousness abandoned her—
"delighted."

Caroline knew what a lamb felt like being weighed and
measured before facing the butcher. "How could you be?
I'm sure I'm nothing that could make such a great lady feel
anything close to delight."

She heard a few shocked sniffs nearby at the comment,
but Lady Fitzgerald's expression merely changed to show
intrigue. "It's true I'm not as easily impressed and swayed
as others. But your humility is very sweet."

"You're too kind, your ladyship."

"Never! I'm far too proud of my reputation for being
difficult to give it up at my age!" She turned back to Ashe.
"Your ward, you say? Is this what brings you back into the
light of day, dear boy? For if she's the cause, I don't care if
she dresses like a turnip. Don't think I won't be boasting to
every acquaintance I have that I am among the first to see
your handsome face and figure out amidst the living!"

"I'm no recluse, Lady Fitzgerald," Ashe said, without a
trace of humor.

"No, of course you're not—not any longer," Lady
Fitzgerald said, smiling again in Caroline's direction.
"And for that, the women of England are eternally in your
debt."

Caroline struggled not to laugh as Blackwell inadvertently presented a pitiable and surly picture behind the
dowager. "All the women of England? I had no idea that
Mr. Blackwell was so popular!"

Lady Fitzgerald laughed, a cascade of cackles that
made several guests attempt to awkwardly join in. "I am
charmed, Miss Townsend! I am completely charmed!
Here, come take my arm and let's enjoy a turn about my
ridiculously expensive salon and learn more about Miss
Townsend of Boston."

Caroline dutifully took the woman's arm, gently holding
the thin offering for fear of bruising the delicate lady. "I'm

afraid you'll find it a boring topic for conversation, your ladyship. Wouldn't you rather tell me about yourself?"

"Nonsense! I know everything there is to know about myself, while you, my dear, are a new puzzle. So"—she led Caroline away from the others—"are you a Quaker, Miss Townsend?"

"Am I . . . pardon me?"

"Forgive me, but your dress! My first impression was that you were in deepest mourning, but—then you wouldn't be out in society, would you?" Lady Fitzgerald laughed again. "And even a woman grieving wouldn't abandon all sense of fashion, so naturally, I have deduced that you are religious!"

Lady Fitzgerald clapped her hands together, as if applauding her own brilliance at deduction.

Caroline looked at her for an instant and then realized that the woman's pleasure was genuine and there wasn't a hint of malice in her game. *Oh, my! I truly look like a Quaker?*

Caroline shook her head. "Your logic is faultless, for I too have noted that any extreme religious fervor seems to accompany odd costumes—and I, sadly, have inadvertently imitated just such a thing." She smiled to make sure the lady was aware of her jest. "I have no eye for fashion, it seems. I fear my personal tastes are too plain even for the Quakers, Lady Fitzgerald."

The lady shook her head. "I have never known them to shun someone for a lack of satin, but what an odd little coup if you'd managed it!"

Caroline replied, making sure her own voice held no hint of disapproval as she tried to lightheartedly brazen her way out of it, "The shopkeeper near Boston assured me that subdued modesty was always in fashion, but now I think I must have misunderstood him." She shrugged her shoulders. "But perhaps it's for the best! English women are so elegant, I cannot think to compete with them."

"What a wretched compliment! But you must compete and you can," she announced with confidence, "for they won't hesitate to ruthlessly compete with you."

"I don't see how a girl easily mistaken for a Quaker is going to ruffle that many feathers, your ladyship."

"Ah! And that is where wisdom edges out over youth, Miss Townsend! You'll ruffle feathers because of that delectable man glaring at us over your shoulder. They'd claw past any woman, from age sixteen to sixty, to stand a bit closer to him."

Caroline sighed and shook her head. "A poor prize for a scratched face!"

"You're not going to fight to fend them off?" she asked.

"I'm sure it's not my place to do so, Lady Fitzgerald. But I'll not sacrifice my dignity for any man—particularly *that* one." Caroline risked a glance back toward an arboretum where Ashe was pretending to admire a rose bush.

"Tell me your interests, Miss Townsend," Lady Fitzgerald commanded.

"I am interested in education, that is, the idea of public education and universities for women." Caroline smiled brightly.

"Public education?" the older woman echoed in surprise.

"It is the foundation of any strong democracy, is it not? A populace that is literate and empowered to understand its own governance?"

"I was expecting you to express something of an interest in botany or the arts—but what a shocking revelation to think I have a reformer in my house!" Lady Fitzgerald's look was pure bemusement. "My late husband would have been enraged."

"I'm so sorry if—"

"Oh, no apologies! Anything that upset George was always welcome. But I had no idea American girls were so delightfully headstrong!" Lady Fitzgerald marveled. "Well, you must see yourself as a representative of your country! You have too much pluck, Miss Townsend, to play the dobbin."

"Thank you, Lady Fitzgerald. Pluck is always a dubious blessing, for I swear I am more often chided for my terrible manners than praised. But I am determined to prove myself worthy without losing my sense of spirit."

"Brava, Miss Townsend! You must not!"

"Then with your blessing, I shall stay as I am, and hope that if nothing else, I make a memorable impression on my new friends." By then, the women had completed the circuit of the room and returned to the arched entrance and her waiting guardian. Caroline's gaze found Ashe's as if to challenge him. *The man is looking absolutely resplendent over there, pretending not to care, but he meant to feed me to the intimidating Lady Fitzgerald alive and kicking, I have no doubt!*

"Let no one say a thing against my delightful discovery, my very own American!" Lady Fitzgerald announced to everyone nearby as she leaned forward and patted Caroline's hand as if she were now a pet. And then it was Ashe who received her infamous look full of admonishment. "She is your ward, Mr. Blackwell! It is certainly your responsibility, sir, to see to your charge's care and comforts! Can you not outfit the sweet thing?"

A muscle in Ashe's cheek ticked and betrayed his frustration, but he managed a polite enough reply. "Miss Townsend is quite unique, as you say, but also quite stubborn, Lady Fitzgerald. I wouldn't presume to tell a woman of such intractable habits how to dress—after all, what do I know of petticoats and other unmentionables?"

His last words were delivered with more of a playful air, and the women around the patio all giggled and colored in a theatrical show of shock. All the women except Caroline, who wasn't as happy imagining how much of an expert the handsome Ashe Blackwell was when it came to the innermost layers of a lady's wardrobe.

"What, indeed?" Lady Fitzgerald finally summoned a reply. "But I'm sure a man of your resources can rely on the expertise of a good couturier when it comes to the more delicate questions of a woman's underpinnings."

"Your ladyship!" Another woman stepped forward, her mouth pinched into a disapproving thin line. "I'm sure another topic of conversation would prove better suited for—"

"Don't be a ninny, Eustace!" Lady Fitzgerald curtly cut her off. "We're talking about acquiring a decent wardrobe for my friend, not debating what color her bloomers and stockings should be."

Eustace looked suitably chastised, and Caroline tried to give her a look of sympathy. A servant brought a tray of drinks out for the guests, and the lively conversation continued, although the elusive and ever naughty Mr. Blackwell was strangely muted.

"My American friend will win over London wearing cabbages, if she must!" Lady Fitzgerald asserted.

"I would rather not wear produce, your ladyship, but thank you for your confidence." Caroline took a sip of her punch, tasting the unmistakable bite of strong spirits in the mixture. Her nervousness faded from a strangling agony to a twinge of enjoyment—if only to see Ashe's disappointment in her small success at not being thrown out or burned in effigy as a mud-dwelling Colonial.

The rest of the afternoon passed in a blur for her as she made new acquaintances with the blessing of her new patroness and managed to elicit only a few more shocked gasps from the elderly Miss Eustace Woodberry before the party's conclusion. Ashe was her shadow, saying as little as possible as she navigated the myriad conversations and did her best to remember everyone's names—if not their ranks and relations. It was a labyrinth of social traps that Caroline was sure she was muddling beyond repair, but with Lady Fitzgerald at her elbow, all was forgiven and each misstep touted as Colonial charm.

Finally, he stepped forward to take her elbow. "I'm afraid we must be going, Lady Fitzgerald. Thank you for your hospitality."

"Your ward is a treasure, Mr. Blackwell. You'll have her matched before Christmas, I warrant," Lady Fitzgerald said.

"Oh, I'm not—" Caroline started to protest, but Ashe cut her off.

"It is my grandfather's fondest wish, your ladyship. Thank you, and good afternoon." He bowed at the waist, forcing Caroline to attempt a rusty curtsy at his side.

"Yes, thank you again, Lady Fitzgerald," Caroline added. "I do hope to see you again."

Lady Fitzgerald waved a farewell. "I'll have an eye on you, my dear, and I'm sure we'll see each other before long. Take care."

Ashe led her away, and Caroline swallowed a sigh of contentment. "What a lovely party!"

He nodded. "Riveting!" he said sarcastically. "Lord Breecher's intestinal issues were far more interesting than I'd have ever imagined. I don't think the man redirected the conversation away from his bowels for more than a minute the entire time."

"You couldn't have politely shifted away to talk to anyone else if it was so tedious?"

"And joined Mr. and Mrs. Claridge's forum on hygiene? Or the endless speculation about whether or not there will be another war affecting the price of their precious textiles?"

Their carriage was brought around, and Caroline took the hand he offered to help her into its interior. Once he was settled as well, she finally responded to his complaint. "Mr. Blackwell, it has always been my understanding that if you don't like the flavor of the conversation, you have the power to contribute your own antidotes and improve things considerably."

The look he gave her was less than appreciative. "The wisdom of youth and inexperience! I'll consider your advice the next time I'm out in society and at a loss for words."

Caroline bit the inside of her lip. "I'm sorry. That was impertinent of me."

His sulk barely lifted as he turned his gaze toward the window and did his best to dismiss her. The carriage ride back to his home was even quieter than their departure, but Caroline finally decided to try once more to break the silence. "It seems that Lady Fitzgerald admires my pluck, Mr. Blackwell."

"Pluck?" Ashe shook his head. "You're damned lucky that Lady Fitzgerald shares my grandfather's odd sense of humor."

"And misfortunate that you do not," she said, defiance making her brave.

"It could easily have gone the other way, Miss Townsend. You may want to keep in mind that as generous as Lady Fitzgerald may seem, that attention can be equally vicious if and when she tires of your *pluck*."

She lowered her eyes to her hands but caught herself quickly in this hint of submission. Instead, she sighed and looked at him directly with her best devil-may-care grin. "You are simply out of sorts because I wasn't the dismal failure you were secretly hoping I'd be."

"That's ridiculous!"

"You look like a pouting child from this vantage point, Mr. Blackwell. Perhaps your grandfather should have hired a nanny instead of a chaperone." It was a terrible goad, but Caroline couldn't take the words back—though she regretted them instantly.

Ashe's blue eyes changed to the hue of a winter sky and he stretched out his long legs to put his feet rudely up onto the seat next to her. "Your suggestion that I am jealous of the novelty of what can only be likened to a hairless cat at a dog show is interesting, Miss Townsend."

Her fingers clenched in her lap, her temper rising. "Is it?"

"Oh, yes. But let's make one thing clear, since our relationship as watcher and charge is relatively new." His look sent a chill down her spine, and Caroline's anger bled away in a wash of cold dread. "I am many things, Miss Townsend, first impressions and ridiculous arrangements aside, but I am not a child. Do not think to press me in that way."

"No, I shouldn't have. . . . No one would ever mistake you for a child, Mr. Blackwell." She took a slow deep breath. "But neither am I a hairless cat!"

The ice in his eyes gave way to a strange heat that made the carriage suddenly airless and far too small. Caroline felt as if she were perched on the seat wearing nothing but her small clothes, the way he now drank her in—a knowing, openly admiring look on his face.

"No, Miss Townsend. You are"—he hesitated, and Caroline was drawn in against her will, wishing he would say something kind and dreading it at the same time—"unpredictable and intriguing."

"Oh!" For once her wit abandoned her as the unexpected compliment left her feeling foolish for arguing with the man. "Well . . . I'd hate to add a lack of character to my list of faults, Mr. Blackwell."

"You're in no danger there. In fact, I'm sure Aunt Emilia would be appropriately shocked at all the delightful flash and pluck you've demonstrated."

"Aunt Emilia?" Caroline felt a new sense of confusion. "I don't recall mentioning my aunt to you."

He shifted back in his seat with a careless shrug, his gaze drifting back toward the carriage window. "My grandfather said something of her, I believe. She sounded like a formidable woman."

It seemed a feasible accounting for his comment, but there'd been something in the familiarity of his tone that made her feel as if he'd hinted at some confidence she'd shared. The topic of her aunt was not one she'd ever bandied about with strangers, far too fearful of repercussions and the petty vengeance that would have followed. Aunt Emilia was not a forgiving soul.

"Yes," she agreed reluctantly. "Formidable."

"Family is often a mixed blessing," he said as he turned back to her, once again the friendly warmth in his gaze as unsettling as the cold, causing a strange flutter to come to life inside of her. "But they're a strength not to be squandered."

Caroline had no desire to discuss her family, finding the subject too complex and painful to bear up to scrutiny. "Mr. Blackwell, do you mind if I ask why you allowed Lady Fitzgerald to think I was husband hunting? Is it really necessary to deceive her in that way?"

"Absolutely," he answered without hesitation. "Every woman under the age of one hundred is assumed to be in the pursuit of a husband, and no offense, but you are enough of a conversation piece without adding the unexplainable wrinkle of *not* seeking one."

"It's not unexplainable, Mr. Blackwell."

He smiled. "Trust me. There is not a dowager or a drudge within a thousand leagues who is going to accept any explanation you care to make, and proclaiming your desire to remain a spinster is only going to fuel the chase."

"I don't . . ." She wasn't sure what to say. Penniless teachers weren't permitted to dream of marriage, but Caroline wasn't going to confess anything to Ashe. It was clear he mistakenly believed as his grandfather did that she naturally possessed part of her family's vast fortune. *I don't desire to remain a spinster! And come to think of it, I don't think of myself as a spinster, Rogue! But the harder I protest the worse it sounds, so I think I'll rely on Sun Tzu again and choose this moment to retreat.* "Very well, I'll trust your judgment."

He raised an eyebrow in disbelief. "Really? You trust my judgment?"

"It's hard to argue with a man who has such a complete understanding of every woman under the age of one hundred." Caroline shook her head. "Besides, I feel compelled to show you that I'm capable of doing more than being contrary."

This time, she wasn't sure what to make of the change in his eyes; his stare was so provocative and stirring that Caroline forgot to breathe for a few seconds. It was a singular sensation to slip within the space of a heartbeat inside the searing cocoon of his attention.

Ashe hadn't moved any closer, but the carriage felt so much smaller as she was suddenly aware of his physical presence. In a rush, the color of the skin at his throat and the male lines and textures of his impossibly handsome face sent a wave of heat across her skin and down her spine, filling a pool between her hips. It was like having hot sand emptied into her stomach, a pleasant, tortuous tingle that made her thoughts scatter.

"I don't think you're aware of all of your capabilities, Miss Townsend," Ashe said, "and that makes your trust an extraordinary gift."

"I . . ." Caroline swallowed hard. "Anyone's trust . . . is a gift."

"I shall strive not to lose yours, Miss Townsend." As he spoke, the spell was broken, as if he'd deliberately pulled back the sensual power he wielded to release her. The carriage began to slow, and the world asserted itself again.

Chapter
5

❧

The following evening brought a different challenge for Ashe. Friends of his family, the Bedfords were less intimidating and expected to be more welcoming, but a dinner party meant his chaperone would have to navigate the delicate rules and etiquette of careful conversation. Lady Fitzgerald was a dragon, to be sure, but Caroline might miss the protective wrap of the old woman's claws.

In what he imagined was one of her better dresses, Miss Townsend hadn't disappointed his dismal expectations in a dark green poplin that promised to make sure every other woman at the party would outshine her. Lady Fitzgerald's admonitions to outfit Caroline hadn't fallen on deaf ears, but there hadn't been time to breech the topic—much less drag the girl to a shop and see to the grueling business.

The greater hindrance was that he'd been avoiding Miss Caroline Townsend like the plague since he'd nearly ravished her on the carriage ride home. The girl had no idea

how close she'd come to having her skirts pushed up and
those creamy thighs spread wide for him. Just the thought
of pressing her back against the cushioned seats and riding
her until she screamed in release was enough to make him
require another cold bath.

Endless daydreams about his sleepwalking houseguest,
and Ashe had endured no less than two cold baths in almost
as many days. The physical exhaustion of his engagement
with Rutherford at the sports club had been a welcome relief, and Michael had expressed some surprise when Ashe
had requested that they meet more often over the next few
weeks.

Ashe was determined to leave nothing to chance. He
would happily allow Rutherford to pummel him on a daily
basis if it kept him from forfeiting Bellewood to a leech
like Winston Yardley. Yardley was exactly the kind of man
who would think nothing of squatting like a toad on a dying relative's doorstep—only to enjoy the spoils and reach
across a coffin to demand his share. He'd insinuated himself into multiple households, becoming mysteriously "in-
dispensable" before his patron or patroness's demise. As
far as Ashe was concerned, he was an angel of death and
deserving of nothing so much as an icy shove out of the
path of humanity.

Defeating Yardley was motivation enough, but now he
had a new spur to drive him forward. *If I can salvage my
pride by not letting this impossible girl turn me into a rav-
ing lunatic before this is all over, I'll count myself a very
fortunate man.*

Michael, as usual, had been quick to lecture him about
the importance of not drawing too much attention this Season, wary of the quiet of the East India Company after their
last efforts to flush out the Jaded's members had failed so
miserably. The Company wanted nothing more than to get
their hands on the source of the Jaded's wealth and uncover
the rest of the treasure that they'd left behind after filling

their pockets in the raja's treasure room; but the Jaded's anonymity wasn't making it easy. Rutherford was completely unaware of Ashe's predicament and was simply reissuing a warning he'd given each of them with regular frequency since their group's return to England. But Ashe refused to live his life ready to jump at every shadow.

He'd calmly told Rutherford, "I've earned my death, like any man. But for once, I can promise you, unless an assassin is in collusion with my grandfather to kill me by depriving me of all my usual entertainments, I am safe this Season."

Most of the others had agreed that Galen's dangerous tangle with assassins over a year ago had probably been the worst of it, and since then, things had seemed to calm until it was Michael alone who remained convinced that they should always be on guard.

Hell, an attempted kidnapping or assassination might be a nice distraction, come to think of it! But I don't think my luck is going to hold for—

"I didn't think Americans bothered with anyone's society but their own," Caroline's dinner partner announced, the staunch old man giving the table a firm thump to underline his opinions and interrupting Ashe's reverie. "Especially since your country is far too immature to have developed much of a social sense, I would say, to even know the basic rules."

Poor Caroline! Mrs. Bedford has unintentionally seated you next to the world's grumpiest and openly hostile American hater in Great Britain, Colonel Rupert Stevenson— and I'd guess right about now, that pluck is about as thin a shield as the crystal on this table.

But the voice that answered Colonel Stevenson was clear and steady, the flat lilt of her accent all the more striking because of it. "Ah, but didn't we begin as Englishmen, sharing a common history? And can't the younger cousin wish to emulate their more dashing older relative—even if it is a bit naughty to try to fit into someone else's shoes after you've stepped on their toes?"

Colonel Stevenson's bluster lost a good deal of its momentum. "Dashing, you say? I'm not sure, but I think you just likened the entire matter to a waltz!"

"Why not?"

He shook his head, a slow smile breaking up the craggy ice of his features. "Better I should ask how it is possible to bring dancing slippers into such a conversation!"

"Well"—she tilted her head to one side, as if contemplating a puzzle—"I'd say when you have two partners who think to take the lead, it's inevitable that someone's toes will get bruised. But if, as you say, the younger of the pair hasn't learned all the nuances of the steps, then it would be the more experienced dancer who would be expected to be more cautious and try not to wound his fair cousin—isn't that right?"

"That would be the rule on the dance floor, but . . ."

"There must be some affection left between the two countries, Colonel Stevenson," she asserted.

"And what makes you say that?"

"Neither party is refusing the next dance."

And then it happened. Instead of throttling her or throwing down his fork, the old misogynist began to laugh at her audacious argument, practically infatuated.

"How is it, Miss Townsend, that you appear to be a woman with great humility, yet hold your own like a duchess? And when I think to dislike you for cheeky pride, you disarm me with the turns of a clever mind that would befit a man better than your soft frame!"

"You ask as if I am in charge of some great scheme, Colonel Stevenson. I assure you I meant only to attempt not to bore you to tears. I fear I am an embarrassment to my guardian when I behave too well."

The colonel threw back his head, laughing wholeheartedly in a contagious show of good humor. The entire table brightened at the exchange, even if they hadn't exactly heard what had amused the dour old man—except for Ashe, who pretended that his soup bowl was too fascinating to allow for distraction.

Seated at his right, Mrs. Lowery leaned forward, her delightful cleavage highlighted by the candlelight. "Your young American charge has quite a way with words, Mr. Blackwell."

"Do you think so?" Ashe pretended indifference.

"I take it you are not so . . ." She leaned in another inch, her voice lowering seductively. "Charmed with her ways as the colonel?"

He openly reassessed the "charms" Mrs. Lowery was pressing in his direction, the low décolletage of her evening gown leaving little to the imagination, smiling at the overt game of flirtation. *Never underestimate a married woman. . . .*

"I hadn't given her charms any notice," he answered, his voice lowering to match hers as if in confession. "I prefer women with more polish and with a bit of experience to match their beauty."

Mrs. Lowery almost purred. "I thought as much! You didn't strike me as the sort of man to bother with a pony when there are thoroughbreds aplenty eager for a ride."

Ah, the joys of a bold married woman. . . .

"Why, Mrs. Lowery! I didn't realize you were a woman who enjoyed the hunt." He deliberately let his eyes drop to the creamy mounds now inches away from his arm. "I confess, I rarely pass up an opportunity to sit in the saddle."

Mrs. Lowery beamed, and Ashe felt the familiar heat in his spine begin to increase at the prospect of a harmless romp. What scandal here, if the lady was willing and discreet?

"Your reputation as a skilled hunter precedes you, Mr. Blackwell." Mrs. Lowery lifted her glass for a ladylike sip of wine that only highlighted the plump curves of her lips.

"I, for one, am pleased to think I might have the chance to see for myself if it is well earned."

Ashe lifted his own glass, discreetly glancing about to make sure that their heated exchange wasn't drawing any undue attention. But the other dinner guests all seemed enthralled in their own conversations, and their host, Mr. Bedford, was expounding at length from his position at the opposite end of the table on the social ramifications of a machine that could make envelopes.

And to think I thought the evening was going to hold no entertainment.

Ashe returned his full attention back to Mrs. Lowery. She was a classic English beauty, golden curls and heavy-lidded blue eyes, though a bit too mature to be mistaken for the porcelain doll that fashion upheld as a standard to be imitated. But Ashe had never preferred dolls.

His tastes demanded something far more alive and distracting.

Before he could voice a reply to Mrs. Lowery's challenge, Mr. Bedford stood to release his guests, either to port and cigars in the library or to entertain themselves in the drawing room with music and cards. "I trust you to find your own pleasures!" he announced grandly, with a cheerful wave.

Ashe bit the inside of his mouth to keep from laughing as his chaperone was almost immediately drawn off by the colonel toward the drawing room for what promised to be the driest lesson on whist any human being had ever submitted to. She gave Ashe a subtle look, pleading for rescue, but he pretended to notice nothing of her dilemma and instead waved happily as if in blessing. *Ah, the delights of civilized company, Miss Townsend! Just try not to slip into a coma!*

"Would you care to join me for a bit of fresh air, Mr. Blackwell?" Mrs. Lowery invited him. "I understood you weren't much of a smoker."

"So true," he said. "It is one bad habit I have failed to acquire, and if given the alternative of an evening stroll, how can I refuse?"

She stood, turning to make sure he could admire more of her elegant figure as she left her chair. "You couldn't, Mr. Blackwell. Not without forfeiting a hard-won reputation as a gentleman."

He stood with her, offering her his arm as they made their way toward the open doors onto the balcony that ran the length of the back of Bedford's town home. He escorted her out into the colder night air and out toward the rail as if to assess the garden below.

"So, tell me, Mr. Blackwell, do all American heiresses dress like servants or is your ward unique?"

"Did you really wish to discuss Miss Townsend, Mrs. Lowery?" He leaned in closer, subtly pressing her up against the balcony railing in a shadowed corner. "If so, I'm going to be terribly disappointed."

"Oh, no! Was there"—she pursed her lips an inviting pout—"another topic you preferred?"

"I thought you were interested in the hunt."

"I am. But to sample your skills as a hunter, does that mean I need to run away?" She batted her eyes, but the imitation of a wary coquette was too clumsy, and Ashe found some of his ardor cooling.

"How fast can you run?" he asked, reaching up to rearrange one golden blonde curl so that it would lightly caress her collarbone. It was an old trick, this touching without touching, but the little gasp it elicited helped to remind him how much he enjoyed the game.

She tipped her face up toward his, clearly not inclined to flee. "In these slippers? This gown? I shall have to forfeit before the race is even begun, sir."

"I like a woman who knows how to yield gracefully." Ashe bent over to claim a kiss, a rote conquest, but he wasn't complaining. *It's been too long, damn it.*

"Ahem." A voice behind the pair interrupted his plans to taste Mrs. Lowery's lips. "How lucky to find you here, Mr. Blackwell!"

He stepped back from the lady with a grimace and turned slowly around to face his current nemesis. "Yes, indeed. How lucky!" he answered, his tone dripping with sarcasm.

A miffed snort from behind him revealed that Mrs. Lowery was equally displeased at the interruption. "Luck has nothing to do with it, if you ask me."

"It seems I have no head for whist, Mr. Blackwell," Caroline went on cheerfully, ignoring the dispositions of her audience. "Perhaps you could take my place at the table and avert catastrophe."

Ashe almost groaned. "I'm in no mood for games."

"Really?" she asked, the barb at the end of the innocent question impossible to miss. "I was sure you thought of yourself as something of an expert."

Mrs. Lowery stepped out from behind him. "I'm sure Mrs. Bedford would be only too happy to guide you, my dear. Why don't you return to the drawing room and inquire?"

"Oh, Mrs. Lowery! I didn't see you there!" Caroline's mock surprise was almost comical, and Ashe had to bite the inside of his cheek to keep from smiling—before reminding himself that the entire scene was hardly a laughing matter. "I believe Mr. Saunders was just looking for you! Shall I tell him I found you? I'm sure he'll be ever so pleased!"

Mrs. Lowery's sharp intake of breath spoke volumes.

The huntress had more than one horse in contention—and this could get ugly very quickly if Saunders catches on. The terrier had teeth!

"No, I'll . . . join him in the drawing room. If you'll excuse me." She curtsied, the crisp speed of it betraying her agitation, before she left them alone without a backward glance.

Caroline crossed her arms as she watched the woman

retreat and then looked back to him, an unapologetic expression on her face. "Well?"

"Well, nothing, Miss Townsend. I'll be damned if we're going to have this conversation now." Ashe stepped forward, holding out his arm. A thread of anger began to weave its way into his tone, spurred by the embarrassment of being schooled in front of a woman. "I'll escort you back so that you can make your apologies and claim to have a headache precipitating our early departure."

"I do not have a headache, Mr. Blackwell."

"No, you *are* a headache, Miss Townsend, but in any case, you will do as you're told or I will throw you over my shoulder and carry you out kicking and screaming if need be." He lifted his arm one inch, daring her to defy him. "Well?"

He thought for a fleeting moment that she would try to rebel, but she withered slightly under his fiery glare and meekly took his arm.

"I should warn you that I am a terrible liar, Mr. Blackwell."

"Then say nothing and leave it to me." He began to lead her back inside. "If you keep your eyes on the floor, they'll assume you're miserable."

"I don't see why I'm the one being ushered out like a child to be punished. It's not as if I'm the one who was—"

"Not. Here." Ashe increased his pace, determined to hold his own until they were safely away. And then he was going to make sure they reviewed the rules of guardian and ward!

The escape was swift and easier than he'd anticipated as he made his excuses and hurried a mortified Caroline out of the Bedfords' home and down to the waiting carriage.

* * *

Once they'd pulled away from the drive, Ashe made his displeasure clear. "A young woman who is posing as a man's ward shouldn't just walk up and imperiously order him about!"

"Rude and boorish men who are in need of a chaperone shouldn't openly play the part of the fool and expect not to get a pinch." Caroline smoothed out the soft gray silk of her skirts a little too forcefully to hide her ire. "A married woman! What in the world possessed you?"

"Flirtation is hardly criminal, and in my experience, a woman's marital status has nothing to do with her delight in the practice," he said, openly unconcerned. "Or her age, for that matter."

"If the measurement for prohibiting a thing is its criminality, Mr. Blackwell, then you've set the bar extremely low for yourself!" she bit back, unafraid.

His hands fisted against his thighs, and Caroline steeled herself for battle.

"Miss Townsend, you overstep!" he growled.

"By asking you to consider how horrifying it would have been if it truly had been Mr. Saunders who had discovered you? Or even the Bedfords? By inquiring what witty excuse you'd have given them for dallying with that woman on a dark, cold balcony when every other respectable guest was accounted for inside?"

He seemed to hesitate, and Caroline watched the mercurial change in his eyes as they thawed with his mood. "Was Saunders truly looking for her?"

Caroline wished she really were a better liar but decided the truth was all she had. "N-no, not exactly, but it was clear he expected her to appear at any moment."

"A good guess, since Mrs. Lowery's reaction confirmed it."

"It wasn't as if the woman was subtle, Mr. Blackwell." Caroline sighed, some of her own frustration bleeding through into her words.

He shook his head. "Subtlety is overrated and stop looking at me like that. I think I had a tutor once who used to give me that look over the rim of his spectacles when I'd failed to memorize a lesson."

Caroline tried not to smile. *How is it possible he can be so disarming when I should be railing against him for so rudely dragging me from the Bedfords as if I'm the one who'd done something wrong? How is it possible that I'm starting to feel as if I'm the one trespassing?* "It's a look you're earning, sir."

"You overreact to a simple flirtation, Miss Townsend."

"Simple flirtation? You were kissing that woman!"

He shook his head. "I was *about* to kiss that woman, and it is sad to me that you cannot tell the difference. A tragedy, actually, that a woman your age could make such a mistake."

She squeaked in protest at the "woman your age," as if twenty-four were some decrepit measure of time. "I fail to see a single element of tragedy in not being able to interpret the subtle nuances of you mashing up against a *married* woman where anyone could have discovered you!"

"Mashing up against?" he asked, lifting a hand to his chest in a melodramatic show of mortification. "I was mashing?"

"You—" She stopped to take a breath and attempt to rein in her temper. "You are entirely cognizant of what you were doing, Mr. Blackwell."

"Not if it looked like mashing! I must be getting rusty." The man displayed no trace of regret but instead was managing to sound a bit hurt at her choice of words. "Then again"—his blue eyes settled on her with an unspoken purpose, and Caroline suddenly found it harder to breathe—"the easiest course may be to repair your lack of education."

"M-my education is not lacking for—"

"Have you ever been kissed, Miss Townsend?"

Oh, God. An impossible question from an impossible man—and I think I've inadvertently answered him by sit-

ting here like a dunce with my cheeks getting warmer by the second. "Yes, I have!" she blurted out the lie, instinctively trying too late to save face, and regretted it instantly.

He didn't blink, but instead smiled, a slow, sensual smile that mocked her proclamation. "Truly and thoroughly?" he asked.

She had no idea what that might mean, but she was too far into the ruse to give it up without sacrificing her pride. "I don't see how that is any of your affair!"

He leaned forward. "You really are a terrible liar, Miss Townsend."

A crisp denial bled away as his proximity unraveled her composure. It was so unexpected to be at the center of his attentions and to feel the first flush of his masculine powers. She'd dubbed Mrs. Lowery a fool, but now, there was nothing foolish about her own desire to understand what it would be like to be "truly and thoroughly" kissed by Ashe Blackwell. Every sensible thought of how inappropriate it was to even allow him to encroach slipped out of her reach as the male scents of sandalwood and cinnamon worked their magic.

He was inches away, and the uneven stones beneath the carriage made every sway and lurch of the compartment his accomplice. She held her place, unwilling to stop him, fear and anticipation warring inside of her. There would be no going back. Afterward, she would have to say something, do something, slap his beautiful face in an antiquated ritual of outrage that she wasn't sure she felt—but all that was for after this kiss.

Her eyes fluttered closed, and the world seemed to narrow to the sweet fan of his breath intermingling with hers.

The carriage stopped and Caroline opened her eyes in a rush of embarrassment as she realized that they'd arrived back at the brownstone and that Ashe was now looking at her with a look of pure triumph as he innocently sat back against the seats.

"You!" She wasn't sure what to accuse him of—but indignation nearly choked her.

He laughed softly. "Perhaps now you'll have a little more sympathy for poor Mrs. Lowery!"

Before she could think of a cutting reply, the footman had come to open the carriage door and Ashe had gracefully unfolded to climb out and offer her a hand down from the vehicle.

Caroline had no choice but to step out of the carriage. She wasn't about to throw a scene in front of the servants, but the urge to shove the man over onto his smug English behind was almost more than she could forbear.

Ashe watched her storm into the house, head held high, and shook his head. Once again, he'd pushed her further than was wise, and truly, he wasn't sure why he'd done it. There had simply been something elusively irresistible about the terrier lecturing him on "mashing," of all things!

Chapter
6

"I apologize for . . . any misbehavior last night." Ashe smiled. "Flirting is like a breath of scented air in a musty closed room for some people. Perhaps I inhaled a bit too deeply."

Morning light flooded the dining room, touching on the silver and china of the elegant breakfast table laid out before them. Caroline had been pushing around her eggs and trying not to look at Ashe, but his apology surprised her. Clearly, he was referring to his encounter with Mrs. Lowery and not necessarily to their fleeting nonencounter in the carriage. Last night after he'd schooled her on his charms, she'd locked herself in her room and spent most of the night pacing.

She'd never felt so foolish in her life. One look from the man and everything she'd valued about herself—her self-discipline, control, and intelligence—had vanished.

Hours of blaming Ashe had given way to the miserable conclusion that she was the only one who could solve the problem. And that was by never again deluding herself that a man like Ashe Blackwell would do more than toy with her. If the rogue had power, it was because she'd given it to him. And as dawn had broken, Caroline Townsend of Boston, Massachusetts, had determined that it was time to reclaim her own independence and remember her place in the world.

"It *was* a musty room," she admitted, unable to stop a smile as Mr. Bedford's endless descriptions of mundane industrial wonders came to mind.

"And you'll be pleased to note that I reconsidered your scolding and I've decided to renew my vows to toe the line," he said.

"Oh, really?" Caroline almost dropped her spoon. "Did I say something profound?"

"You must have." He shrugged his shoulders, a man disarmed. "Or the ghost of Mr. Withers, my old tutor, must have, for I've awoken with new determination."

"Well, I should thank Mr. Withers, or more likely, Mrs. Lowery. She's reminded me not to become too distracted to leave you alone for moonlit strolls." *Not that you were alone, scoundrel!*

"Was Colonel Stevenson such a distraction? My goodness, I didn't think the old bird had it in him!" he teased.

"Oh, please!" She tried not to laugh. "Truce, Mr. Blackwell."

He held up his right hand, as if to add to the weight of their détente with a wry oath. "Truce, Miss Townsend." He refilled her teacup, serving her as naturally as if they were the oldest and dearest of companions. "So, let's see if we can start over on a more cordial note and pretend to have met under more ordinary circumstances."

"I would like that." *As if any meeting with Ashe Blackwell would have felt ordinary.* "Was Mr. Withers a bit of a tyrant?"

"He tried to be," Ashe said. "But once I learned he had a penchant for brandy, we became the best of friends."

"Did you ply your own tutor with brandy?" she asked in astonishment.

"Of course not! I was ten!" His protest was humorous. "But I knew enough to have a bottle secretly sent to his rooms on the nights before I knew the weather would be fine enough for fishing and games."

"If it were anyone else, I'd not believe a word of it." She stirred her tea. "I once had a teacher, a Mr. O'Connor, who was well-known for sleeping through his lessons, except now I'm wondering if one of the other students didn't have your same clever ideas."

"Ah! Every young man's dream of the ideal instructor is one who can snooze through a Latin lesson!" he said.

Caroline smiled over the rim of her teacup. "I take it you were not the ideal student then?"

"Hardly!" he confessed without a trace of guilt. "I take it you *were* an ideal student then?"

"It was such a gift! My male cousins hated their tutors, but I remember counting the hours until they would come again. Every minute I could steal away with my books was . . . heaven." She spoke without thinking, instantly aware of how odd she sounded. "I took advantage of whatever education I could seize upon."

"Why? Wasn't your life and fortune advantage enough? Why not paint teacups and learn how to embroider?"

Caroline shook her head, accepting his natural curiosity but wishing to deflect it without revealing too much of her personal woes. "Not every woman is fulfilled by painting on porcelain. My situation is unique, Mr. Blackwell, but suffice it to say, I would prefer to make my own way in the world. My parents always stressed the value of independence and self-reliance, and after they died, those traits have served me well."

"We have something in common, you and I."

His response surprised her, and Caroline could feel her

face warming at the lack of censure in his eyes. "And what is that?"

"Besides losing our parents, I'd say that neither one of us has shied away from seeking our own path. My grandfather may grumble, but I have never wanted to rely on his wealth or his approval for my happiness." He then reached over to offer her a tray of kippers. "Would you care for a kipper?"

She laughed softly, the change in conversation to a mundane offer of fish too strange not to strike her as funny. "Yes, thank you!"

"Ah! There, you see? It never fails! Nothing cheers a woman like kippers for breakfast."

Caroline felt some of her good humor evaporate at his inadvertent reference to the endless parade of women who had undoubtedly enjoyed a more scandalous breakfast with the man. It was enough to bring her back to reality with a cold snap.

"They're very delicious," she intoned quietly.

"Now, there's a solemn endorsement," he said, heaping his own plate high. "I'll have Godwin tell the cook to make sure you have them at every meal."

"I'm sorry. They *are* delicious, Mr. Blackwell, and please don't torture dear Ellie. She might miss the subtle sarcasm and you'll spoil her menu for the week. I understand from her assistant she's gone to a great deal of trouble to try to impress you on your return."

"Ellie?" he gave her a quizzical look then smiled, and Caroline's breath caught in her throat at the strange power of it. "I'd forgotten that my grandfather had mentioned that you have a talent for getting to know the staff. He was very struck by it, Miss Townsend, as am I—so long as you don't go instigating rebellions!"

"It was never my intention, Mr. Blackwell. But only tyrants need worry about revolutions, isn't that right?"

He laughed outright. "You are too quick for me! God help the man who thinks to outwit you, Miss Townsend."

Is everything with this man about conquest and contests? Caroline's eyes dropped to the kippers, unwilling to challenge him and end the strange truce between them.

"I've arranged for a ride this afternoon," he went on, pushing his own plate aside. "The weather is unseasonably warm and, after all, what is a social Season without a ride through one of our famous parks?"

Her hands fisted so tightly beneath the table, they began to ache. This time she would be forced to admit an inadequacy to him—and there was no softening the news. "I cannot ride, Mr. Blackwell."

"Pardon me." He cleared his throat. "Not at all?"

"Not at all."

The flash of stunned horror in his eyes was something to behold, but he mastered himself well and rallied to ring the bell on the table. "I'll have Godwin tell the stableman to arrange for an open carriage instead."

"Is the carriage open to allow me to look at London's finest, or for them to look at me?"

"A mutual study is inevitable," Ashe agreed with a wry grin. "And what do you think so far of London's elite?"

She shrugged. "They seem ordinary enough, and perhaps that's a pleasant surprise."

"Ordinary?" he asked in astonishment. "You cannot be serious."

"Of course I am. I've not found anyone to be inherently superior, Mr. Blackwell—not in taste, or conversation, or education. They seem to think more highly of themselves than is warranted, but then that's hardly their fault. Everything seems arranged for them to believe that blood alone determines worth."

"That confirms it—you are a revolutionary."

"I'm an American."

"Ah! It's the same thing!" He laughed. "And I suppose

at home, only the most tasteful, witty, and educated people rise to power and wealth."

"Life is never so fair, Mr. Blackwell. Human nature doesn't vary with geography."

Ashe sighed. "Now, there's a pearl of wisdom. My friend Darius will want that carved over every Jaded's doorway."

"Jaded's?" she asked.

"A silly term for a social circle consisting of a few boring men in my acquaintance." Ashe waved the question away. "On a different and brighter note, I also thought we might consider another excursion for tomorrow morning. What do you say to a bit of shopping, Miss Townsend?"

"Shopping?" Caroline set down her fork, feeling instantly wary at his friendly tone. "What sort of shopping?"

"The sort I understand young women enjoy," he replied as he rose from the table to stretch his legs. "A new wardrobe for your first visit to Town!"

"Clothes?"

"You say the word as if I'd just asked you to taste eel oil." His blue eyes darkened a bit, and she knew she'd surprised him . . . unpleasantly.

"No, clothes are—hardly fish oil. It's just—"

"I thought it would please you. I've made inquiries into the best shops and arranged for appointments for you tomorrow morning."

"I realize my wardrobe isn't exactly"—she took a deep breath before going on—"up to your standards, but I can assure you, Mr. Blackwell, that I couldn't possibly allow you to buy me clothes."

"Why in the world not?"

"It isn't proper."

"I'm getting lectures to the contrary everywhere we go, Miss Townsend. What the hell isn't proper about a man buying clothes for his ward?"

"I am not your ward!"

"Well, since you're the only one who knows that besides my grandfather, that logic isn't going to hold, Miss Townsend!"

Caroline's arguments stumbled as she realized that he was right. Even so, it was difficult to allow him the liberty. . . . "You're right. But if you are doing it to please me, then I shall release you from that burden here and now. I don't need new clothes."

"Like hell you don't!"

"Language, Mr. Blackwell!"

"Very well." He let out a long, painful sigh. "Since you are determined to rob me of my diplomatic approach to the subject, I shall be extremely direct and frank about this matter."

"As you wish."

"You look like a mud wren, Miss Townsend, and have been mistaken more than once for a servant. Now, while this may suit some perverse American sense of martyrdom when it comes to fashion, I have to beg you to see reason. You are in my care, whether you like it or not. And your appearance reflects on that care. At this point, everyone seems to think I'm the cruelest and most frugal guardian they've ever met."

"They cannot possibly think such a thing!"

"They can, dear little Quaker, and it will certainly only get worse as we proceed," he corrected her. "And since you are supposedly determined to prevent scandals connected to my name, I am finding it hard to believe that you would fuel this particular danger."

"It's not that I wish to fuel any rumor! But . . ." She lost her thought, caught in a miserable web of embarrassment and pride. She had no money of her own, but admitting such a thing to Ashe was out of the question. "I don't care what anyone thinks about my bonnets, Mr. Blackwell."

"My grandfather expressly instructed me to see to you." He crossed his arms, his expression one of quiet resolve.

"Perhaps"—she took a deep breath—"if you allowed me to repay you for the expense."

One eyebrow raised before he replied, "No. And I say no only because I'm going to find it distasteful to negotiate every damn bit of cloth with a woman who by the looks of things doesn't comprehend the value of sundries and silks. There will be nothing practical in this new wardrobe, Miss Townsend, and may I say, you are the first woman I have ever met who required an argument to go shopping."

"I don't want to be in your debt, Mr. Blackwell."

"You won't be."

Caroline felt a strange stop in the conversation at the unlikely turn. "I won't be? How is it that you are going to buy me a new wardrobe that you will not let me repay you for, and I won't be in your debt?"

"You'll be doing me a favor by giving in. And so, technically, I will be in your debt when this business is over."

"No one else would see it that way. And if . . ." She bit her lower lip, but then went on determined not to leave anything unspoken. "I won't turn a blind eye to any more flirtations, Ashe, in exchange for this *favor*. I won't be purchased with a few yards of fabric."

"I'm not trying to buy you, Miss Townsend. I'm trying to dress you so that you don't look like a woman freshly escaped from a workhouse."

"You're exaggerating!"

"No, I'm being direct and frank. And since that approach seems to have the greatest advantage when it comes to your Colonial sensibilities, I'm determined to win the day."

And once again, it's a contest between us. "If I submit to do you a favor, it's a hollow victory, Mr. Blackwell."

"I'll take victory on any terms when it comes to you."

Somehow it was a compliment when he spoke the words, and Caroline knew she'd already yielded to his wishes. "Very well." She smiled. "You win."

"You are a unique woman, Miss Townsend."

"I hardly think so."

"You manage to be passionate about so many things, yet instead of being abrasive, you make it refreshing—as if arguing about the nature of a woman's character is the very essence of charm."

"You're not used to women offering you a lively debate now and then?"

Ashe laughed. "Women of good breeding do not debate, and those that do aren't of a certain class or station. . . . Well, let's just say, I don't think I've wasted time with any woman who wasn't agreeable to my proposals."

Caroline felt some of her good humor fade. She stood from the table, preparing to retreat. *Ah, all those agreeable women . . . He's too handsome to gain an argument from any sporting woman and I doubt that's what he would have paid them for anyway. As for the others, who could blame them?* "How sad for you, Mr. Blackwell. Well, I think I'll head upstairs and explore your library for a while before our carriage ride."

"Wait." He took a step closer, his eyes darkening with regret. "I've done it again. The instant you start to let down your guard, I speak without thinking and ruin it."

"You ruin nothing." She swallowed hard, hating the lump in her throat and the effect his sympathy had on her. "I'm glad I can provide you the free entertainment of a good argument now and then."

"You do more than that, Miss Townsend."

She sensed there was another meaning to his words but didn't dare ask. The truce was forgotten, and Caroline turned and left him to head to the library, wishing that mud wrens would stop secretly hoping to transform into cardinals.

* * *

The carriage ride through the park hadn't been as painful as he'd expected. Not that he'd worried excessively about the ever "charming" American Quaker sitting across from him wearing that same wool coat and wretched straw bonnet she favored. She was the most eccentric creature he'd ever met. Instead it was his own skin he'd worried about most. It was an unseasonably pleasant day, and he'd forced her out to make the best of it. To be seen riding in Hyde Park was the most mundane but palatably public activity he could undertake and it had put him squarely in the sights of his peers as a man reformed and apparently returned to good society.

They'd avoided the worst of the congestion on Rotten Row, but everyone seemed to be out to make sure that they could see who else was out. The polite stares and arch nods made him feel like a prize bull on the auction block, but Ashe distracted himself with Caroline's refreshingly strange opinions on everything from liveries to political reforms. He deliberately allowed the conversation to flow away from the emotionally charged topic of their arrangement—and was rewarded with a more relaxed and animated companion for the afternoon.

Like Colonel Stevenson, he'd been thrown off by how surprisingly self-possessed she was, and he'd forgotten to be shocked or affronted by her forward manner and unfashionable ways.

You're more of an entanglement than I ever envisioned, Caroline—and if I can survive having you as a chaperone, I think I can withstand almost anything.

But as the carriage rolled slowly down the manicured drive, Ashe watched the passing pedestrians and riders with new eyes, wondering if the solution to his problems with the cumbersome Miss Townsend wasn't in front of him the whole time.

Lady Fitzgerald had assumed they were husband hunting, and there was no reason to deny it. But perhaps he had a reason to give the rumor more credence—or at least, appear to make an effort. After all, as her guardian, it was only right that he'd be on the lookout for potential husbands, so perhaps instead of warning his friends off, he should have looked at them as viable distractions for the terrier. Galen's wife could even step in on occasion as a chaperone to augment their mission.

The terrier deserved a bit of fun, didn't she? And if it meant he could abstain from a few bone-dry outings, Ashe was all for it. He doubted she would protest, but then, he hardly needed her permission. And if all went as he envisioned it, she would simply see all of the introductions and activity as part of a London Season.

Truth be told, he really had had a revelation after almost kissing her last night. He'd initiated the game to demonstrate his mastery and power over her, only to end up putting himself through hell. It was one thing to have her teasing him as she wandered in her sleep, but he had no such excuse for putting himself in the fire wide awake and in control of his faculties. He'd angered her, but at no small personal cost. He'd ended up putting himself through long punishing hours of sexual frustration that had forced him to fist his own randy flesh to release no less than three times before dawn.

Ashe had finally concluded that there was too much at stake to allow for any more nonsense. *My desire for the lady is beginning to cloud my judgment and it's time to get control of the situation.*

He'd made his amends this morning, and no matter how the terrier squeaked, he was going to see her dressed as befitted her station and his plans for her. Warring with her was winning him no ground, and he'd decided in a state of grueling exhaustion that it was time to apply more subtle tactics.

He didn't want to present any real suitors since he didn't know how his grandfather would stand on the matter—and he certainly didn't want Miss Caroline Townsend permanently part of his world. *Not if I cannot have her. . . .* She was unsettling enough in passing without thinking of running into the unlikely siren at every single turn of the seasonal wheel. Instead, the idea of tasking someone he could trust with an innocent attempt to draw her off and keep her better entertained was far more comforting.

Darius.

Darius was the candidate that came immediately to mind. He seemed to love his books more than other men loved wine and women—and he would be perfect for her. He was a practical scholar who could while away endless hours in happy debate and gift Ashe with a few hours of peace.

And he would keep his hands to himself if I asked him to. And why I'm going to ask is something I'm not going to dwell on. It's not as if I'm in any position to make a claim—but the thought of any other man touching her, enjoying what I can't, is impossible.

Impossible!

From the moment I agreed to this Season, I should have known that nothing would be easy.

He couldn't say what she was or was not. Terrier, eccentric heiress, siren—Caroline Townsend was a formidable obstacle and there would be no ignoring her. But Ashe was determined not to make the mistake of underestimating her.

Chapter

7

❧

"It's too late at night for a game of chess, so if you've summoned me for one of your escapades"—Darius held up his hands defensively as he came into the first-floor study—"then I'll save you the trouble and let you know that I'm not interested."

"No escapades, my friend. I have decided to abstain from immoral excursions for a while and see how the world looks from your eyes." Ashe moved over to the sideboard and poured them both a glass of port.

Darius shook his head. "I'm no paragon of virtue, so whatever game you're playing, I'll go ahead and yield."

"You're too quick to capitulate. Though I do have a favor to ask, so it's encouraging to know you're in such a winnable mood." Ashe held out one of the glasses as if it were a small peace offering. "Nothing shocking or dishonorable, Darius, you have my word."

"You are many things, Ashe, but you were never dishonorable." Darius accepted the glass, his forest green eyes reflecting the simple sentiment. They'd been best friends since their imprisonment in India, and while opposites in many ways, theirs was an unbreakable bond.

"Thank you, Darius." He squared his shoulders. "You see, it seems I'm to make a civilized appearance in society this year. I have vowed to avoid all traces of scandal and attend every boring function and party a man can stomach."

"And what does Michael think of your new vow?"

"Rutherford would prefer if we all moved to remote parts of Scotland and kept to ourselves until the next century, just to be safe. We need to find the man a new hobby, Darius."

Darius laughed. "True. And while the life of an eccentric hermit might suit some of us more than others, I don't think the Jaded will be retreating any time soon." His smile faded as the topic brought back painful memories. "There was talk at White's about the Company's eagerness to top their gift of the Kohinoor to the queen. The prestige and wealth of it has given them a taste for more and fired up more than one man's imagination in a direction that is making Michael unhappy."

The Kohinoor was the world's largest diamond and was "acquired" by the East India Company and given as a gift to Her Majesty several years before. It was the size of a man's fist before it had been recut to become part of the crown jewels.

The lore behind the stones of India was the stuff of fairy tales and myth, but it did make Ashe think about his own cache hidden away beneath the floorboards under his mother's pianoforte.

God, wouldn't those star sapphires suit the terrier?

He'd never given even a fleeting thought to bringing them out for anyone else, but the idea of it coalesced into an unbidden sexual fantasy about shocking the prim American right out of her clothes and into a necklace dripping with sapphires to stretch her out across his bed. Then a hundred erotic images followed, each more taboo than the last. . . .

Unaware, Darius continued, "The Company does like to recover 'lost treasure' whenever they can. And now it seems Galen's old nemesis, Rand Bascombe, actually intends to personally mount an expedition to India."

Ashe cleared his throat and forced himself back to the topic at hand. "He'll faint after a week in the heat and humidity, get some fever, and limp home proclaiming himself a hero," Ashe said, dismissing the dangers. "To hell with Bascombe! If he's on the other side of the globe at the bidding of his cronies in the East India Company, then he's not here. What could be more perfect?"

"All right, enough of Bascombe! Tell me more about this favor. Does it have anything to do with your recent reforms?"

Oh, yes. The favor—let's try the direct approach.

"I've taken on a ward, at my grandfather's request, and I was hoping you could lend a hand. The role of guardian is new to me, but I was thinking that the girl deserves a cheerful Season, and you're a man I could trust to entertain her without any difficulties."

Darius's look of shock was priceless. "A ward? And you wish me to entertain her?"

"Just attend a few of the same functions and act as a friendly face in the crowd." Ashe finished his port. "I'm not asking you to court the creature."

"The creature?" Darius expression became more grim. "Ashe, as much as I owe you, I don't think—"

"Her name is Caroline Townsend and she's charming! She's American and she has an intellect that will keep even you racing to keep up! And she's"—Ashe took a deep breath—"very pretty once you get past her propensity to wear clothes that make my housekeeper look like a dancing girl in comparison."

Darius shook his head slowly. "She sounds delightful,

but wouldn't Josiah be a better choice? He has that mournful artistic disposition that ladies seem to swoon over."

"No. Caroline is far too cerebral to be bothered with a man who sighs too much. You're the smartest man I know, Darius, and not uneasy on a woman's eyes. Surely you can keep her occupied with endless banter about the structure of ancient religions and their correlation to architecture and whatnot."

"I'm flattered," Darius said, in a tone that made it clear he wasn't. "However, I'm not sure. This feels . . . deceptive, somehow."

"Nonsense! There's nothing more straightforward than introducing a friend to my current charge."

Darius smiled, openly skeptical. "If it were a straightforward situation, you'd have simply invited me to something and made a casual introduction. Instead, you've summoned me late at night to ask me a 'favor' and requested that I 'entertain' this girl—obviously to achieve some unspoken goal of your own."

Ashe realized he may have underestimated his friend's perceptive powers. "I thought it would be wiser to speak to you ahead of time, rather than surprise you with the situation in public and risk a misunderstanding. I'm not trying to make a match! I just want to create an innocent diversion."

"A diversion from what?"

"Damn it, Darius! Are you going to help me or not?"

Darius sighed. "I will, but I'm not going to dishonor myself and cavort around like an idiot. If you're asking me to play with this young woman's affections, then I'll excuse myself and wait for the next requested favor to prove my loyalty."

"I don't want you to toy with her, Darius. Just meet her and present yourself as an ally. I'm not . . ." Ashe wasn't sure how to phrase the strange dilemma he was in. Caroline was far more than a thorn in his side—she was becoming an eminent threat to his sanity. If Darius could distract her and mute their conflict, it was worth any price. "I am not in a position to be her friend."

"Don't misinterpret what I'm about to say, Ashe, but this diversion . . . Do you have designs on the girl?"

"God, no!" Ashe blurted out, surprised at the intensity of his own tone fueled by the lingering fantasy of those pert breasts divided by a gold rope of sapphires while he spent himself against her silky ass. *I'm losing my mind!* He closed his eyes and took a slow deep breath and then tried again. "It's simple, really. I'm honor-bound to behave, Darius, and frankly, without going into details, trespassing with Miss Townsend would be tantamount to the worst kind of self-sabotage."

"I see," Darius nodded slowly.

"Not to mention that she dislikes me and I'm in no rush to remedy the situation."

"Really? A woman who dislikes you?"

"Oh, stop!" Ashe stretched out his legs. "She's as proper a thing as you are, if not more so, and you remember what extreme circumstances it took to cement *our* friendship."

"A year or two in a dungeon." Darius smiled. "But you're right, I don't think I'd recommend it to the lady."

"Then it's settled." Ashe sat up in his chair. "We're attending a ball at Worthley's in four days and I'll see that you have your invitation in time."

Darius squared his shoulders, a man facing his execution. "I hate balls."

"Perfect! Because although I haven't asked the girl, if my luck holds, she shares your sentiment," Ashe said, holding out his hand to his friend, ultimately sealing their bargain. "I'd bet a thousand pounds she can't dance, Darius, so you've nothing to fear."

Darius took it slowly, accepting his fate. "I'll count the hours."

As will I, dear man. As will I.

* * *

An hour or so after they'd parted, Ashe considered his friend's sense of honor and felt a twinge of remorse. He was in this tangle for all the wrong reasons and it had been too long since his own sense of honor had stirred him to action. *For all the good that it had done me.* The memories were too painful to sustain, and Ashe wasn't going to allow them to overpower him. God, he was aching for release, a mindless surge of pleasure that would wipe out the ghosts of the past, if only for a moment. Ashe pondered a discreet trip to a bordello, weighing the risks against the potential benefit of possibly achieving a good night's sleep afterward.

One thing was inescapable. He'd played at the part of the rogue before India, but after, there'd been no more pretending. Ashe knew he'd deliberately tried to drown himself in pleasures of the flesh—if only to distance himself from truly feeling anything at all.

I've made my own prison, and I'm still self-aware enough to know it. So does that make me a wiser man or more of a fool?

He glanced back down at the invitations on his desk, vaguely aware of the door opening behind him. He spoke without looking up, "Nothing else tonight, Godwin. Just make sure Mrs. Clark has things in hand for—"

"I had the strangest dream."

Ashe groaned before turning around to take in the sight of her in his doorway. Her hair and skin were damp from an evening bath, though he couldn't imagine her asking to have one drawn at this hour. Even so, he wasn't sure whether to laugh or cry at the delectable sight of her.

I should say something immediately about how you'll catch a chill, dear Caroline. But instead, I don't think I'm going to be able to say anything at all for a moment or two. God help me, but I'm going to ask Godwin to start locking your bedroom door.

She presented an erotic offering that ricocheted fire through his frame. Her thin cotton nightgown clung to her body, the white fabric even more sheer to show off the dusky pink tips of her breasts and the irresistible dark blonde curls at the juncture of her thighs.

"What did you dream about?"

"I dreamt I wasn't myself." She reached up to touch one damp tendril, tracing it with her fingertips.

"No one is themselves when they dream, Miss Townsend. But you—somehow I suspect for you it is even more pronounced." Ashe smiled. Her nightly transformations were nothing short of miraculous.

"I was definitely taller," she provided cheerfully, stretching her arms upward to demonstrate and forcing Ashe to keep his seat as his body responded to the visual treat the movement provided. She was an unashamed nymph cavorting just out of reach, and his body surged with heat and fire ready to join in the dance.

His grip on the desk tightened until his knuckles showed white. "Miss Townsend, you need to go back to bed." *Before I rip that gown off your ripe little body and have you in a raw, unbridled fuck that's going to rob me of the last semblance of civilized humanity I have left.*

And there it is . . . I don't want to be civilized. God help me. I never wanted to be civilized again after—India. After her . . .

Another woman's face began to form at the edges of his thoughts and Ashe moved to his feet to shake it off. "Let's get you back to—"

"I'm on my way to the library. Mr. Blackwell said I could borrow any book I wished."

"You read too much."

"You sound like Aunt Emilia."

"She doesn't approve of your literary pursuits?"

She shook her head, smiling brightly. "She doesn't approve of anything. I feel very sorry for her sometimes. Don't you?"

"Yes, poor Aunt Emilia," he said, without any effort toward sincerity. "Bed."

"As you wish."

Ashe's relief at the easy concession was fleeting. Instead of turning on her heels and ending the tantalizing encounter, she breezed past him toward the sanctuary of his large four-poster bed. Before he could protest, she'd climbed up to crawl across the coverlet, presenting that beautiful round little ass he'd admired before. It was like watching two halves of a ripe silky peach sashay toward the pillows, and Ashe's breath caught in his throat.

She collapsed in a giggling feminine heap, rolling over to sprawl across his bed. She pulled one leg up, baring her thighs in a wicked gesture that would have made the best skills of a courtesan pale in comparison. "I find that I like being taller."

This isn't happening. I'm going to ask Rowan for a sleeping draught to keep the damn creature out of my room!

His intention was to gently drag her off the bed, but the ankle he gripped was ice cold, and Ashe's attention shifted instantly. As sexy as his damp siren looked, she was in real danger of pneumonia or fever, and Ashe wasn't having it.

He knelt on the edge of the mattress and pulled the covers back as swiftly as he could. She offered no resistance when he reached for her, encircled his arms around her, and lifted her easily up against him. She was as cold as marble but so beautiful he struggled to think. Caroline put her head against his shoulder with a sigh, her damp hair sending a sensual shiver across his skin and pebbling it with goose bumps.

She was light in his arms but all womanly curves and firm flesh. The instinct to warm her was overwhelming.

Propriety was nothing, and the rules meant less as he weighed out the dangers and tried to ignore his desires.

He set her back down, then slid his hands up the outside curves of her thighs to push her gown up over her hips. "Lift your arms," he whispered, his voice rough with need.

She obeyed him without hesitation. Her fingertips stretched gracefully to the ceiling and her eyes met his, a veil of dreams giving their color golden depth in the low light of the room.

He peeled off the damp garment, up over her head, smoothly and swiftly, drinking in the vision of her bare breasts with their impertinent rose tips puckered and pouting for attention. Her skin was cream and honey, the burnished gold of her hair set off to perfection against his ivory bed. Her hips were wide and inviting, and she faced him, kneeling with her plump bottom balanced on her heels, without a hint of modesty.

He took a deep breath to try to clear his head and instead was rewarded with the heady scent of her sex—a sweet musk that rivaled any perfume. He turned away as his cock threatened to tear open the front of his trousers, and he quickly laid her gown over a chair by the window to help it dry.

Damn it! Only the worst kind of cad would take advantage of a woman in such a state! Let's warm her and then get her back to her own bed before the worst happens and Godwin does decide to knock on the door looking for the girl!

He turned back and in two strides returned to the bed to press her backward onto the bed, covering her in the warmth of down and silk. He began to strip off his shirt, ignoring the wicked suggestion of a lustful whisper in his head that if he lost his pants as well, the warming would go much faster.

Her eyes never left his, her expression a drowsy smile of pleasure. He hesitated briefly. *What if she wakes up now?*

Hell, if an ice-cold bath isn't going to stir her, then this shouldn't cause much of a ripple!

"This isn't celibacy," he ground out softly, pulling his shirt from his shoulders. "This is purgatory."

He climbed into the bed as carefully as he could, drawing her against his side and pressing the fire of his bare chest to hers. Her nipples brushed up against him, growing harder as the sensation of the contact with his chest hair stimulated them. Her legs entangled naturally with his, and Ashe was convinced that no man had suffered more than the sweet knifing pleasure-pain of her soft thighs and damp sex nestling against him through the cloth of his pants. He reached down to adjust her position, and made the strategic mistake of cupping her delectable ass; the round curves filled his palms and nearly sent him over the edge. His cock throbbed and pulsed with every shuddering breath he could manage, and Ashe had to close his eyes to fight for control.

He ran his palms up her back, working the friction of his fingers against her smooth skin to try to draw the chill from her core. "The next time you want a bath, miss, you must ring the bell and ask Daisy for some warm water."

He glanced down to see if his words had registered only to have her tip her head back, her brown eyes hypnotic in the candlelight and shadows as she looked up at him. "Is it better to be clever or tall?"

"That's a child's question." His tone was brusque, but her gaze never wavered as she waited for his reply, and Ashe found himself softening his resolve at the trusting patience in her eyes. "I'd say a bit of both doesn't hurt if you're a man, but for you . . ." He drew her closer, savoring the feel of her body against his. "One of us should keep their wits about them, so I'll say it's better to be clever, my American."

She reached up, cradling his face within the cool blades of her fingers, her breath sweet and warm against his lips, and arched up against him to kiss him lightly, a brush of light silk against the sensitive curves of his mouth. Ashe savored the amazing boon of what was undoubtedly her first kiss, awed by the power of it. He tried to resist the temptation to deepen the kiss, allowing his slumbering siren to have her way with him. But when her tongue darted out, wetting his lower lip only to playfully bite him, Ashe abandoned his reserve.

The sweet friction was intoxicating and Ashe meant to drink his fill. He seized control, answering her gentle exploration with a more commanding one of his own. She was warm honey and potent as any wine, and Ashe had been too long without the taste of a woman.

But even so, Caroline was a delight he couldn't remember experiencing with any other. Each lingering caress of his tongue to hers was an electric storm of sensation and desire, and Ashe reveled in the ebb and flow of need that fueled a fire within him that defied control.

Ashe's arms tightened around her, shifting to press her into the down mattress beneath him, sliding effortlessly into the world of the intoxicating solace of a woman's body. Being partially clothed afforded no shield, but instead intensified the sensation of her wet core and lush nest of curls against his leg. Instead of shy resistance, Caroline was an eager press of artless excitement that made his blood clamor for conquest.

I could have her, and what man breathing would blame me?

For a telltale instant, his conscience failed to respond, but even over the roar of lust pounding through his frame, the unwanted answer finally came.

My grandfather, and every man of good character, would be all too quick to point out my error—right before they flogged me and hung me.

Damn.

He lifted his head, trying to keep his eyes closed so that

the sight of the siren beneath him didn't ruin his valiant effort at chivalry.

Damn chivalry! What an idiotic invention! If I ever met the rusty knight that came up with it, I'd wring his neck and accept the accolades of every man walking.

She sighed and lowered her face to snuggle against him, her hands making lazy trails across his chest in wide sweeping circles. "Hmmm, purgatory is lovely."

It was all he could do to look away to the clock on the mantel across the room and count the minutes while she slowly warmed against him. Her breathing slowed to a steady rhythm that betrayed that she'd fallen fast asleep, and Ashe marveled at the ironies of life.

I could lock her in her room from now on.

But his chaperone wasn't going to stand for it during waking hours, and he would guarantee himself a poisoned letter to his grandfather about the matter.

I could lock my door.

Every shred of manly pride rose up against the notion of trapping himself in his own home. *I'm the master of this house! Not some errant child to be shut up for bad behavior!*

Ashe let out a long, tired breath. *At this pace, I'll behave simply because I'm too exhausted to think of straying!*

He waited until he was sure the crisis had passed and then extricated himself to retrieve her gown. His body ached from pent-up lust and he only hoped he didn't limp in the morning. For now, he carried her in a blanketed bundle back down the hall to her room. He didn't risk dressing her again, for fear of his luck running out.

It will serve you rightly, Terrier, to wake up to a mystery of your own making.

* * *

It was a strange bit of torture to stand still on a dais while endless measurements were taken, withstanding the assessment of strangers as if she were a life-size doll to be made over. She'd have put off the morning's excursion if she could, but Ashe had insisted that she couldn't go to any more functions in any of the gowns she'd brought with her. And it was impossible to explain that she wasn't feeling like herself after awaking before dawn to the odd realization that she was stark naked. Her dreams had been a strange tangle of dancing in waterfalls and swimming into Ashe's arms, and awaking to her nightgown strewn across the foot of her bed and a broken water pitcher on her floor had been unnerving.

Am I losing my mind and cavorting around my room in my sleep?

The attendants in the shop moved in a complex choreography, circling her and handing the shop's owner, Mrs. Simms, everything she needed before she even had to voice her desire. At the moment, Caroline was being pinned into an elaborate dress that had more in common with Lady Fitzgerald's garden than any garment she'd ever seen.

"I don't think I like all these flowers." Caroline tried to keep her tone gentle, but firm.

"No? I think they are charming, mademoiselle!" the dressmaker protested, rearranging the skirts to show off the organza blossoms that trailed from her waist down her skirts to the hem.

"I appear to be imitating a flower pot," she groused softly, beginning to wonder if any of her opinions mattered in the slightest as the woman simply tried pinning even more flowers along the dress's edge.

"You look like spring," Ashe intoned from the doorway, sending Caroline's heart racing at the sight of him leaning there, assessing her. "Like Persephone in bloom."

"Mr. Blackwell, I can see why women are often likened to flowers in poetry and prose, but I'm not sure it's an analogy I'm comfortable with." She used her most scholarly tone, deliberately trying to fend off the effects of his gaze. She was rambling and she knew it.

"What could be wrong with such a comparison?"

"The implication is that women are objects to be admired, sniffed, and ultimately plucked." She regretted her cheekiness the instant she'd spoken the words, as his entire expression changed from fleeting shock to pure delight—as if she'd challenged him.

Even the dressmaker on the floor squeaked in amused horror, but Ashe stepped forward with a wicked smile. "You, Miss Townsend, have a wit that defies analogies, but I find myself wondering what kind of flower you would be."

For a moment, she was speechless, and he went on relentlessly, his voice a seductive spell.

"Surely not a hothouse flower or an exotic orchid. But something just as enticing. Gardenia? Lily? Something—"

"I am not a flower! Any more than you, Mr. Blackwell, are a—" She bit her lower lip, cutting off her impetuous protest.

"Any more than I'm a . . . What am I in this game, Miss Townsend?"

"A gardener," she mumbled, her face staining with a blush.

He laughed, and with a wave of his hand dismissed the seamstress to ensure that they were entirely and improperly alone.

Caroline felt a flash of panic to see the woman go and tried to hold her ground. "Call her back! It isn't seemly that you should be here without . . ."

"A chaperone? Ah! But I have my chaperone right here, and so I can see no rules being broken." Ashe circled the dais, eyeing her from every angle. "Besides, you can always indicate that I wished to reprimand you privately for your wretched attitude, as any proper guardian would do if his little blossom insisted on acting the stinging nettle."

Caroline stomped her foot in an ineffective gesture but

one that made her feel marginally better. "You twist this arrangement to suit yourself from moment to moment!"

"Thank the gods my grandfather wisely chose a woman who is not so changeable." He sighed. "My Miss Townsend never forgets her purpose . . . does she?"

My Miss Townsend. The intimate implication of his words sent a shimmer of heat across her skin and she marveled at the ease with which he exercised his powers. *What woman wouldn't crave to be at the center of his attentions? To wish for him to—*

"Does she?" he prompted again, taking a step closer until he was next to the dais, looking up slightly at her. "Ever forget her purpose?"

"No." She squared her shoulders, ignoring the bite of the pins at the movement. "She *never* does."

But his eyes mocked her, as if he could read her thoughts and knew that they were of anything but her vows to mind her duties. A fleeting image of being pressed against Ashe's bare chest drowned out a practical protest, confusing her with its power and intensity. She took a slow deep breath to regain her composure before adding, "Never."

"I am a lucky man to have such a tenacious chaperone."

"Mr. Blackwell—"

He cut her off with a cavalier wave of his hand. "Mrs. Simms!" he called the seamstress back, ending their private conference and forcing Caroline to hold her place.

"Yes, Mr. Blackwell," Mrs. Simms answered quickly, her arms full of a stack of fashion plates for his examination. "I've brought a few views for your selection."

"Thank you, Mrs. Simms. And I've decided that Miss Townsend may have been right."

It was Caroline's turn to swallow a shocked squeak. "Really?"

"She is far too beautiful to need anything too overwrought and I think this color is overwhelming. Miss Townsend should shimmer in color, but not drown in it. The pale sapphire blue, and that coral—we'll have a gown in each. And yellow, but not the butter. I don't want her looking like a dandelion. Something in burnished gold with a hint of pink."

"Something more creamy to set off her skin and hair?" Mrs. Simms suggested, and Caroline marveled at the way she was instantly dismissed from the conversation yet the center of the pair's attention at the same time. It was like being caught in a maelstrom of fabric and color that she had never imagined.

"Yes, exactly. But nothing sweet! As you've seen, my American has no patience for frippery and flowers. A few layers and flounces to keep her fashionable, but only enough to frame her figure and draw a man's eyes."

"I'm not drawing anyone's—" Caroline began, only to be soundly ignored as Ashe held up a roll of green silk in front of her face.

"There, now that suits! This for a riding habit, and a darker jade green for a day dress." Ashe spoke with such authority and confidence that Mrs. Simms simply nodded and took notes while he flipped through the plates at lightning speed. "This one, not these, but this in the coral organza, but no bows, and we'll take all of these. And undergarments to match each dress. She'll need everything from the skin out, Mrs. Simms."

Caroline took another deep breath. "I don't need a riding habit, Mr. Blackwell." *Much less new undergarments!*

Ashe shook his head. "You'll learn. Or at least have the proper outfit if you ever wish to give the appearance of a woman who knows how to sit astride a strong mount and hold her own."

The dressmaker squeaked again, but this time she was smiling, openly enjoying Ashe's unorthodox comments.

Caroline was not as amused. "You are deliberately being provocative. Mrs. Simms is going to think the very worst!"

"Oh, no!" Mrs. Simms interjected. "I am the soul of discretion, young miss."

"There, you see?" Ashe settled into an ornate chair in the corner, like a man taking a box seat at the theatre. "Mrs. Simms has heard far more shocking things, I suspect, as ladies chatter about their selections."

"Mr. Blackwell, I don't require this many gowns! I don't see how I'm going to possibly wear all of them!"

"Ladies of quality change their ensemble at least three times in a day, Miss Townsend."

"And have no time for anything else, I imagine!" she protested.

"Precisely!" he agreed, rewarding her with an impudent pirate's smile. "Dressing and undressing are the secrets to a woman's happiness."

"That's the most ridiculous thing I've ever heard." Caroline crossed her arms primly.

"Only because you've never been properly dressed," he countered, and then added, "or undressed, for that matter."

Caroline gasped at the inference but wasn't about to argue the point in front of strangers.

He went on smoothly, "Consider this a way to give your poor ladies' maid something to do besides dust your desk and books."

It wasn't hard to imagine Daisy's delight at new dresses, and Caroline was cheered by the thought of leaving her young friend a few lovely prizes after she'd returned home. "For Daisy, then."

"Mrs. Simms, we'll also need to see anything you have ready-made for alterations. We have a ball to attend in three days and I cannot take Miss Townsend in brown wool no matter how she fusses. Naturally, we'll pay for the rush."

"My best dress will do for—" Caroline bit the inside of her cheek at the quelling look she got from Ashe for her efforts to save poor Mrs. Simms some hard labor and Ashe some of his fortune.

Mrs. Simms looked as happy as a child at Christmas. "We'll bring in what we have and see to it that your ward is a vision for the ball, Mr. Blackwell!"

"And if you can recommend a hairdresser and arrange for them to attend Miss Townsend at this address later today"— Ashe handed over his card—"I would be ever so grateful. Her ladies' maid can observe and ensure that the necessary final touches can be duplicated for future outings."

"And shoes?" Mrs. Simms inquired, a greedy bird enjoying the feast.

"Without a doubt! We're going to the milliner's next, but I'll trust you to immediately send the shoemaker our color palette to see that Miss Townsend has everything she needs."

"I'll take care of everything, sir!" Mrs. Simms curtsied and bustled from the room, no doubt visions of the bills she would send to that same address he'd provided already warming her heart.

"Oh, and Mrs. Simms, one last thing." Ashe stopped her just at the door. "A half a dozen nightgowns of the finest quality with matching wraps. Beautiful things to improve her sleep, if you will."

"Yes, Mr. Blackwell!" Mrs. Simms curtsied again, merrily closing the door behind her.

Caroline stepped down from the dais, ignoring the bite of a few pins left at her waist. "It's too much!"

"It's the bare minimum, and you promised to sweetly accept this without argument."

"I did?"

"Well." He shrugged his shoulders, unfazed by her sputtering and foot stomping. "I haven't your memory for conversations, so it may not be a direct quote, but that was the gist of it after breakfast."

"I thought agreeing to be outfitted for my visit here meant two or three gowns! But you're outfitting me for a lifetime, Mr. Blackwell, and frankly, not for the life I'm likely to lead." She sighed, and tried a gentler tone. "I'm very grateful for your generous gesture. But isn't it a bit of a waste to—"

"It's never a waste to fulfill a promise and I believe I'm in enough control of my faculties and fortunes to decide what I will and will not do. If you're grateful, then I could have sworn the proper response was something along the way of a thank-you."

"Thank you. B-but nightgowns? I fail to see what my appearance in public has to do with you buying me . . ." The heat flooding her cheeks made her words falter a bit, amazed that she was about to argue about nightgowns of all things. "I *have* a nightgown, Mr. Blackwell, and I am sleeping just fine!"

And there it was again. A look from him that spoke volumes she couldn't decipher. That strange heat in his gaze that made her knees feel unnaturally weak and her skin shiver with a sensitive and lazy streak of lightning.

He's looking at me as if he's fully aware of the state of my nightdress! But that's impossible! He's at some game, that's all! Could he somehow know that I awoke without it this morning after a night of fitful dreams? Is he . . . spying on me? She couldn't believe that even Ashe Blackwell was capable of such a vulgar thing.

"No doubt," he finally spoke, then took a small step closer, the blue in his eyes darkening like a summer storm. "Indulge me, Miss Townsend."

Indulge me. She was a bird staring up into the sun, too dazed to protest. Every intelligent reason for argument evaporated in the heat of his presence, but Caroline stiffened her spine. "You expect every woman to indulge you without argument."

"Never you."

She shook her head slowly. "Never."

Without another word, he turned on his heels to follow Mrs. Simms out the door to add whatever he pleased to the day's order, leaving her to wonder how any woman could deny him anything when asked.

The rogue likes shopping. And frankly, I'm beginning to grasp its appeal.

* * *

Ashe left the carriage for her so that she could get back to the brownstone safely alone later, along with an alerted footman who would be waiting at the door of the shop to escort her out, and he made his way down the street to try to clear his head.

He'd accompanied her only because he feared that on her own, she'd have come back with more gray wool. Keeping his distance was taking its toll, and after another long, restless night without real sleep, he sensed he was reaching his limits. Even as he'd teased her, he was the one who'd felt the sting.

Because there she'd stood—his prim American chaperone, tight-lipped and protesting every luxury meant to elicit her smiles—and all he could see was the siren who'd sprawled naked across his bed, shameless and sweet, so irresistibly sexy and impossibly asleep. She'd been fiery magic in his arms, and he was having trouble banishing the illusion from his thoughts.

Ashe had found himself deliberately pushing the conversation to see if Caroline remembered anything of her nocturnal adventure, but it was difficult to tell. She'd blushed and seemed a bit flustered, but any flirtation could have elicited the same reaction.

Seducing an unmarried female guest under your own roof was as cliché and foul a mistake a man could make, and once again, Ashe had to question his grandfather's true intention. *Is the old man deliberately testing me by placing the delightfully challenging Miss Townsend within reach?*

He took some small comfort in his restraint, knowing that a hundred other men would simply have taken what was offered and blamed providence. But to Ashe, it smacked of rape to take a woman unaware of herself, and as difficult as it might be to face the terrier if things came to light now, he could still defend his behavior.

If not actually take pride in it.

Is the woman who kissed me last night some hidden part of her? Is it real in any way? When he could get Caroline to smile or laugh, it was easy to see a glimmer of the playful minx he'd encountered, but her reserve was formidable and gave Ashe pause. *What a revelation it would be to awake that part of her! To see Caroline come alive as she was in her dreams and wield that power!*

Ashe's mood turned black, frustration whipping through his frame. *It's a fool's daydream and an idiotic fantasy that's going to yield me nothing but a miserable outcome with my grandfather and an onset of blue balls likely to put me in my grave!*

Impossible creature! I'm damned no matter what I do!

At least he'd seen to her wardrobe and could now rely on Darius to bear the brunt of her company. And frankly, it might be time to take an evening to himself and vanquish some of his tensions in a harmless bit of fun.

If last night was a test, then I can honestly claim to have passed. But I'll be damned if I'm walking through that fire again!

Chapter

8

🌑

"You're out of sorts this evening, Ashe."

"That's a hell of a greeting to give a friend after a miserable night at the tables at Clives!" Ashe threw himself into his favorite overstuffed chair in Rowan's study. "And I'll have you know I'm as cheerful as a meadowlark!" he growled.

Rowan smiled and held out a glass of wine for Ashe. "How could I have missed it? But then most meadowlarks don't look like they've had a burning coal shoved into their—"

"For a physician, I'd expect a bit more tact and consideration," Ashe cut him off, his better humor asserting itself as the magic of the Jaded's sanctuary took hold. There was simply something about Dr. Rowan West's cluttered library and study that made the world retreat and lose its bite.

The room was filled with strange souvenirs from his family's travels and academic adventures that yielded odd statues or leather-wrapped scrolls valued only by obscure specialists. It was a mismatched jumble of various cultures and styles, but the owner's character overruled the chaos, and Rowan's small brownstone was the sanctuary and unofficial headquarters of the Jaded's membership.

It wasn't the finest of homes, though it was situated in a comfortable enough neighborhood to inspire Dr. West's richer clients' confidence. They wouldn't have trusted a man too far down on the social ladder, nor tolerated one who seemed to have risen too far up it.

Tonight, Ashe had been relieved to find Rowan still awake, apparently just returning home less than an hour before, according to his manservant, after a late-night call on an elderly patient.

"After your note warning us off, I wasn't sure I'd be seeing you until the spring, but Darius said you were having a unique Season. Not that he elaborated on what constituted a unique Season, but you can imagine how it makes a man wonder." Rowan took the chair opposite, stretching out his long legs. "Just assure me you haven't done anything too insane."

Ashe shook his head. "There's nothing to tell. My grandfather has requested a favor of me, and I've undertaken a ward for the next few weeks. Though at the rate we're progressing, she'll either run home or I'll inadvertently kill her, so I expect it's a temporary imposition."

"Well, that's unique enough," Rowan said. "And does this ward have a name?"

"Miss Caroline Townsend, and don't pretend you haven't heard about my American problem."

"A rumor here and there, but I didn't give it much credence. Frankly, you're not exactly the sort of person I can imagine anyone entrusting with the care of a young woman of any nationality."

Ashe winced. "There's a bitter tonic to swallow! I'm not the devil, Rowan."

"I'm sorry. Didn't you just say something about killing this girl?"

"Inadvertently!" Ashe corrected him quickly, shifting guiltily in his chair. "I'm not plotting her murder."

"A relief for Miss Townsend," Rowan jested, "but I'm not sure I'm convinced of her safety. What sort of girl is she, Ashe?"

"The worst sort! Humorless thing, prim and prudish and stubborn! She has more opinions than any man I've ever met. In other words, I've asked Darius to distract her if he can."

"Poor Darius!" Rowan leaned forward and added a little more wine to his agitated guest's glass. "She's pretty, then?"

Ashe almost denied it out of rote habit, but the memory of caramel brown eyes and the beauty he'd seen unfold before him in the last week choked off his response. The taste of her still lingered on his tongue, and Ashe drank some of his wine to try to banish it. *Pretty? She is like a star sapphire that seems a dull blue stone of no consequence until it is polished and the light strikes it just so. . . . I'd have never looked twice or even noticed her, but now I'm having trouble looking away.* "Some might think so."

"And your thoughts?"

"Irrelevant." Ashe tipped his head back onto the chair's pillows to make an evasive study of the room's ceiling. Inset pressed tin tiles painted copper added to the room's strange elegance, and Ashe's eyes traced the intertwined patterns to gain a bit of control. "Better to think of her as a gargoyle."

"Rather than an angel?" Rowan finished, intuitively sensing his friend's dilemma. "Ah, the joys of being the sober and careful guardian of a young woman's virtue!"

Ashe laughed, abandoning his meditation on West's ceiling. "Sober and careful—these are words I had never aspired to."

"I shouldn't mind seeing a sober and careful Ashe Blackwell—even if it is a passing novelty."

His humor faded at the familiar words, and he wondered if his grandfather hadn't somehow gotten the word out about his hopes for the Season. "I'm always careful, and sobriety is overrated."

"You're no drunkard," Rowan countered.

"No, but I'm not a teetotaler! I have my reputation to protect!"

Rowan laughed. "One bout of babysitting is not going to tarnish *your* reputation! It's not as if you've thrown on monks' robes and sworn off whorehouses!"

Ashe struggled to maintain his composure, his friend's jest coming far too close to the painful truth. "Any more signs of trouble for our merry band? Rutherford was quick to give me another round of dire warnings about keeping a close watch, especially with London invaded by so many tourists this time of year."

The doctor's eyebrows rose at the quick change of subject, but he allowed it out of respect for his friend. "Nothing of note, and I believe I received the same speech from him last week. I'm hoping that after a bit of time, we can stop worrying about every shadow and go on with our lives. If the Company is really that interested in treasure, they know enough about the Jaded to make a more direct case than breaking windows or bothering with subterfuge, don't you think?"

"Rutherford's been more than a little frenetic in his watch lately. Even Darius hasn't escaped a dire word of doom and gloom—as if Darius needs it, living the quiet life of a scholar!"

"Darius isn't as disconnected from the world as you imagine, Ashe."

"And I'm grateful he isn't! Tomorrow, we're attending the Royal Museum with Galen and his bride, and then in another two evenings to Worthley's, where Darius will make his charming debut. If all goes as I have planned, the rest of the winter will evaporate like a bad headache, and my life will go on undisturbed."

Rowan nodded, reaching up to massage the back of his neck in fatigue. "I won't ask exactly what your plans are, but I'll wish you luck."

"I don't need luck, Rowan." He looked over at his friend and recalled the hour. "Well, I'm off for the night, Dr. West! I'll leave you to your well-earned rest." Ashe stood up in one fluid movement, grateful for the brief reprieve and good conversation.

"Stay out of trouble, Ashe."

Ashe rewarded the comment with a devilish grin. "Easier said than done," he replied and made his way back out into the night.

*   *   *

It was a restless night as Caroline turned the events of the day over and over in her mind, wishing to take most of it back. She kicked against the coverlet with a sigh and then froze at the sound of a carriage pulling up in front of the house.

Curiosity overruled all else, and Caroline left the bed to quickly take a look from her window. Ashe's silhouette in the lamplight was unmistakable as he made his way up the stairs and into the house.

Fury and disappointment warred within her, but also a growing realization that she was on a mission of folly. His grandfather couldn't possibly expect her to keep an eye on him at every moment, could he?

How in the world can anyone stop a grown man from doing as he wishes? And if I'm not here to guide or halt his baser nature, then all of this is for nothing.

"Miss?" Daisy asked tentatively from the doorway. "Would you like some warm milk? I've brought up a small tray."

Caroline turned, instantly remembering that she'd put off questioning her maid in a belated onset of guilt about using Ashe's servants against him. But recent events and Ashe's late return diminished her reluctance. "Thank you, Daisy." She picked up a wrap for her shoulders and moved away from the window. "I'm sorry to have kept you up at such an unreasonable hour."

"Oh, there's no worry there," Daisy said as she set the tray down on the small table next to the bed. "I was still awake."

"Really?" Caroline drew closer to accept the cup of milk. "Were you having trouble sleeping as well?"

"Oh, no!" Daisy bit her lower lip self-consciously. "It's nothing like that. It's just . . ."

"Yes?" Caroline said, hoping to encourage the young girl to confide in her without seeming too eager.

"My beau is one of the coachmen, and I admit I like to keep an eye out for him." Daisy smoothed out her apron nervously. "Not that it's not all proper and that. Mrs. Clark isn't one to allow for shenanigans under her watch! And it's just a walk on our day's off to—"

"I don't see anything improper with wanting to know that he's safely returned," Caroline said. "In fact, I think he'd be touched to know of your concern."

Godwin is too clever and there I have it—the means to know of Ashe's every outing. But it feels so underhanded, and now that I'm looking into her eyes, I don't think I can ask it of her.

"You're so kind, miss!" Daisy beamed. "Was there anything else I can do for you?"

"No." Caroline shook her head. "Not tonight."

Daisy bobbed a curtsy and left her to her milk and her sleep, and Caroline took her warm cup to bed, wishing she had a more ruthless nature. There would be no reward for her at the end of the Season if he fell into his old habits and set the tongues of London wagging about his ignoble feats.

But the true source of her pain had nothing to do with the risk to the bargain she'd made with the elder Mr. Blackwell. She'd stood at the center of his attention and scrutiny today and allowed him to dress her as if she were his. And she'd secretly gloried in it. But no matter how pleasurable and forbidden it all felt, Caroline's isolation and loneliness had only increased when she'd realized that he'd left her at the shop and gone out. Her pain was in knowing that Ashe's flirtations meant nothing to him, and that whenever he wished, he was free to seek his entertainments without any care of her.

Whereas I am not so lucky. . . . I cannot escape the growing sense that if the blackguard beckoned, I would abandon my own conscience and every rule I ever thought to hold to.

But that is my dilemma, and not his.

Caroline sighed and set the cup aside. She hadn't indulged in a nightly cup of warm milk since her departure from Boston, and she was comforted by the return of this simple ritual. She liked to have a cup before bed to help her sleep, a habit she'd picked up in childhood as a way to prevent sleepwalking. Caroline knew she'd outgrown the malady, but the cure made her feel better all the same. She sighed again and leaned over to blow out the candle next to her bed.

He gave me his word. He's outfitted me like a princess. I have no evidence that he's done anything wrong. So I'm not going to ask Daisy to play the spy.

At least—not yet.

Chapter
9

"Ah, miss! Look at how exquisite it is!" Daisy lifted the jade green day dress from its wrapping of tissue paper, her eyes shining with excitement for her mistress. "That's a color like a dream!"

Caroline fingered the hem, smiling. Daisy's euphoria was catching despite Caroline's fatigue. "It is pretty, isn't it?"

"You should wear it today to the museum!" Daisy laid it out across the bed and went back to the box. "Gloves to match! And shoes! And even a sweet little bonnet!"

"It seems a bit much for a simple tour of an art museum," Caroline teased.

"Not at all! The Royal Museum's all the rage and all the blue bloods are there, rubbing elbows and lording it about! The paper said it's all the finest milling around and admiring how grand it is to live in an enlightened age." Daisy sighed with envy.

"Have you ever been, Daisy?"

"No, but when I get my chance, I'll be there with my best bonnet on!"

A knock at the door signaled the arrival of a few more of the previous day's purchases, and Caroline gave in to the pleasure of watching Daisy's reactions to each box's contents. Each hatbox and ribbon made the maid clap and squeal, but when the ball gown was discovered, Caroline feared Daisy would swoon at the sight of it.

"It's the prettiest thing I ever thought to see!" Daisy sighed, a girl overwhelmed, her eyes filling with tears. "You'll be a vision in it—an angel, that's what!"

Ashe had left her at the shop before the gown was selected, and Caroline had been more than a bit leery of making the choice on her own. Shimmering pale blue silk with lace flounces, the overskirt opened on the sides to reveal an embroidered gold satin underneath, all balanced by the delicate lace and drapery of the décolletage. Mrs. Simms had assured her that the dress was not too sweet, but alluring. "The color will stand out because it is so pure, and it sets off your beautiful hair and eyes," Mrs. Simms had cooed, and Caroline had given in.

"Let's just hope Mr. Blackwell agrees and isn't embarrassed to be seen with me at the ball," Caroline said, helping Daisy to pull it free from the large box it had arrived in.

"He'll glow with pride!" Daisy beamed, hanging the ball gown on the wardrobe door. "I can't wait to see everything you bought!"

The boxes of undergarments were pure decadence, and Daisy eyed them with awe but diplomatically refrained from too many comments on the delicate luxury of French lace camisoles and silk-layered petticoats in six colors, or the ribbon quilling on the whale-boned corsets.

Her old dresses were quietly packed back into her trunks to make room for the new purchases, and Caroline couldn't help but experience a touch of shock at the sheer amount of all of it. *And there are so many more to come!*

Ashe was generous to a fault, and despite his assurances, she still didn't believe that she would wear a fraction of the purchases he'd made. But as her fingers traced the soft organza and sumptuous silks, fur-lined cloaks and cashmere wraps, it was harder to believe that a mud wren could have such things. The transformation they offered was a dream, and Caroline only hoped that she could manage it—and not prove the old adage about sows and silk purses.

* * *

She descended the stairs for their outing to the exhibition, new bonnet in hand, a cool queen in jade, and Ashe had the first inkling that he'd gotten away with nothing. She carried herself like a duchess and made a man feel like a peasant for daring to stare at her. He acknowledged that she may not be a conventional beauty, but he couldn't see anything about her that didn't appeal—a fact at the very core of his dilemma. And why he wasn't about to betray just how much the very sight of her affected him.

He pulled on his gloves nonchalantly. "You're not late."

"I'll interpret that as a compliment." She reached the bottom of the stairs.

"It was," he said, "and you look quite lovely, Miss Townsend."

"Thanks to you, Mr. Blackwell," she said, turning to allow him to admire his purchase.

"Not at all. It is always a pleasure to dress a woman." He deliberately kept his eyes focused on hers, and nothing else, refusing to take in too much of the flattering ensemble and the way it made her waist look smaller, setting off her ripe figure. Daisy had done her dark blonde hair up in an intricate fall of curls encircled by tiny braids, and wound a matching ribbon through it all. "Are you nervous about meeting my friends?"

She rewarded him with a starched look of disdain that almost made him smile. "Not at all."

Good, we're back where we started, you and I.

The ritual of a guest's arrival interrupted whatever argument might have occurred, and Ashe gratefully turned to see his friend Galen coming into the entryway with his wife at his side. As one of the Jaded, he trusted Galen like few others, and Ashe was hoping that the addition of Lady Winters to the party would offer Caroline a better ally and confidante in the weeks ahead. But he also knew that he'd mercilessly ridden Galen in recent months about falling so quickly and happily into the matrimonial yoke with what he considered a minimal and less than manly struggle—so he braced himself for any ribbing in return about his current predicament.

Although, with dear Caroline giving me looks like daggers, I'd say Galen won't have too much fuel for this fire.

"Miss Caroline Townsend, may I introduce my good friend, Lord Winters, Mr. Galen Hawke, and his lovely bride, Lady Winters."

"God, that sounded pompous," Galen groused, extending his hand with a warm smile. "Ignore Ashe, he's just trying to make sure you have the impression that not all his friends are ne'er-do-wells."

Caroline smiled in return, her entire stance relaxing at the jest. "Or simply impress me with the idea that he *has* friends."

Galen laughed heartily, elbowing Ashe. "I like her!" He sobered slightly to complete the ritual. "It may be dangerous to allow you ladies to form an alliance, but I suspect it's already too late."

"Indeed, it is!" Lady Winters beamed, then stepped forward to offer her hand to her newest acquaintance. "You must call me Haley and pay as little attention to these two as you can."

The carriage ride to the museum was a merry trip, though Ashe deliberately played the part of an observer rather than joining in the lively conversation. Lady Winters asked about Boston and Caroline's life there, and for Ashe, it was a revelation to watch the subtle evasions as Caroline made his friends laugh with several clever antidotes but revealed very little about her personal self. She was a petite little mystery, sitting across from him, her new bonnet framing her face and dark gold curls.

I've assumed so much of her, this eccentric woman, and avoided asking too much—hell, I didn't want to know her, did I? At first, because I wanted her gone, and later, because everything I learn about her only adds to her appeal.

"And what does your family think of your solo adventure to London?" Haley asked in friendly curiosity.

"I'm sure they think it yet another sign that I am far too headstrong and beyond all hope," Caroline replied cheerfully. "But since that was unlikely to change no matter which side of the Atlantic I am on, it is hard to fault them."

"You are not homesick, then?" Haley said.

Caroline shook her head firmly. "My life will be there, just as it was, when I return."

"*If* you return," Haley offered. "You may find yourself married before spring, if Lady Fitzgerald is to be believed."

Ashe almost growled involuntarily at the announcement, but Caroline's quick reply captured his complete attention.

"Lady Fitzgerald is entitled to her speculation, but I did not come to London to find a husband," she protested.

"Did you not?" Galen laughed. "No one will believe it!"

"I told her as much," Ashe said and bit the inside of his cheek to keep his expression sober. "But I don't think Miss Townsend believes anything *I* say."

Caroline made a point of ignoring him and looked directly to his friends for support. "Please excuse our ongoing debate. My guardian and Lady Fitzgerald want only the best for me, but I seem to be causing nothing but trouble when I forget to censure my opinions on husbands, hairless cats, and hat ribbons."

"Not at all! I admire your . . ." Galen began, then hesitated, as if searching for the right word.

"Pluck?" Caroline supplied with a mischievous grin.

"Yes, exactly! I admire your pluck, Miss Townsend," Galen said, only to notice the expression on his friend's face. "Don't you, Ashe?"

"Oh, yes," Ashe echoed, swallowing the urge to reach across the carriage and either kiss her or shake her for her impertinence. "Miss Townsend has no shortage of pluck."

* * *

The museum was a revelation for Caroline. She guessed it would take more than a single afternoon to see it all, and even then, a person could likely visit every day and still discover something new. The gallery exhibits were fascinating, each one a demonstration of some great master or the treasures of a lost civilization.

Lady Winters pulled her aside to stroll through an Egyptian display of glittering wealth and golden statues. "All this to accompany someone into the afterlife . . ."

Caroline smiled. "I can't help but wonder about all the people who would have sacrificed anything to possess such things while they were alive."

Haley sighed at her elbow. "And here it sits, for a dead pharaoh who has no use of anything at all."

"Here it all sits . . ." Caroline hesitated to voice anything that might seem critical.

"A pretty waste," Haley supplied with a smile, then leaned closer to a small statue of a beautiful woman with her arms outstretched. "I wonder if she minds all of these stares."

"Anything is better than the cold and dark of some for-

gotten vault." She wasn't sure why she felt drawn to an in-
animate object, but for all the figure's proud features, it was
easy to imagine her feeling a bit forlorn in her glass prison.
"Even if it's not the future she imagined for herself."

"No future ever is," Haley said softly. "Though it's the
surprises in life that make it all worthwhile."

Caroline doubted they were still talking about statues.
"Surprises are often unpleasant, Lady Winters."

Haley leaned in, as if the stone beauty might also share
an opinion on their philosophical discussion. "Has Mr.
Blackwell surprised you?"

"Not at all." Caroline straightened up instantly, aware
that the answer had come too quickly and a little too
breathlessly to be believed, so she attempted an amend-
ment. "Although I did expect him to be fatter."

"What a confession!" Haley said with laugh. "But truly
now, what is your opinion of your guardian?"

"Why?" Caroline countered. "If you know him, then
you know that my opinion would hardly matter in the
greater balance."

Haley shook her head with a quick smile. "I'm not sure
that's true, but I wish to hear it all the same."

Caroline considered her words carefully. "Any answer
I gave you would be misunderstood. If I speak in neutral
terms, you'll see some greater mystery behind my words.
If I praise him, you might accuse me of being smitten. And
if I complained . . ."

"Do you have complaints?" Haley asked, her brow
furrowing with concern. "I don't mean to pry, but you're
here alone, without family or friends, and . . . while Galen
would trust him with his life, I'm not sure I would trust
Ashe with a young woman's reputation."

"I have no complaints," Caroline asserted as confidently
as she could. "And you shouldn't waste a moment of worry.
What Mr. Blackwell most wants of me is to see me setting
sail for home—if only to be free of the trials of an unin-

vited guest. But his grandfather and mine were business partners and close friends, and so we are each honoring them by making the best of this Season. And, of course, by not murdering each other."

"You're telling me what you think *he* wants. But you've yet to answer my question."

"Very well." Caroline took a deep breath. "I think he's exactly the sort of man who is going to try to seize on all the wrong things for all the wrong reasons—like the poor soul in that sarcophagus over there. I think he's too handsome for his own good and he is his own worst enemy, but I'm not foolish enough to underestimate him for it."

"You don't think he's simply in need of reform by the right sort of woman?"

Caroline shook her head. "I would pity the woman who makes the mistake of that assumption. True reform is a choice, not something to be imposed by someone else." Her own words were no sooner spoken and Caroline grew pale at the ridiculous irony of it. *Yet I am here to do nothing less, aren't I? To offer some strange calming influence on him by my presence and my moral character and keep him on a restrained path for a Season—how is that different than what she is insinuating? Have I not agreed with his grandfather that I can somehow "manage" him?*

Lady Winters gave her a strange look but then nodded. "I can see there is nothing to worry about. I shouldn't have pressed you." She held out her arm. "Why don't we rejoin the men?"

* * *

"Your ward is quite the young lady," Galen said as the men spoke together while the women walked through the Egyptian exhibit.

"Whatever you're about to say, don't!" Ashe crossed his arms defensively. "Rowan's already made the same play. She's nothing to me but an inconvenience."

"You're a liar." Galen smiled. "Your eyes follow that inconvenience's every movement."

"Keeping track of her in a crowd is simple courtesy."

"You're deluding yourself, but I'm enjoying it too much to argue."

"You're the one so besotted with his own wife he's forgotten how singularly annoying it is to be a beleaguered bachelor." Ashe readjusted his hat. "Besides, you're forgetting our reputation. The Jaded have no interest in the treacherous company of women beyond their temporary uses."

"Oh, yes. I'd forgotten." Galen's grin belied his words. "Miss Townsend certainly looks treacherous from here."

"Oh, for God's sake! I'm not so far gone that I can't sidestep one woman—especially this one!"

"*Especially* this one?" Galen's look was pure delight. "You, my friend, are in a sinking boat and are too stubborn to even think of looking for the shore."

"She is unmannered, unpredictable, and impossible, Galen. The woman remembers every word ever uttered in her presence and has a persistent habit of appearing where she is least expected. Trust me. At the first sign of a deserted island, I'm marooning her."

Galen said nothing, looking out over the fashionable crowds, and Ashe allowed the silence. He'd protested a bit too much and knew it. But Galen had the good grace to drop the matter, at least for the moment, and Ashe was grateful.

I can only hope that Lady Winters isn't having a similar conversation with Caroline. The last thing I need is a female alliance forged over my shortcomings or, worse, my missteps the last few days.

But when he caught sight of the pale green feathers of her bonnet as she strolled back toward him, he forgot the argument. Next to Lady Winters's striking height and brunette coloring, Caroline's diminutive size gave her a dainty look, he thought. Her gait was natural and pleasing to him.

There was nothing mincing or practiced in the way she moved, no attempt to play the little porcelain doll. Even with her new clothes, she had a style all her own.

The women rejoined them to continue touring the crowded halls, and Ashe began to finally relax and enjoy the day. Caroline was a bright and cheerful companion, her enthusiasm contagious. And he was secretly taking pleasure in the sight of her in a beautiful gown of his choosing, drawing stares for all the right reasons as they moved from exhibit to exhibit. It was a simple thing, to have a woman on your arm—but he'd never given it any thought before or savored the gentle—

"Blackwell, you naughty thing!"

Ashe recognized the voice but couldn't fathom why he would be hailed in such a casual manner in such a public place.

Margot. She wouldn't dare!

"What a deliciously wicked man! To kiss and run and force a woman to happen upon you in such a public place!" she cooed, a striking vision in bright lavender and yellow in a dress that clung to her every curve, the décolletage on the brink of indecency. Margot always managed to make an unforgettable impression.

She dares.

It was one of the most singularly awkward instances of his life.

Galen did his best to pull his wife out of the line for introductions to avert disaster, but Haley had instinctively stepped closer to her new friend, closing ranks against the intruder in a motherly gesture.

"But then public places are always more interesting when I am lucky enough to run into you!" Margot continued, giving him a shameless look of invitation.

"Miss Stillman, what a surprise," Ashe ground out softly. "If you'll excuse us, we were just off to the view the mosaics."

"Oh! I wouldn't wish to interrupt!" she purred, her eyes passing over Lord and Lady Winters, only to linger on Caroline. "Is this the little American ward we've heard so much of? You didn't do her credit, Mr. Blackwell, when you described her." She curtsied. "Well, enjoy the museum! Good afternoon." She curtsied again and then made her way at a leisurely saunter off toward the stairs leading down to the main floor.

Well . . . that was damaging.

Galen cleared his throat. "My darling," he addressed his wife, "come look at this painting with me for a moment."

Haley looked as if she would protest, but a quick glance at her husband's face ended the debate and the pair discreetly withdrew to give Ashe a moment alone with his ward.

"She was very friendly," Caroline noted. "Though that was a bit more conversation than I was led to expect from a woman of your preference."

Damn the woman's memory!

"I am not going to discuss a woman like that—here!"

"You won't discuss her," Caroline echoed, looking after Margot as she disappeared down the stairs before turning her focus back to Ashe, "but you'll enjoy her company when it suits you. How sad!"

"Margot hardly needs your sympathy," he said, then winced at his inadvertent use of the courtesan's first name. It was an implicit confession he'd never meant to make.

"I meant to say how sad for you, Mr. Blackwell. You value your company less than your conversation."

"In this instance, Miss Townsend"—Ashe tried to keep his tone low to not draw any more attention from passersby— "I value my reputation and privacy."

"But only in this instance?" she asked pertly.

"Mr. Blackwell," the unmistakable voice of Lady Fitzgerald cut into their exchange, and Ashe began to wonder if he hadn't earned some kind of curse. "What have you done to my American?"

"Lady Fitzgerald, do you not approve of the changes?" Ashe held his ground.

Caroline had also turned at Lady Fitzgerald's unexpected appearance and had the good grace to blush.

"You look like a dream in that color, Miss Townsend," her ladyship noted, just as a haggard Miss Eustace Woodberry caught up with her friend. "Doesn't she look wonderful, Eustace?"

"L-lovely," Eustace agreed, desperately trying to catch her breath.

"We are here to see this new modern style of painting on display for ourselves," Lady Fitzgerald continued. "Naturally, I don't intend to return in case my interest is misinterpreted as an endorsement, so I'm determined to take in everything I can to form an opinion in a single afternoon."

Eustace nodded miserably behind her and Ashe had to bite the inside of his lip at the inconvenient urge to laugh. "Well, then we are lucky to meet you, even briefly, Lady Fitzgerald. Since you recall Miss Townsend, may I introduce Lord and Lady Winters?"

"I know your father, the Earl of Stamford, Lord Winters, and it is a genuine pleasure to meet you at last." The dowager gave them a courteous nod before signaling Eustace to prepare to keep walking. "Lady Winters, I am charmed. If I recall, you were a Moreland before your marriage, were you not?"

"Yes." Haley nodded. "I was."

"A very old family," Lady Fitzgerald pronounced with approval—as if her word were final in all matters. "Well, if you'll excuse us, we have much to see and Eustace is eager to proceed."

Lady Fitzgerald set sail with a nearly limping Miss Woodberry in tow, bringing a comical touch to the strange interlude.

Galen put a hand on Ashe's shoulder, his voice low

enough that only his friend could hear. "You certainly have no shortage of interesting women in your life."

"You have no idea," Ashe said under his breath, his gaze fastening on the one woman who stood primly and unapologetically at the center of the chaos that had become his life.

* * *

The day ended without further upheaval, but Caroline wasn't sure if the quiet served her nerves any better. She was humbled by the sweetness of Lady Winters and the casual humor of her husband, and she truly hoped she'd found a friend in Haley. Caroline tried to remind herself that only she knew of the strange twists in her relationship with her "guardian," but it was hard not to allow the turmoil of her emotions to show. Miss Margot Stillman was a beauty, without question, with her jet black hair and pouting lips. And while she'd naturally known that he had dozens of women, that his indiscretions were the reason for his grandfather's threats, meeting the courtesan had hit her far harder than she'd expected. The woman was like a bird of paradise, and she'd suddenly felt foolish in her new dress—a mud wren putting on airs.

I'm jealous. My God, I bristled like a woman with something to claim—and why? Because he's toyed with me? Almost kissed me? Occupies my every waking thought?

It was an indefensible situation to be in. Jealousy came tangled with a dozen other admissions she wasn't ready to face, but she was far too proud to pout about it in front of Lord and Lady Winters.

When they reached the brownstone and made their farewells, Caroline braced herself for yet another disagreement with her charge. But as she pulled off her new bonnet, Ashe simply headed upstairs without another word.

"Did you enjoy the Royal Museum?" Godwin asked as he took the bonnet from her numb fingers.

"Yes, it was . . . extremely enlightening." She watched Ashe's retreat, unsure of what to say. "If you'll excuse me, Godwin, I need to ask Mr. Blackwell about something."

She followed him up the stairs, wanting more than anything to apologize and heal the rift between them. When she reached the open doorway of his rooms, it was clear he was preparing to go back out. "Please don't go out, Ashe."

"You have enough for ten letters to my grandfather, Caroline. There's no need to worry about me instigating anything at this hour."

"We had such a lovely day. I was hoping that we could talk and—

"A lovely day? Allow me to summarize. We were publicly accosted by a whore of my past acquaintance and if that didn't sting enough, you decided to turn it into an open debate about character upon which Lady Fitzgerald chose that moment to appear unannounced and make my 'lovely day' complete."

"Is that what she really is? A whore of your past acquaintance?"

"Say what you mean to say, Miss Townsend."

"She seemed extremely . . . familiar with you."

"She once was—extremely and intimately familiar with me, Miss Townsend." She knew he was being deliberately provocative, but it stung nonetheless.

"But not now."

The storm in his eyes became ominous. "You overstep, but then, I should be used to that by now."

"I want your word that you aren't seeing her, or anyone like her, on these excursions of yours." *God help me, I sound more like a jealous woman than anything else!*

"And what would my word be worth? Would you trust anything that I might say?"

She hesitated for a heart-stopping moment and instantly regretted it. His look was scathing as he walked past her, heading out into the hall and down the stairs out of the house.

Chapter

10

🌰

After lunch the following day, Caroline stared at the blank paper beneath her fingertips, doing her best to compose her thoughts before laying the point to the page. She wanted to send a letter to the elder Mr. Blackwell and reassure him that all was well, but she wasn't sure how to sound convincing.

I am enjoying my time in London and your grandson's hospitality.

Caroline sighed. It wasn't a lie, but the note would be miserably short as any additional details seemed inappropriate. It was hard to imagine how his grandfather would interpret a description of her misadventures to date. She'd started enough arguments to qualify as a harridan, yielded control of her wardrobe, and discovered that she may be just as susceptible to Ashe's charms as any other woman— despite all her resolutions to the contrary.

And had misplaced a second candlestick from my room, somehow broken a water pitcher, and woken up without a

stitch on. Thank goodness Mrs. Clark is a woman of such
good humor when it comes to the house's furnishings!
Even so, I can't help but worry. If either Blackwell gentle-
man learns of my poverty, petty theft would be just the
minor incident to seal my fate and lose my chance for an
independent future.

So far, everyone's assumption that she had inherited
some of her own dear grandfather's wealth had gone un-
challenged. It wasn't in her nature to betray her family's
small cruelties to the outside world and it was hard to imagine what Ashe's reaction would be if he learned that she
had a profession. Ladies from good families were allowed
to do charity work so long as it didn't interfere with the vast
portion of their lives or overexcite their passions to qualify
as a "cause," but a profession was out of the question. She'd
always understood the rule, even if she didn't accept it, and
had never said anything of her teaching position in her cor-
respondence with Mr. Gordon Blackwell.

I am enjoying my time in London and your grandson's
hospitality. She tried the sentence out again in her mind.
Your grandson's hospitality. His home was lovely, and his
servants extremely attentive. But Ashe still refused to eat
most meals with her, avoiding her company whenever he
could, which made the erratic moments when they were
together even more potent and unsettling.

I am enjoying London and even did some unexpected
shopping the other morning.

At last, Caroline abandoned delays and began to pen as
straightforward and entertaining a letter as she could manage, without betraying any unsettling details. She described
her impressions of the people and places and assured her
patron that kippers had been the best surprise so far.

"Making a report to Grandfather Walker, are we?"

She looked up, instinctively covering the page with another blank sheet of paper. "I thought he'd wish to know
how much I'm . . . enjoying London."

"Really? Enjoying London?" Ashe's expression conveyed his skepticism, his eyes dark with some unnamed foul mood. "Don't forget to mention the lovely weather we've been having."

"Would you like me to convey any message from you?"

"I'm sure you're being thorough enough that I'd have nothing to add."

"You're pouting." She set her pen down. "If it's any comfort, I kept the indiscretion with Mrs. Lowery out of my recounting—"

"By all means, don't leave anything out! What kind of dutiful chaperone and spy would you be if you began editing your tales?"

"You're trying to goad me into some kind of quarrel, like some guilty adolescent!"

"Damn it! I am not a child!"

"No, you are not!" She stood, hands on her hips, squaring off with him and fearlessly ignoring how he towered over her. "You are a grown man who was crowing about his wicked reputation when I first met him, so why you're roaring at me like a wounded lion is beyond my understanding! I'm writing a letter to a dear old man who has treated me like family and was kind enough to send for me and request my help! I'm dutifully sending him word, just as he'd asked, and if you have issue with it, speak plainly or write your grandfather yourself!"

"I'll speak plainly! I'm growing tired of this ridiculous charade! I've demonstrated that I can manage myself. Why don't you write and tell my grandfather that there's no need to continue?" Ashe held his place, refusing to step back. "He'd be happy to have you back at Bellewood and you can congratulate yourself on a man reformed!"

"You've demonstrated nothing of the kind! You behave when it is in your better interest to do so, but you're a notorious flirt. And I'm hardly confident you're managing yourself when you leave the house alone at all hours!"

"I made it clear when you arrived that I will come and go as I please!"

"You can make whatever rules suit you, Mr. Blackwell. It doesn't mean I'm going to turn a blind eye to your strange propensity to make social calls late into the night—and return at any hour!"

"My God, what are you doing? Standing at the windows all night?" he asked, his voice dropping with an icy chill.

"No!" Caroline hated the heat that flooded her cheeks, aware of the telltale color that accompanied it and made her look like a guilty spy. "I have trouble sleeping. . . ."

"*You* are having trouble sleeping," he repeated, an ominous look in his eyes.

She suddenly felt wary of him. "It isn't unheard of."

"I'll tell you what's unheard of." Ashe leaned just an inch or two closer, and Caroline's heart skipped a beat—but not out of fear. "What is unheard of is a man with any measure of a spine putting himself through all of this."

"Is it truly that difficult?" she spoke quietly. "Parties and dinners? Afternoon socials and teas? Are they so horrible to endure? Or is it my cumbersome company that stings your pride the most? Am I such a wretched harridan that I drive you to behave like a rude oaf out of sheer defense? For you certainly avoid me as often as you can!"

"I'm going out for a ride, chaperone, and I'm *not* asking your permission or making any promises to return before next Thursday!" He turned, stalking off in a rage. He called over his shoulder, "Keep up if you can, Miss Townsend, but otherwise, stay the hell out of my way!"

Caroline stomped her foot in frustration, loathing the man for his stubborn pride and unpredictable moods. *One moment he's playing the generous guardian and being attentive and playful and the next . . . he's storming off as if it's my fault that he's in this mess!*

"I'll keep up with you, Rogue! You're not in charge of

me, you big bully!" Her words echoed in the empty salon. Caroline looked down at the unfinished letter, wishing she had more courage. A clock ticked on a side table and the decision to follow him was made in a single reckless breath. Caroline marched out of the room, determined to teach him that she was not some lapdog to be kicked aside whenever he pleased.

She reached the stable yard just behind Ashe, in time to see him mount a sleek brown stallion in the courtyard and ride off.

"Is there a horse saddled that I can take, James?" she asked the groomsman.

"I . . . I was about to give Juno a walk-up, but—"

"I'll take her."

"Are you . . . sure?" He eyed her plain dark green day dress with its full skirt and crinoline. "I mean, if you'd like, I can hold her while you—"

"James, I'll take her now. Thank you." Caroline eyed the gray roan mare stoically. The animal was far larger than she'd anticipated. But she wasn't about to back down. Riding seemed a simple thing. You sat on the horse and held the reins and held on. *How difficult can it really be? People do it all the time! Even my cousin Mary Louise, who has the intellect of a house cat, rides!*

"Y-you don't have gloves or boots, Miss Townsend," James pointed out miserably. "Not even a proper coat!"

"Please help me up, James!" She stepped up onto the little wooden stool next to the mare. "I have to catch up to Mr. Blackwell! Please, hurry!"

"Miss Townsend, I . . ." James tried again to delay her, but she gripped his arm in panic.

"James, please!"

The young man's shoulders sagged in defeat as he reluctantly gave in to her unorthodox pleas and helped her up into the saddle. Her skirts and petticoats were no small encumbrance, but once she had the reins, Caroline wasted no more time in worrying about the details.

You're not going to escape me this time, Ashe!

* * *

He never expected her to follow. He'd left the salon like a man with all the demons in hell at his heels. And suddenly, it was as if they were.

Wisps of memories long banished tangled with recollections of the dungeon that the Jaded shared and the strange balance he was sure the universe had kept by punishing him there. He'd been too fractured for recovery and hated the cause of all of it—his own weak and wanton nature.

"All misfortune is earned, either in this lifetime or a previous one, and a man must taste each drop of misery with a smile before he can achieve growth," an old shaman had intoned when he'd first arrived in India, and Ashe had laughed because life was about pleasure—not pain! And then, the universe had enjoyed the last laugh as the floodgates of agony had opened up on his head. . . . He'd fallen in love for the first time and brought nothing but misery and death to her doorstep in return. If there'd been joy, it was too fleeting to bring any comfort, and he'd lost the ability to feel anything before he'd been caught and hauled off to that dungeon. *All misfortune is earned.*

The American siren had brought it all to the surface with her dreamlike kisses and looks of disapproval. *I'll write my grandfather myself and see if there's any chance of packing the puritan off before—*

"Ashe!"

He heard her calling just as he started to gallop down the drive and realized with a shock that she'd taken him at his word. He reined in his horse and turned, struck with the horrifying sight of Miss Caroline Townsend wrestling with her horse as the mare took fright from Caroline's full skirts flapping about its neck. The animal bolted in panic and he knew Caroline wasn't going to make it past the stable arches. He spurred his own mount to try to reach her in time but could only watch helplessly as the grooms desperately ran forward to aid her—but not before she fell.

The world slowed, and Ashe felt severed from reality, the only sound his own ragged breathing in his ears as he closed the distance and jumped from his horse before it had even stopped running to try to get to her faster. "Caroline!"

He was at her side instantly, pulling her into his arms, fear choking him.

She pushed against him, an impatient and unwilling victim. "I'm fine!"

"I'm going to dismiss that groomsman for ever allowing you to—"

"You can't! Poor James was nearly in tears when I practically stole that horse, and I would feel directly responsible! Please, don't!" she pleaded.

"Poor James can keep his job then, but he'll get a lecture from me about letting strange American women steal my horses," he conceded begrudgingly.

She shifted away from him again and only managed to sit more squarely in the ice-cold muck. "*This* was not at all how I imagined it!"

He bit the inside of his cheek to keep from smiling as he took in the delicious sight of a spitting-mad Caroline Townsend, ignobly landed on her ripe derriere in a mud puddle—unharmed. "How did you imagine it?"

"Oh, the usual!" she moaned, trying to pull her ruined skirts back down over her ankles. "Wind in my hair, gracefully chasing you down to kick you in the shins!"

"Ah, yes! The *usual* . . ." He lost his battle of self-control and grinned at her signature candor. "Perhaps you can kick me later."

"Don't think I won't!" she said, a small smile echoing

his as her humor returned. She examined her bloodied palms, scraped from her untrained landing on the drive's gravel. "Mrs. Clark will fuss about these!"

Ashe had had enough. He swept her up off the ground into his arms and lifted her to carry her toward the house.

"I'm perfectly capable of walking!" she said breathlessly, forced to put her arms around his neck for balance. "Mr. Blackwell, put me down!"

"No." The brief answer irritated her, but Ashe didn't care. Relief was powering a surge of possessiveness that he couldn't deny and didn't want to.

She began to kick and twist in his arms, but it was all too easy to tighten his hold and capture her more tightly against him.

"Is everything all right, sir? Should I send for Dr. West?" Godwin offered as Ashe marched back into the house with his uncooperative prize.

"Everything is fine, Godwin. Miss Townsend was just enjoying her first riding lesson. Please inform Mrs. Clark to draw Miss Townsend a hot bath and send up a bottle of brandy." He turned back to speak to Godwin, as if carrying American women through the house was an ordinary occurrence. "Also, send word to Foster's we won't make dinner tonight."

She stopped kicking, but Ashe knew he hadn't won the day as he headed up the stairs.

"It wasn't that big of a puddle, Mr. Blackwell. I'm not sure that a bath is in order," she argued primly, the color in her cheeks turning to a dusky pink. "It's the expensive dress you purchased that bore the brunt of it."

"You'll think differently when your muscles and joints start to protest later—not to mention your backside."

She squeaked in outrage at his indelicate mention of her bruised bottom, and Ashe's chest tightened at the dear little sound. He was becoming far too fond of Miss Townsend's unguarded expressions.

As he reached the door to her bedroom, he set her gingerly down on her feet, noticing as he did that she'd lost one of her new shoes in her brief battle with Juno. "There, I've put you down."

"You are an imperious and infuriating man, Mr. Blackwell."

"I'd apologize, but I think I should wait for just another moment."

"Another moment for what purpose?"

"For this."

He leaned over and, in an instance of pure impulse, kissed her. He credited shock for holding her in place, and then there was nothing of thought or strategies. Instead of a tender first kiss, this was about reclamation and possession of the sweet delights he'd already sampled. Her lips parted for his, a spontaneous surrender that was made all the more potent in its unpracticed passions. Soft and succulent, her mouth became a feast of sensation and taste that made him drunk with raw lust. As his arms tightened around her, pressing her against the heat of his frame, there was nothing left of reason. There was only hunger for her and the scalding dance of her mouth against his as she matched his needs, never pulling away but instead proving that his reserved little chaperone was a tempestuous thing—warm and willing.

It was the heady confirmation that the chemistry between them the other night wasn't a fleeting dream or misguided game. A small sound escaped from her, a purring sigh that added to the strength of the storm inside of him. His cock was a searing weight that ignored civility, and Ashe's hands slid down her back to cup the ripe curve of her ass and lift her up against him. Even through untold layers of petticoats, he could feel the delightful fire between her thighs and he knew he was lost.

At last, she began to pull her mouth from his, gasping for air as she wriggled to try to achieve some distance between them. "You . . ." she whispered.

"Would you like that apology now?" he offered, releasing her slowly to set her back on her feet.

Before she could summon her wits to answer, he stepped back at the first echoes of Godwin's footsteps coming up the stairs. If he'd thought it would feel better to reveal that the woman who visited him as she dreamt was truly the same one that irritated him so consistently when awake—he was mistaken.

Instead Ashe felt like the worst cad.

He'd overstepped in both realms and made himself a depraved cliché.

"I'm sorry, Miss Townsend. You have my word, for whatever weight it still holds, that that will *never* happen again." He kept his voice low, grimly grounding out his confession. "I have likely been in the wrong since we first met at Bellewood, and didn't realize . . . I am apparently so far into the dark woods, as my grandfather phrased it, that I have forgotten myself. Please forgive me." He gave her a curt nod and walked away, unwilling to withstand the devastation and hurt in her eyes.

* * *

She leaned against the closed door and tried to catch her breath. It was the first time she'd ever been kissed and Caroline was stunned at the revelation of it. And there was no denying she had been truly and thoroughly kissed, and even worse, that she'd welcomed it.

Welcomed it. Reveled in it. Gotten lost in it.

It was one thing to find her host attractive and distracting, but this was different. This was a hunger she'd never experienced before, a longing so powerful she'd yielded up everything she was to him—and she'd wanted more. Only to discover that whatever had made him reach for her had also caused him untold pain.

If he were simply toying with her, she'd have expected some laughter or a continuation of the sarcastic lesson he'd initiated in the carriage after the dinner at the Bedfords'. But he hadn't looked like a man amused by a game or gloating in his superiority over her. . . . The heartless rogue had looked lost somehow.

But I'm the one with the heart to lose.

A gentle knock on the other side of the door interrupted her thoughts.

"Miss Townsend?" Mr. Godwin inquired from the hallway. "May I come in?"

She opened the door to a very worried-looking Mr. Godwin holding a tray of refreshments, including a very out of place bottle of brandy. "In a panic, Cook has thrown every sweet she had on hand onto a plate but then thought to add a bowl of broth, so I'm not sure what you'll make of this, miss."

"You can just set it on the desk, Mr. Godwin, and tell her I'm overwhelmed at her thoughtfulness." She stepped back to allow him access, wishing she weren't so much trouble for the house. "There's no need for panic. I just introduced myself to a mud puddle."

"And to Juno," he added with a smile, setting down the large tray. "Cook will send up heartier fare for your dinner, and in the meantime, Mrs. Clark is making sure the water is heated for your bath."

"Will Mr. Blackwell be dining in this evening?"

Godwin shook his head. "He has made other plans."

"Oh." Caroline practically winced, dreading another quiet dinner in her room spent worrying about where her handsome charge had gone and when he would come back. She felt increasingly helpless and useless in her role, and the day's events had only added to her confusion and anxiety. *Is Ashe friend or foe? I cannot say which would worry me more. . . .*

Mr. Godwin continued, "Oh, and Mrs. Clark wanted me to reassure you that the candlesticks were recovered. I'm not sure what the message means, but Daisy was eager that you should hear the news."

"Where did she find them?" Caroline felt breathless with relief.

"Mrs. Clark didn't say."

"I've come up to ready you for your bath, miss!" Daisy hailed from the open doorway.

Caroline started to reassert that she didn't need a bath but caught sight of her reflection in a mirror on the wall. She'd smeared mud and blood on her cheek reaching up to push her hair off her face, and she resembled a derelict with her chignon falling down and a splatter of mud across the front of her white blouse. *He kissed me looking like that?* "Oh, dear! Yes, perhaps a bath . . ."

Mr. Godwin nodded. "I'll leave you in good hands then, and of course, you'll ring if there's anything else you need."

"Yes, thank you, Mr. Godwin."

He closed the door behind him, and she was immediately enveloped in Daisy's lively chatter and gentle ministrations. "What a fuss they're making downstairs! My poor James! He got an earful from Mrs. Clark about not taking as good a care of you as he should, and then they was all giving him such a dressing-down I thought he'd melt into a puddle!"

"Oh, no! You must tell Mrs. Clark the fault was entirely mine! I wasn't thinking!"

Daisy nodded, guiding her to the chair in front of the vanity table. "A man'll do that to you, mark those words! My cousin Jenny used to get so angry at her beau that she'd just start swinging pots and pans at the man. Her aim became so deadly, she knocked the sense right out of him. Regrets it to this day! Course, he earned a cracked skull bein' a worthless scrap of a man, but . . . she's forgotten all that now that he's as meek as a lamb. Just smiles and does whatever he's told! An improvement, some might say." Daisy picked up the silver comb to begin taking down the rest of Caroline's ruined twists and braids, releasing Caroline's muted gold curls to fall down her back. "Not that we were eavesdropping to know about your quarrel with Mr. Blackwell."

Caroline wasn't sure what to protest against—that Ashe had robbed her of her senses or that the entire house had overheard their terrible exchange. "It was a simple misunderstanding."

Daisy's silence spoke volumes as she set the comb aside and picked up the brush. "As you say, miss."

Caroline's eyes dropped to the vanity's marble surface, wishing she could remember propriety *before* she started raising her voice and allowing her temper to get the better of her.

"Mind you," Daisy went on, her tone friendly and full of comfort, "I think it's good for a man like Mr. Blackwell to have someone who's not afraid to speak her mind. With his wealth and pretty looks, there's not many a woman that would square off to give him trouble, and my mother always used to say that adversity makes the man."

Caroline smiled. "Your mother sounds very clever."

"She was! And she had a lot of experience squaring off with my father, so there you have it!" Daisy set the brush down and went over to the wardrobe to retrieve Caroline's dressing gown. Daisy helped her undress, her fingers nimbly making quick work of the numerous buttons and ties. "Mrs. Clark just had them carry up a bit of hot water from the kitchens to make sure everything was ready for you."

"Thank you, Daisy."

Within minutes, Caroline was in the wash room, ensconced in the claw-footed tub, up to her chin in steaming luxury scented with lemons and sweet water. Despite all her protests, the bath's magic was instantly apparent and every ache and pain began to dissipate. *The distance from Juno to the ground looked much scarier once I was on the dear mare than it had from the yard. I can't believe that was me, ordering servants about and trying to gallop down the road without a single hint of a plan.*

"Oh, well." She sighed. "At least I didn't hit him with an iron pan."

Daisy stepped back inside with a tray of soap and warm cloths. "Men have earned worse."

"Oh!" Caroline blushed. "Well, lucky then there wasn't a pan at hand."

"Miss? If you don't mind me asking . . ." Daisy set the tray down and knelt next to the bath. "Not that we was eavesdropping, mind."

"Well noted. I would never accuse you of eavesdropping."

"But if you're to keep an eye on him—and it's at his grandfather's request, well, I mean, it's the comings and goings that sounds like trouble, I'd have to agree." Daisy spoke without looking at her directly, instead rearranging the lotions and soaps on the side table. "But James, well, he's much beholden to you for defending him and I am, too, for keeping my man in service. And if you wished to know where his carriages go . . ."

"Th-that would be incredibly helpful, Daisy."

"Mind, it's no help when he rides off on his own, but we'll do our best. Especially if there's a bit of a warning. Harder to say when the master leaves in a rush, but at least James could give you an idea of where they'd been." Daisy looked at her directly, her cornflower blue eyes shining with concern. "They'll be no mercy for either of us if Mr. Blackwell finds out, miss. But you've been so kind, I know you'll not say anything to him."

So much for being too embarrassed to ask her. . . . Caroline shook her head. "I'd see myself turned out first, Daisy."

"I knew you'd say something like that, and that's what I told James. And that it was only right to help you." Daisy held out one of the cloths. "I understand you're not going to the Fosters' dinner."

"My undignified stunt caused Mr. Blackwell to cancel our engagement, but I can't say that I'm truly disappointed."

Caroline wasn't sure she could have faced the scrutiny of strangers after the day she'd had. Even now, the lingering memory of his kiss and abrupt withdrawal afterward made her feel vulnerable and on edge. "Mr. Godwin said he's made plans to go out again tonight."

"We'll see." Daisy sat back on her heels. "For now, he's locked himself in his study for the night, prowling about in there like a caged lion. If James hears differently, I'll let you know."

"Thank you, Daisy." Caroline sighed. "I . . . I don't need anything else for now."

"Yes, Miss Townsend. Ring if you think of something and I'll come straight away." Daisy stood with a smile and left the room to allow her some privacy.

Caroline sank back into the warm water until it touched her chin.

She tried to convince herself that nothing had really changed. She was still charged with watching over him and still committed to her promise to Grandfather Walker. But everything *had* changed.

I am undeniably not *immune to Mr. Ashe Blackwell's charms.*

Chapter
11

Worthley's grand mansion was filled to capacity with a glittering whirl of London's elite, each vying to outshine the other as they reveled in an extraordinary social Season. Ashe could only watch in wonder as "his American" was sought after for every dance, garnering admirers and holding her own as if she'd attended hundreds of grand balls. Her dress was a revelation, and their playful exchange at the dressmaker's came back to haunt him. The shimmering silk was an ethereal shade of silvery blue that evoked an icy waterfall. The draped fabric of the generous skirt was elegant without any of the lace flounces and flowers the other women drowned in, accenting her tiny waist and generous curves. She was a breathing confection of muted gold and blue, his Indian star sapphire brought to life.

This is no wallflower, shyly waiting for attention. She's something else entirely, and I'm the fool who cannot seem to go a single day without wanting to kiss her or

strangle her. Although lately, it's been far too much about
wanting to kiss the creature for my comfort!

He'd practically locked himself in his rooms since he'd
"mashed" her outside her bedroom door, banishing all but
Godwin to bring him trays on the condition that the man
didn't utter a single word.

Ashe hadn't trusted himself to go out, entirely too aware
that his sexual frustration had gained a ravenous edge that
defied logic. He was no longer confident that it was absti-
nence alone that had given his desires such stinging tenacity. Especially since his fantasies now all revolved around
one petite and impertinent American who was as alluring
splattered with mud as she was swathed in silk.

Mrs. Grantley, an acquaintance of his grandfather's,
had met them at the event to oversee Miss Townsend's
attendance and play the matronly chaperone, and Ashe
hadn't resented the interference. Tonight, he was going to
demonstrate once and for all his self-control, discipline,
and power to ignore sleepwalking sirens—or kill himself
in the attempt.

"Mrs. Grantley," Caroline began again, "I don't really
dance. Perhaps if you explained to some of these gentlemen
that they are risking their personal safety it would—"

"Tosh!" Mrs. Grantley huffed. "Of course you can
dance! Besides, no one expects you to know all the latest figures, being hindered as you are by your American
upbringing!"

"I'm not sure I would describe it as a hindrance to be
Amer—"

"You'll dance!" Mrs. Grantley was an immovable object, and Ashe had to bite the inside of his cheek to keep
from smiling as the color in Caroline's cheeks betrayed
her ire, but she fanned herself and gave up the debate. She
looked at him to see if he might prove a potential ally, but
Ashe quickly looked away.

"Is Mr. Blackwell dancing?" Caroline asked Mrs. Grantley, as if he weren't standing at her side.

Ashe shook his head curtly, and Mrs. Grantley's brow furrowed as she answered, "I-I'd say it seems unlikely."

Caroline's fan slowed and she squared her shoulders. "What a pity! Just think of all the disappointed women who will regret missing their chance. . . ."

Ashe cleared his throat, unable to stop himself from responding. "I hardly think they'll grieve."

"Really? Lady Fitzgerald made it clear that every woman in England was eager to take her turn in your arms," Caroline said archly.

Mrs. Grantley gasped, and Ashe grinned despite his vows. "Are they? *Every* woman?"

"Clearly, Lady Fitzgerald has an exaggerated impression of your influence." Caroline's look was ice-cold dismissal. "I can't speak for Mrs. Grantley, but I'd wager that I know of at least one lady who would rather embrace a beehive."

"She sounds like a very sensible creature. I shall have to make a point of introducing myself and commending the lady."

She didn't reply, instead closing her fan with a snap. "You'll earn a scratched face for your efforts, Mr. Blackwell."

He smiled, a humorless thing. The impulsive vow he'd made after kissing her yesterday still tasted like poison on his tongue, but his resolve and pride were all he could hold to. *Or forfeit my sanity.*

He spotted Darius in the throng, making his way toward them in his best evening clothes, but instead of relief, a surprising new emotion gripped him.

Damn!

"May I introduce Mr. Darius Thorne to you? Darius, this is Miss Caroline Townsend of Boston." Ashe made the introductions, his tone clipped and emotionless, and then briefly bowed. "If the two of you will excuse me, I just spotted an old acquaintance I should speak to." Ashe walked away to quickly put some distance between himself and the pair, quietly cursing the anxiety and jealousy that had attacked him when he'd seen Darius dutifully crossing the room.

Well, here's a twist! This was my brilliant idea, and by God, I'm not going to stand here and pout like a miffed schoolboy. Thorne's a man of his word and he's only here as a favor to me.

Ashe's displeasure snaked inside his chest, and he let out a long, slow breath to embrace the pain. "All misfortune is earned," he whispered to himself.

* * *

Caroline watched Ashe walk away with stiff steps, his back ramrod straight as he retreated so unexpectedly.

"It's a pleasure to meet you at last, Miss Thomspon."

"At last?" Caroline smiled as her newest acquaintance managed to look even more uncomfortable in their surroundings than she felt. Tall and striking, his green eyes were kind, as he bowed over her hand.

"I am an old friend of Ashe's and he spoke very highly of you."

She laughed. "Did he? Nothing of his reports can be good if they are accurate, so I'll just pretend to be flattered, Mr. Thorne."

"That can't be true." Darius shook his head.

"What exactly did he say, then?"

Darius hesitated long enough for them both to start to smile. "I couldn't repeat his praise verbatim, but I'm sure he mentioned that you were incredibly clever."

"Clever is his way of saying difficult, I should warn you. Mr. Blackwell doesn't appreciate a woman with opinions of her own."

"Mr. Blackwell doesn't appreciate anyone with opinions of their own," Darius countered, "but as his friend, I've learned to ignore his more troublesome traits and render my opinions as I wish."

"Exactly the approach I was taking!" Caroline fanned herself, marveling at how comfortable she was with Mr. Thorne. "Have you known Mr. Blackwell for many years?"

"A few, but I would boast that from those brief years in his acquaintance, I know more of him than most." Darius shrugged. "Ashe is . . . complicated."

"Is he?" she asked, her voice soft and careful. "I suppose he must be."

"Must?" Darius gave her a curious look.

"The man would have it that he is just as you see, but he's as changeable as quicksilver and as difficult to contain." She shrugged. "Is that not complicated enough?"

"I'd say you have a firm grasp on the man." Darius held out his arm to escort her toward the dance floor.

"How did you come to know Mr. Blackwell?"

"We met abroad. I was traveling to study the linguistic links between ancient Sanskrit and Arabic, but also to survey some of the architectural design of the local temples."

"How fascinating!"

"You'd be one of the first to think so, I'm afraid. My scholarly pursuits rarely make for interesting parlor conversations."

"Do they not? I cannot imagine a better subject than one that shares knowledge or enlightens the mind." Caroline shook her head. "Perhaps that's why my parlor conversation is never very entertaining."

"Ashe said you were well read." He stopped at the floor and swung her into position to join the other dancers. "Shall we dance?"

Caroline took a deep breath. "I can only promise to do my best not to injure your toes, Mr. Thorne."

"A generous promise," Darius said with a smile. "And one I'll try to uphold myself."

He swept her onto the floor, his own awkward steps disguising hers as they both did their best to navigate the crowded room with some semblance of grace. After a minute they were both laughing at their subterfuge, hiding amidst the other more skilled dancers and trying not to trade pinched toes.

"Tell me the truth, Mr. Thorne," she said. "Should I mercifully lose my dance card and hide behind the drapes for the rest of the evening?"

"And deprive your other partners of this test of chivalry?" Darius did his best to turn her in time to the music, narrowly avoiding a collision with another couple. "Never!"

Caroline meant to say something clever about misguided knights, but a man approached from behind Darius and tapped him on the shoulder at exactly that moment.

"Pardon," the man began, his expression congenial. "But may I borrow your delightful partner for the remainder of the dance?"

Darius stopped, the intrusion unexpected but not out of bounds when it came to the rules of etiquette. "If Miss Townsend has no objections, I suppose that would be acceptable."

Caroline shook her head, privately disappointed to lose her newest ally so soon, but she acquiesced. "Yes, though I hope to hear more of your studies, Mr. Thorne."

"Absolutely, I'll make a point of it." Darius bowed to her and then courteously allowed the other gentleman to take his place.

Fashionably pale, the interloper's cravat was an elaborate and exaggerated concoction that seemed to highlight the fact that the man seemed to have no chin, but his smile was friendly. "Miss Townsend! You cannot imagine what a pleasure it is to have this chance to meet at last!"

"At last?" She tried not to laugh. "Everyone keeps saying that and I cannot see how anyone deserves such anticipation."

"Oh, I'm sure you are deserving, Miss Townsend. I am a relative and friend of the Blackwells and delighted to learn of your arrival. If you'll permit me, I am Winston Yardley."

He guided her back into the swirling crowd, his hold much lighter than Mr. Thorne's and less protective. What had been amusing with Darius felt unsteadier now, but Caroline did her best to brazen it out.

"Of course, Mr. Yardley."

"You are from Boston, are you not?" he asked. "I knew, of course, that the elder Mr. Blackwell had partnered with an American some years ago, but when I heard that the connection had endured and that your family had entrusted you to English friends for a time . . . it was a happy surprise."

Caroline's mirth faded. There was something about the gentleman that didn't set well, but she couldn't name it. "Yes, from Boston."

"You are not what I expected, Miss Townsend."

"What did you expect, Mr. Yardley?" Caroline asked as she barely missed having her instep crushed by the man.

"I'd heard you were inevitably awash in gray wool and gabardine. But you seem as fashionable a woman as any here!" He beamed at her. "I have often said that I wished to travel to America and explore some of your wilderness, but alas! I am needed here and cannot shirk my duties to go off on selfish adventures."

"A shame." She kept her eyes on his shirt front, thinking her first impression of Mr. Winston Yardley hardly allowed for him roughing it in the American West.

"And how are you finding London? Is it . . . satisfying?"

Caroline's heart skipped a beat. His tone made the polite question seem anything but polite. "It is a great city."

He grinned as if she'd made some lively jest. "You have a reputation for a quick tongue, Miss Townsend. I'd expected far more of an anecdotal reply."

"I hate to disappoint, but surely you've heard too many clichés about London to desire another tourist's tales."

"There is nothing cliché in any of your reported speeches, but what of my cousin? Any good anecdotes about him?"

She tried to hide her shock at the brazen inquiry, but before she could think of a response, he went on.

"No, no! I wouldn't dream of asking you for gossip about your guardian!" he said with a theatrical flourish of his eyebrows. "After all, gossip about Ashe is easy enough to come by, isn't it?"

"I wouldn't know, Mr. Yardley." Caroline stiffened, beginning to pray that the dance would end before she disgraced herself by making a scene. "I am not—"

A hand on Mr. Yardley's shoulder interrupted yet again, but this time the touch was not gentle and it was no chivalrous request to cut in. Ashe stood behind Mr. Yardley with an expression of fury that made her blood run cold. Relief at finding her rescuer so close at hand was matched by the sudden fear that Mr. Yardley might not survive the evening.

The music concluded, and while the other dancers retreated from the floor or hesitated as new partnerships were made, the three stood like a strange island in a glittering sea. Caroline almost forgot to breathe, but at last, Ashe spoke. "Miss Townsend has promised the next dance to me, Yardley."

Mr. Yardley stepped back, retreating with an awkward bow. "Naturally."

Ashe reached for Caroline, moving in front of Winston Yardley without a second glance, pulling her away farther onto the dance floor.

"Mr. Blackwell, I—" she began, but his hand tightened around hers and Caroline lost her train of thought.

And then the music began again and she was in his arms, and she was alone in the world with only Ashe to cling to. She forgot to worry about her toes or the steps of the dance because there was only Ashe's strong arms, guiding and holding her. Caroline felt graceful and weightless, and all her resolve to show him nothing but the practical and detached chaperone he deserved vanished.

She risked a glance up at his face and met his gaze, drowning anew in the deep blue she found there. Since they'd met, she'd experienced so many of his moods, but now, it was impossible to read him. He was fire and ice, desire and scorn, and Caroline felt a renewed sense of fearlessness as she faced him. *I am not afraid of you, Ashe.*

The room spun with each sweeping turn of the waltz, and the small distance between them became charged with an unspeakable energy. The simple dance transformed as the connection between them grew palpable. The rhythm of his body moving with hers, the fleeting touch of his hard thigh through her skirts sent shimmering arcs of heat up into her hips and back. Caroline became aware of each breath she took and every inch of her skin.

"Did I . . . do anything wrong, Mr. Blackwell?" she asked.

He shook his head but didn't speak.

Caroline nervously pursed her lips before trying again to divert herself from the havoc his touch was wreaking on her composure. "I thought you weren't dancing."

"And disappoint you?" He smiled at last, and Caroline marveled at the power it wielded, her knees weakening at the gleam in his eyes.

"Did I look disappointed?"

"You looked like a woman in need of a better partner."

She could feel the blush that bloomed on her cheeks. *Are all my feelings so transparent? Can he read me even now?*

"I only hope I didn't offend anyone if I'm so obvious."

"It's not possible, Miss Townsend. But did you enjoy meeting Mr. Thorne?"

"He was very amicable."

The gleam in Ashe's eyes darkened. "And Mr. Yardley?"

"Mr. Blackwell, are you jealous?"

"No." His next turn was a little faster, forcing her to cling to him in response. "Not of Yardley. But you should know that if I fail in my wager with my grandfather, it is the delightful Mr. Winston Yardley who stands to gain in my stead."

"Yardley inherits? If . . ."

"Yes."

It was too monstrous to think of, and Caroline's fingers trembled. She'd suspected that there were terrible consequences to his wager, but she'd never directly asked for fear it would affect her judgment. Suddenly all she could feel was sympathy for Ashe. Whatever his sins, it would be an injustice to forfeit his fortune and holdings to a man like that.

She felt new shame at her role in the sordid game. After all, she knew what it was to live without means at the discretion of someone else.

He went on, "It makes no difference, Miss Townsend. When I was younger, the world's fabric was woven of one passion or another—like a cloak that protected and insulated me from the dark cold of the world. And even when I learned that passion was no shield, I refused to change."

"And now?"

"I'll change because I choose to," Ashe said softly, "not because I'm compelled by the threat of a troll like Yardley." He swept her into another turn. "Tell me, Miss Townsend, did you mean what you said to my friends about not looking for a husband?"

"Yes, Mr. Blackwell."

He shook his head. "It's too simple an answer. I thought

most women considered matrimony an ideal state to achieve . . . happiness."

"Is that the case for men? Is it essential to their happiness?" she countered, enjoying the intricate steps of their quiet discussion as much as the dance itself. "Are you not questing for a wife, Mr. Blackwell?"

"Not now, but I will marry when I must, for all the usual reasons."

"And what reasons are those?" she asked.

"Duty, fortune, and family. I'm sure my grandfather has already selected some suitable young lady to occupy her place at Bellewood when the time comes."

"Are you not master of your own fate, sir?"

The smile he gave her never lit the melancholy blue of his eyes. "Is anyone?"

"You speak so readily of passion, Mr. Blackwell. But never love."

"Love is far more dangerous, Miss Townsend, than passion."

"Do you speak from experience or the cynical vantage point of a man too worldly to bother with such a dangerous emotion?"

He shook his head. "Experience is the best teacher. Isn't that the old saying?"

"Then you . . . you have been in love?" she asked, suddenly hoping desperately that he hadn't, that somehow no other woman would have such an intimate part of him.

"Once."

"And?"

"Once was enough and I'm not in the mood for confessions, Caroline. I prefer passion. No one gets hurt."

Except me . . . Each time you touch me and then push me away, she silently replied.

"Though I should warn you that as your guardian and one currently denied all distracting passions, I actually had visions of murdering my best friend tonight. My best friend who I would have joyfully sacrificed my own life to protect, but the sight of the two of you dancing together, conversing so easily and laughing . . ."

It was an admission that stunned her into a temporary silence, the flattering power of his jealousy too new for her to comprehend. *He is jesting. He is saying these things to tease and torment me, simply because he can.* "How lucky for him that you aren't prone to murder!" She blushed and smiled. "Thank goodness men no longer wear swords to formal occasions."

"I wouldn't need a sword. I was thinking that strangling Darius would be satisfying enough."

"Ashe," she said, his name sweet on her lips. "Perhaps you shouldn't introduce me to any more of your friends if—"

"Thorne is a good man. A better man than myself. And if I had any last shred of decency, I would simply step back and allow—"

She interrupted him. "I'm not a horse to be handed over, Mr. Blackwell."

He swept her into another turn. "Must everything be an argument?"

"No." She slid her hand down to touch his arm, an unconscious gesture of comfort and reconciliation. "Not everything."

But Ashe pulled away as the music ended, and he left her alone on the dance floor.

Chapter
12

Much later that night, Caroline nervously made her way to his rooms, unwilling to retire with so much unsaid. He'd retreated yet again behind a sullen wall, watching her dance with various partners until she was sure she'd done enough damage to her country's reputation to ensure a war. And then, at last, he'd sent her home with Mrs. Grantley overseeing her safe delivery into Mr. Godwin's custody. She'd waited by her window, keeping watch for him and his late solitary return. She was determined once and for all to have a straightforward conversation with the enigmatic man and put an end to the misunderstandings between them.

No more cat and mouse. I will tell him honestly of my position, and then he will give up the chase and I won't have to worry about my own weak inclinations when it comes to Ashe's charms. No man of his status will continue to bother with a schoolteacher—and we can finish the winter holidays without conflict.

She knocked softly on his door and waited for his hail

before entering quietly. "Pardon the late hour, Mr. Blackwell, but I—"

"Not again," he moaned softly, squaring his shoulders as he turned to face her, an unashamed Adonis with his unbuttoned shirt and open dressing gown. His long legs were still encased in black tailored pants, but his feet were bare and he looked every inch the reckless rogue. "I don't have it in me tonight to turn you away, miss. You have spent all your chances at virginal escapes."

Caroline hesitated, confused. *Again? Did he refer to the kiss? To their arguments? Virginal escapes?* "I didn't come to . . ."

"What do you want, Miss Townsend?" He poured himself a generous brandy from the sideboard. "Another session of nocturnal torture? For I will have to admit that I am at my limits. You give me those stern looks and cheeky lectures on how I should behave during the days and then . . . you present yourself in soft silk with that ripe little naked body underneath and pretend you haven't the foggiest idea of how your eyes drive a man past reason." He took a deep draught from the crystal glass. "You make a man wonder things he should not, Miss Townsend."

For Caroline, the world came to a dreamlike halt. "What kinds of things?" she whispered.

"You make me wonder if you'll close your eyes when I spread your thighs, or if you'll look at me just as you are now. You make me wonder if those lashes will lower when I taste you, or if the color will appear to change when you spend yourself against my mouth and my cock."

She gasped in shock, a spasm of wet heat between her thighs responding instinctively to his words as her inner muscles clenched in an unspeakable need.

"Even that little show of protest makes me want you." He set down the glass. "I don't have the strength to play this evening. Go, Miss Townsend. Or this time, instead of delivering you untouched back to your rooms, I'm going to finally prove myself the worst villain and ruin us both."

Torture him more? This time? He alluded to previous nocturnal visits, and God help me, I think of dreams and I blush. . . . Have I been sleepwalking again? Is it possible?

"You're hesitating, chaperone. I said go now." He walked toward the bellpull. "Damn the consequences! I'll ring for Mrs. Clark, and she'll see you settled innocently enough."

"I am not . . ." Caroline took a steadying breath. "I can see myself to my rooms, Mr. Blackwell."

He hesitated and turned slowly, looking at her with an intensity and new awareness that made her skin burn and her breasts feel heavy.

"You're—awake."

"I am awake, Mr. Blackwell."

"How extraordinary . . ." He didn't look away, holding her in place with the raw desire in his eyes. "Not extraordinary that you are awake, Miss Townsend, but that you're still here—for I would think a sensible woman would have fled several minutes ago."

"You don't seem to admire sensible women, Mr. Blackwell."

"You're wrong. I admire them very much and demonstrate that admiration by keeping my distance. You should go now, Caroline. I don't think one of your rousing debates is going to deter me for long."

She didn't move—she wasn't even sure she could. There was something so surreal about the exchange, and every part of her felt alive and hungry for whatever it was that sensible women ran from. "Deter you from . . ." She swallowed hard, wishing she could summon her wits enough to voice an unimaginable request. "I don't want to go."

He shook his head. "You have no idea what you're saying."

"Then perhaps I should make a confession of my own." She could hear the soft whisper of his breath stop in anticipation and surprise, and she summoned what courage she could to go on. "When I look at you—I wish for the most . . . lurid and preposterous things, and I don't care if I get hurt, Ashe."

"You don't know what you're saying."

"You must be right. For I think I have as much to lose, if not more, by this—but I can't seem to remember any of it now."

He held up a hand. "It's not possible, Miss Townsend. You could not have more to lose than I do. But here is where we stand. If you so much as twitch in my direction, I will not be held accountable for my actions."

"I want—"

"You'll want to flee now while you still can, or I'm going to demonstrate just how lurid and preposterous things can get. I am strong, Miss Townsend, but not strong enough to . . ."

She said nothing, but everything in her wished he would finish speaking. Just when she knew he wouldn't, he continued, his voice even rougher with raw emotion.

"I am already ruined, Miss Townsend. But you have the power to make me wish that I were not. Please, show mercy."

"Ashe," she whispered, "mercy is an easy thing, for I could ask the same of you."

"Damn it, woman!" He shook his head. "You should insist on an apology. I spoke earlier without any thought to your delicate nature and—"

"I am not that fragile. It's not as if I've threatened to swoon or run screaming."

"Why is that? Why haven't you?" He took a step closer, and her heart hammered in her chest. "You accuse me of playing games with women's affections, but it is you, Miss Townsend, who is toying with me. Have you discovered that you like the sweet taste of power? You hold the reins, as you yourself have pointed out more than once. Does it suit you to let me catch your scent only so that you can chastise me for responding?"

My scent . . . How is it that those words make me want to beg him to teach me a thousand indiscretions? How did I come to this moment?

"I wouldn't do such a thing. I have no illusions of holding any power over you. I'm not running because"—she hesitated, a blush coloring her face—"I'm not afraid of you."

"Of course you are, and you should be."

Her stomach fluttered with a dozen molten butterflies that began to alight in the cradle of her hips, a molten wet heat blossoming at the potent threat of his words. "And why is that?"

"Because you know I'm no gentleman." He took another step toward her. "Don't press me, Miss Townsend. An oath will only carry a man so far."

"Are you really so monstrous that you have to keep yourself hidden away from civilized folk? What sins have you committed, Mr. Blackwell, to earn exile?"

"What do you want from me, Miss Townsend?"

"I want you to tell me why you work so hard to be so . . ." Caroline hesitated, unsure of how to describe his self-imposed exile. "Why do you punish yourself, Ashe? Why do you despoil your own character?"

"Every misfortune is earned," he whispered.

Caroline shook her head and had to catch her breath before responding, as the sight of him so vulnerable and honest made her heart ache to touch him. "That is a philosophy that I cannot ascribe to, Ashe. You're intimating that you have the power to summon suffering, and while men may think of themselves as masters of the universe . . ." She prayed his humor would warm at the jest.

Ashe's smile was a wicked and wonderful thing to behold. "How is it that we're now discussing philosophy in my bedroom, Miss Townsend? You would make seduction a debate when I am seconds away from demonstrating just how ungentlemanly I can be. I'll only offer you one final chance to run, Caroline."

She held her breath before she shook her head. "No."

"For all your talk, you cannot be this much of a reformer, even with a fortune at your fingertips. You make a brave enough show of not wanting a husband, but I don't think you want to throw your chances for a good match away, Caroline. Not for me."

"Not for . . . you." Caroline tried to think of the words that could frame the storm of desire and desperation that raged inside of her. "You were right, earlier tonight, when you said that none of us were masters of our own fates. We're so different, you and I, but we have that much in common, Ashe. I have a fate and future of my own waiting in Boston when I return. And there is no match to ruin."

"You don't know that, Caroline."

You've known love and have no use for it, Ashe. But what I wouldn't give for a small taste of it . . . Aloud, she answered him as calmly as she could. "I want to stay because I want to be daring. For once, I would like to be brave."

The space between them evaporated and he gently framed her face with the warm, strong blades of his fingers, his eyes gazing deeply into hers. "Tell me what lurid and preposterous things you imagine, Miss Townsend."

"I cannot."

"Can't you?"

She wasn't sure she could speak at all but finally managed. "Kiss me."

"Not if that's all you want, Caroline." He spoke through clenched teeth, his voice a low, threatening rumble that made her knees feel weak and numb. "I swear, woman, you—"

"You swear a great deal, Mr. Blackwell," she cut him off. "If I've tormented you, if I've caused you pain . . . I won't be the one to betray you, Ashe. But if you don't kiss me again, I think my heart is going to stop."

For a single moment, she feared he wouldn't—but then she was in his arms and his mouth covered hers in a warm press, and it was a revelation.

She had never been kissed before Ashe had done so after her first disastrous riding lesson, and she had always imagined that it would be a strange thing to have another person pressing his mouth to hers. It had always looked like a pedestrian and ridiculous thing, but she had only seen the most polite and cool exchanges amidst her cousins and their relatives. But this—this wasn't mundane or polite.

This was the first tendrils of an electrical maelstrom as the silk of his lips touched hers. This was a connection that unraveled her ability to reason as he suckled her lower lip and introduced her to a storm of hunger, tasting and savoring the fire and texture of Ashe's passion. He pulled back to coax her into opening her lips in protest only to invade the intimate chamber of her mouth with his tongue and demonstrate that even now she had yet to be "truly and thoroughly" kissed.

Every nerve ending seemed to stretch out like eager reeds toward the sun, and Caroline knew that the time for command and discipline was lost. She reached up, her hands sliding up over his shoulders, and absorbed the heat of his body through the barrier of linen. She felt like a vine clinging to a solid rock wall, her grip tightening as her knees began to buckle at the waves of unfamiliar need that radiated through her frame. There was no thought—no logic—just a sea of sensation and heat and an introduction to a primal world of instinct and desire.

His mouth left hers, only to trail down her bare throat, and Caroline moaned. *This is like pushing away from a cliff wall, and instead of falling, discovering that you can fly.*

He released her briefly, only to turn her so that she was

facing away from him, and then his kisses returned to the
sensitive curve of her throat, the warm indent behind her
ears, and to uncover the point where her neck and shoulder
met to send molten fire down her spine. She moaned again
as his breath fanned over her skin when he lifted her hair
to move it aside and give him access to the back of her
neck. She squirmed at the powerful arcs of fire that traveled down her spine to pool between her hips until she was
sure that nothing of her body was now bone—for she felt
transformed into a creature of liquid and molten flesh.

One of his arms held her in place from behind while
his free hand began to unlace her ball gown, the teasing
brush of his fingers against her back making her writhe
with wicked anticipation. Caroline tipped her head back
against him and closed her eyes in surrender.

*This. This is what I wanted when he looked at me in the
carriage. All of this.*

He pushed the dress slowly off her shoulders and began to taste and tease every new inch of bare skin along
her shoulder blades that was exposed for his attentions.
His mouth was magic against her skin, and every caress
of his lips only made her want more. The expensive garment pooled at her feet and she kicked it away, mindless of
anything but Ashe.

Her corset lacings proved to be no hindrance at all for
his deft fingers, and Caroline sighed as the confines of the
undergarment fell away to join her gown on the floor, allowing her to inhale deeply and savor the sweet ache of her
ribs expanding again. With each layer lost, she felt more
free and strangely more brave.

His hands slid down her shoulders and then across the
curves of her back to encircle her, his fingers splayed as
they traveled up her rib cage and soothed the bruised flesh
only to cup her ripe breasts and lift them in his palms. Her
nipples hardened at the shocking contact, the thin material
of her chemise making the touch even more wicked. She

arched back against him, offering herself up to his hands, and was rewarded as his fingers circled the sensitive coral peaks, drawing them out and teasing each tip until Caroline was bucking against his hands, writhing at the lightning he invoked.

Ashe's breath quickened in her ears and one of his hands dropped to grip her hip, holding her in place against him as he moved against her to increase the friction of cloth and flesh. She almost cried out when she realized that the rock-hard shape pressing against her bottom was his unmistakable arousal. Even through the clothing that remained to her, she could feel the daunting size and shape of his erection, its searing heat making her shudder.

Suddenly, he twisted her around to lift her from the floor in a flurry of petticoats and Caroline's eyes fluttered open in shock to be cradled against his chest. She looked up and was instantly lost in the blue storm in his gaze. *I should be afraid, shouldn't I? But how can any woman experience fear when you look at them like that, Ashe?*

He carried her to the bed and set her down in its center with a playful throw. Her teeth teased her lower lip in nervous anticipation. "Ashe . . ."

He shook his head, a new energy encompassing them both as he stood next to the bed and began to unbutton his white linen shirt. "No talking, Caroline. Not this time."

Not this time. The implication that there would be other times made her aware of the damp, slick need that seeped from her body, a new wave of hunger almost making her whimper. She couldn't believe that it wasn't a dream; that she was in his bed in her underclothes, shamelessly watching him disrobe and impatiently waiting for him to ruin her.

He shrugged off his shirt, and before she could marvel at the planes and chiseled shape of his chest, he'd unfastened his pants and shed everything to bare himself for her inspection. Caroline gasped at the delicious display, mentally comparing him to the only male figures she'd seen—although unlike the classic statues she'd seen with their modest fig leaves, he was a living, flesh-colored example of male beauty with nothing to disguise his now rampant erection.

She knew she was staring, but the sight of him was far more than any ignorant fantasy had prepared her for. Here was male power at its peak, and her confidence wavered.

I am to manage—that?

Ashe climbed up onto the mattress next to her, kneeling to begin relieving her of her petticoats, each stroke of his hands across her skin soothing her nerves and reigniting the fire inside of her. Caroline kept her eyes on his, drinking in the approval she saw there as he spread her out like a feast for the eyes.

She lifted her arms as he dragged her chemise up over her head, tossing it away, and then pushed her back onto the feather mattress. Completely naked, she stretched out for him to survey at will.

Caroline was a woman transformed and she relished it. Everywhere his eyes swept over her, her flesh marbled and then flooded with tingling awareness. She was starving for the heat of his hands on her body.

Now was the moment when she should shy away and protest her innocence, but she'd already crossed the Rubicon. She wanted more than kisses from this man. At last, his hands moved over her body, his fingers splayed to tease and torment. The palm of his hand swept over the gentle swell of her belly, then across her hips to hover over the triangle of curls, skimming across the juncture above her thighs as if to divine her very essence—an erotic wizard casting a spell over her body.

She wanted all of him and all that went with him. She wanted ruin and rapture.

His body covered hers and she instinctively lifted one of her legs to increase the tantalizing feel of his skin working against hers. Her breasts felt swollen and heavy, the coarse silken hair of his chest teasing her nipples until they were like pebbles to the touch. His arousal pressed into the soft swell of her belly and fed a sharp ache that was growing between her legs.

He kissed her again, this time as if he would consume her very soul. Caroline held nothing back, clinging to him and riding the crest of each impulse that guided her desire.

Caroline's hands roamed over him in gentle conquest and exploration—daring to touch him as she wished; unwilling to be passive in this adventure. His cock had a wild attraction all its own, and she blushed at the raw power of it, dipping her hands down to seize it, pulsing and hot in her hands. It was heavy and fever-warm but silky smooth like suede against her palm, jerking and pulling at her lightest caress as if it had a separate will. The head of it was shaped like a plum, mounted atop a thick, rigid mast of flesh that pushed up as if demanding more.

His breath hissed through his teeth and he captured her hand with one of his, covering her fingers as they tried to encircle him. "You'll kill me with pleasure, Quaker," he whispered. "Here . . . like this."

He guided her hand, demonstrating the stroke and pressure that he needed, and Caroline's heart skipped a beat at the delicious knowledge that she could affect him so easily. His breathing changed with the speed of her fingers and she smiled at the victory.

His head dropped to capture her breast with his lips and Caroline nearly fainted in surprise. His tongue circled the swollen taut flesh, grazing her with his teeth and teaching her an entirely new lesson about the ways his mouth might yet send her over the edge.

She twisted beneath him, bucking in innocent ecstasy and unknowingly adding to Ashe's urgent need to complete this conquest. "Enough." His voice was rough with passion. His hands centered her beneath him, parting her thighs with his. Caroline closed her eyes as one of his hands slid between her legs and delved into the damp well, stroking the soft flesh there. It was heaven to feel him there, but then his thumb moved across the tight little pearl of her clit and Caroline cried out as a new kind of bliss overtook her. With feathery strokes of his fingers flickering across her sensitive flesh, he created a paralyzing tension within her, mounting it like a coil preparing to unleash untold force. Caroline instinctively welcomed it and tried to remember to breathe.

It was a relentless pressure that finally released the force inside of her, a wave of ecstasy making her cry out. She rocked her hips up into his hand as shudder after shudder of pleasure began to whip through her frame, until she was sure she was lost to it.

Ashe pulled his hand away, but before she could register the change, he'd positioned his thick cock against her entrance, pressing into her as she continued to come. Caroline threw her head back as she felt herself fall apart, the last vestige of control slipping away as her world became the sensation of her core stretching and tightening around the thick, hot velvet sheath of him. He drove into her, each stroke a revelation as her body shook, her inner muscles clutching at him with shameless greed, wordlessly begging him for more.

Caroline's heart pounded in her ears as he responded, plunging into her, deeper and deeper, harder and faster, until she was dizzy with the pain and pleasure of it. He lifted her hips to fill her completely and she cried out as the base of his cock worked against her clit at the same instant he rocked against the very entrance to her womb.

He moved into her, and she began to counter him, drawing against him, her primal hunger yet unsatisfied. She wanted nothing more than for the connection between them to remain unbroken. It was intoxicating to see him above her, to watch his body come into hers, and to feel her muscles contracting around him, milking him and pulling him deeper and deeper inside until she couldn't feel where she ended and he began.

More. God help me, I would have more of him—even now.

The red-hot coil inside of her tightened again and her eyes widened in shock as she realized what was happening.

Ashe must have sensed it as well, as he took command of her, pumping into her faster and faster until she screamed in release. Caroline felt him tense in her arms as his scalding sweet crème jetted inside of her and Ashe groaned as the world stilled and he spent himself at last.

After several minutes, he gingerly freed himself and Caroline winced at the strange ache at the loss. He drew his fingers across her brow, his expression sincerely concerned. "Are you in pain?"

She shook her head, marveling that only now did she feel shy with him. "No. It was . . ." Words escaped her. *How would anyone describe such a thing?*

He kissed her, a gentler echo of his previous touch. "Be honest."

"I cannot say." She blushed furiously. "Perhaps another attempt and I'll come up with the proper description?"

His smile warmed her all the way to her toes, and she had to look away for fear he would think her daft. "You are not nearly the rogue you imagine, Mr. Blackwell," she spoke softly, her voice drowsy as she began to drift off.

"And how is that?"

"Because if it's true I came to your rooms unaware of myself, you never took advantage of me."

"*If* you came to my rooms?"

She pushed against him in a lazy, playful protest. "You are not a cad, sir."

"I cannot make you out. You're a puzzle to me each and every minute—awake or asleep. You argue my every assertion, ruin my ability to think straight, and you would still champion me?"

She answered him with a kiss, sweet and soft, with the first hint of skills that he alone had taught her. "Tell me the truth, Ashe. You never did answer my questions before."

He shook his head then pressed his lips to the soft pulse at her temple. "Another time, my lovely Quaker. Another time."

* * *

To hell with the consequences!

Ashe tried to summon a sense of remorse or even distress at the risk of bedding this woman, but something different was happening.

He wanted more.

How much suffering did a man have to do before the balance of the scales might allow for some small taste of happiness?

Have I paid for my sins?

Surely the answer was yes. Because instead of scrambling to recover his balance and hide the evidence of this indiscretion, Ashe felt a flash of triumph at possessing her. If they were discovered, there could only be one conclusion.

She would be forced to marry him.

The idea failed to shock him.

Why not the terrier? She pleases me and I would be guaranteed a life without a moment of boredom or quiet. She's stubborn enough to hold her own and she challenges me. We get along well enough and the house is already running better with a woman in it. Hell! Even my grandfather likes her and approves of her character.

It couldn't be that hard to convince her, could it? I'm not such a dreadful catch, no matter what she's heard.

But she'd spoken of a future awaiting her in Boston, and Ashe wasn't sure what that entailed. It was difficult to compete with an unknown, and he didn't like the idea of a rival waiting back in Boston to enjoy her kisses.

I'll prove to her that I'm the better man. And when she's forced to admit an addiction to my kisses, she'll have no more thoughts of returning to America.

His brow furrowed, his own conscience stinging at the direction of his thoughts. *I can't trap her or force her to do anything. If I've learned anything about my chaperone, I've at least learned that much.*

And proving that I'm a better man . . .

Caroline's no fool.

I'll have to tread carefully to let things unfold—without a scandal, without hurting her, and without letting her go.

Chapter
13

In the dark gray hour before dawn, before the house was awake, Ashe stared at the woman sleeping in his arms by the light of the candle by the bedside. She'd defied every perception he'd had of her and proven that however fetching she'd been while sleepwalking, aware and alive in his arms she was incomparable. Her reserve had fallen away as gracefully as the silk from her body.

As if sensing his scrutiny, her eyelashes fluttered open, her brown eyes a molten caramel in the low light as she focused on his. "You're thinking and not sleeping, Mr. Blackwell."

"I'm trying *not* to think about your next note to my grandfather," he said with a wry smile.

"Oh!" Her expression held a flash of alarm and she tensed against him. "Now it is my turn to think."

"Nonsense," he assured her softly, placing a kiss on her furrowed brow. "This is the sort of dilemma that is never solved by thinking."

She opened her mouth as if to protest but closed it just as quickly as the irony of preaching reason in her current state of delectable compromise struck home. Ashe reached up to smooth her cheek with his fingers, marveling at the precious gift of her innocence and genuine concern for consequences. He cleared his throat, redirecting her attention from the panic stirring behind her eyes. "Caroline, it was a jest. There is no harm here."

"I hardly think this . . . I mean . . ." She pulled the coverlet around herself tightly, looking shy and unsure of herself. "I would never wish to see you hurt by . . . my actions."

Her actions? Does she think to take the blame for this?

"Shouldn't I be the one making that speech? But if you're referring to the business with my grandfather, wagers and contracts have nothing to do with us, Caroline."

She smiled, shaking her head. "Wagers and contracts have everything to do with us, Mr. Blackwell, but when you—touch me like that, you make it difficult to recall the particulars."

"Let the world stay outside the gates, Caroline. The servants will say nothing and so, for now, my life is in your hands. But"—he kissed the soft indent of each of her palms—"I find I'm not fearful. I've lived in fear for too long to let it rule me in this."

She smiled, her expression pure disbelief. "What fear has ruled you until this moment, Ashe?"

Ashe closed his eyes for a second, rueful of his unguarded admission. *I am far too comfortable with you, my American, and I'm forgetting to watch what I say.* He gave her his most cavalier smile, trailing his fingers across her collarbone to distract her from the topic. "I think I have a deep fear of chaperones."

She struck him playfully on the arm. "You aren't afraid of anything!"

Ah, if only you knew, Caroline, but I have more than my share of demons.

"For now, it's your reputation that we have to protect at all costs."

Her mouth fell open in shock before she realized it and regained her composure. "*My* reputation? I don't think anyone would think . . . I am too sensible a woman for your friends to suspect you would even look twice, Ashe."

"You're naïve if you think they aren't already placing wagers on how soon I'll have you thoroughly corrupted. I should hire a chaperone for you."

"If I wasn't in need of one before, wouldn't another set of eyes only add to the . . . risk of exposure?"

"For a woman new to subterfuge, you have a gift for the details. You're probably right."

"Then perhaps this woman of subterfuge should return to her room, Ashe."

She began to slide off the bed, retrieving her wrap, but Ashe gently caught her hand. "Wait."

"The servants may already be up. I cannot . . ."

He pulled her back onto the bed, gently capturing her beneath him and cradling her face in his hands. "Caroline, whatever else you believe about me, please believe this one thing—I said I was thinking about your notes to my grandfather this morning, but I care nothing for it. My first concern was for you. I would not have you wronged by what has begun between us. I am humbled by this . . . change. Don't retreat from me, Caroline."

"I'm not sure what to feel, Ashe." Eyes that she'd averted met his at last, and he could read the uncertainty and raw emotion reflected there. "It isn't that I would abandon— this. But I am unpracticed at seductions and games."

"I would not have you any other way, my dear Miss Townsend."

Her cheeks colored beautifully at the compliment, her squirm of embarrassment making Ashe's body respond at the delicious friction. "I . . . I don't think I can face a withering look from Mr. Godwin," she whispered. "Please, Ashe."

Something in her voice gave him pause, and Ashe realized that her shame was tangible and almost sweet. She was so different from the parade of callous creatures who had graced his bed that it made his breath catch in his throat. She wasn't exaggerating her discomfort but trustingly confessing it to him as her protector. Any thought of overriding her concerns and keeping her abed bled away. Instead, Ashe wanted to erase her fears and prove that even now he could shield someone from harm.

"Godwin's silences can be a little daunting," he agreed softly. "Mind, I don't pay him much attention anymore. But if you prefer to return to your room, I'll escort you there and make sure that we avoid discovery. Agreed?"

She nodded slowly, accepting her wrap from his hands. "Thank you, Ashe."

Thank you? Ashe wasn't sure how to feel about the strange and delicate truce between them. He'd taken her virginity and, by every measure, ruined the girl with unapologetic raw lust. It was unfamiliar territory, even for an avid hunter, and the polite ritual of locating one's clothes, helping her dress, and bringing her to her room felt awkward. Part of him wanted to seize her and drag her back into bed until she'd spent herself so much she didn't care if all of London strolled by for a glance.

But another part of him acknowledged the folly of it and the need for discretion.

I want to protect you. But how do I protect you and let you go after last night?

He tied his own dressing gown and quietly walked her down the dim hallway, all too aware that there wouldn't be an answer. At her door, he kissed her again, a slow, sweet farewell that felt like a brand on his skin.

"There is no retreat, Caroline," he whispered, and she shivered against him.

"No." She sighed. "No retreat."

* * *

She crawled in between the cool, soft sheets of her own bed, curling around one of her pillows while her thoughts churned. It was a tangled moral dilemma that would have been easier to solve if she weren't so irrevocably blind at its center. She'd given in to her desires and destroyed her chances for a better life. But the panic she'd felt had been for Ashe.

I'm a fool. I've forfeited everything in a single night and all I can think to worry about is protecting Ashe. There is something he's not telling me, and it has nothing to do with wagers. But whatever holds him, I cannot deny my heart now.

Or deny her body . . . Even now it clamored for more of his touch and ached at the strange, lonely expanse of her bed. She covered her eyes with her hands and wondered what kind of woman failed to mourn the sacrifice of her virginity but instead felt only elation and longing. *I've abandoned my reason.*

But I cannot abandon my honor.

The urge to confess the full truth of her agreement with his grandfather had been unbearable. But telling Ashe about the twenty thousand pounds meant risking more than his censure. It meant that he would see her like all the other women in his life who took payment for their time. All her talk about honoring their grandfathers' friendship would look like a lie. And he would realize that her eccentricities pointed toward nothing more than poverty.

Impossible!

But if she kept the secret of her seduction from his grandfather, she would be no better than a thief.

An honorable woman would end it and walk away.

Caroline struck her pillow with her fist in frustration. *I'm not going anywhere! Because I want him so much I can't breathe and I'm too weak not to beg him to touch me again. I want more. I want to know every forbidden thing he's mastered and experience it all at his command.*

"So much for the Quaker." She sighed in the dark.

But each illicit encounter would mean living a lie and risking his fortune.

She shifted restlessly and then became very still as she seized on her decision.

I'll keep his secrets to protect him but I won't be rewarded for . . . loving him.

She kicked back the covers and climbed out of the bed to find a lamp. Caroline then settled in at the small desk with her books and laid out her pen and ink.

I'll forfeit Grandfather Walker's reward since I've learned that I am such a wanton woman, but I'll phrase it so that I don't reveal what's happened to damage the older man's trust. Grandfather and grandson deserve a new start and a successful Season.

It was harder and harder to think of the college—to think of a future without her dreams. She'd given in to her emotions and she wasn't sure what her future held. Once he had his fill of seduction, then she would have nothing to look forward to but a return to the grueling poverty of her life in Boston, cold classrooms and loveless years.

No retreat.

He'd asked her not to retreat and spoken of change . . . but he'd made no promises and no declarations of affection beyond the moment.

Not that she expected anything of him except what he'd honestly admitted he was capable of—passion. Ashe wasn't a man to give his heart away after losing it once, and Caroline was too pragmatic a woman to hold her breath waiting for it.

But my heart is my own, and I'm not going to squander his kisses.

She pulled out a fresh sheet of paper and began her note to the elder Blackwell with a soft sigh of surrender to the Fates.

Chapter
14

The music room was an oasis of calm and Caroline felt very brave as she sat at the piano and slowly and sound-lessly depressed the keys. If his mother's spirit were present, Caroline had no desire to offend by actually making an amateur noise on the beautiful instrument. It was a stately monument with inset rosewood flowers along its gilt edges—a lady's instrument evoking a grace and sense of self-possession that Caroline longed to feel.

The morning had been worse than she'd anticipated when she'd been informed that Ashe had left the house for his usual appointment with Mr. Rutherford at their sports club.

Caroline's nerves were on edge. *Of all the mornings for him to disappear!* She'd longed for some reassurance from him, some show or action that would make the previous night's dream more real. Instead, all her fears and doubts had threatened to send her running until she'd walked past the music room.

Now, she communed with spirits she had never met and took comfort from orderly polished surfaces and the faint smell of oranges and honeysuckle.

"Pardon, Miss Townsend, but there is a Mr. Yardley to see you," Godwin announced from the doorway. "I have asked him to wait in the green salon downstairs."

"To see *me*?" Caroline stood up from the bench in surprise. "I . . . suppose that's . . ." She swallowed, hating the flood of awkward emotions that threatened to turn her into a babbling idiot. "Yes, thank you, Mr. Godwin. I'll be right down."

Within moments, he was before her, openly enjoying the effect of an uninvited visit. The man was even more pale and overblown in daylight, in a bright green morning coat embroidered with flowers at the cuffs. He made a deep bow, only to look up with a wry grin. "You look very lovely this morning, Miss Townsend, though I should apologize for calling so early after such a late and exhausting evening."

Caroline forced herself not to groan at the thought of the nature of her late and exhausting night but smiled instead and prayed her color didn't give anything away. "Mr. Blackwell is at his sports club this morning and will regret not seeing you, I'm sure." The lie tasted like tin in her mouth, but she wasn't going to admit that she knew there was no affection between Ashe and his cousin.

"At his sports club? Well, that's for the best since I'd hoped to call when we could talk, just the two of us, uninterrupted."

"I can't imagine what conversation we could have that would require such privacy, Mr. Yardley. I mean"—she took a steadying breath, wishing she had a better command of English etiquette to politely send the man away—"since we've only just met, it seems an odd request."

"I didn't mean to give offense, Miss Townsend," he said, gesturing for her to be seated. "It was because of our new acquaintance I thought to make my case."

Caroline sat down carefully on the chair's edge. "Your case?"

"I'll be as direct as I may." Winston took the chair across from her in a theatrical flourish. "I am all too aware that my cousin holds me in poor regard, Miss Townsend. And I was eager to ensure that your view was not altogether prejudiced against me."

Caroline kept her hands firmly clenched in her lap. "My opinions are my own, and Mr. Blackwell has kept his to himself, so you've no concerns on this subject. W-was there anything else?"

"Oh, please! If you think to heal some familial gap by politely pleading ignorance, I can assure you there is no need. Ashe thinks little of ordinary men like myself who strive to stay on a moral path of discipline and self-sacrifice." Mr. Yardley placed his hand on his ostentatious waistcoat just over his heart. "I hope only to better myself, Miss Townsend."

My God, he thinks I'm a Quaker!

"A noble goal, Mr. Yardley, but I'm not sure I understand your point. After all, my good opinion can't be worth all this fuss if—"

"I am aware of your odd situation, Miss Townsend. You see, I think my great-uncle, Mr. Gordon Blackwell, thought it best to rely on as many safeguards as he could to ensure that the best man would ultimately be named as his honorable and capable heir."

"My situation?" Caroline wasn't sure how to respond. "I'm not sure I—"

"Oh, it is still a secret to the rest of the world, for I am no gossip!" Winston held up a hand as if to ward off any interruption she would have made. "When my dear uncle let the truth slip in a recent conversation, I had no choice but to rush to London to see for myself the young lady who would attempt to restrain my cousin. And after meeting you, I knew you would be relieved to know that you have an ally and friend on hand should you need one."

It was impossible to say what he knew, and Caroline struggled not to sputter in protest at the unpredictable turns in the conversation. She stood to end the conversation, forcing him to follow suit. "Whatever you may have inadvertently been told, frankly, Mr. Yardley, you have rushed to London for all the wrong reasons. But I will be sure to convey your concern for my well-being to your cousin."

"Whatever my great-uncle has offered for compensation, I'll double it. Though naturally, the payment would have to be delayed until I received my fair and just inheritance."

"You'll pay me for what exactly?"

"For helping me to expose my cousin's weak character to the world and ensuring that he loses this foolish wager." Winston's smile was as benign as if they were discussing the weather. "I'm no villain, Miss Townsend! And I know it may seem that greed is an element in my plot, but let me say in complete honesty that it has nothing to do with the money."

Caroline shook her head in astonishment. "Does it not?"

"Not at all! Ashe is a wastrel and he would squander his inheritance on vice and self-indulgences! But I"—he squared his shoulders as if preening—"I would make the most of Bellewood and restore the family's honor. I had no hope or thought of this windfall until I learned of Ashe's recent folly and wager, and now I cannot help but think that it's a moral challenge I mustn't shy from."

"Windfall? You wouldn't accept it, knowing that it meant another man's downfall!"

"Naturally, I would! And if the man is a worthless waste, I cannot help but think a woman of your moral fiber must find Ashe as abhorrent as I do."

Caroline stared at him in amazement. "I can assure you nothing of the kind! The only thing abhorrent to me is a bully who thinks to manipulate the moment to his own advantage!"

"Ah! There's that spirit I've heard so much about!" He beamed merrily and then retook his seat as if she'd asked him to stay for tea. "Come now, Miss Townsend! Ashe's sins are too tawdry to examine in your presence, but you cannot be completely unaware. He's kept half the whores in London well employed this last year, but it is a truly public scandal we require if we're to unseat him."

"*We* don't require anything of the kind!" Caroline fisted her hands at her waist in frustration. "*You* can make your own way out, Mr. Yardley."

He went on as if she hadn't spoken. "You can ensure his failure by simply using his weaknesses against him. From what I garnered at Worthley's, he is not disinterested, is he? It's a bit obvious, but you should make yourself available to him."

Caroline held her ground, fury making her movements stiff and ungraceful. "Forgive me for being obtuse, but I believe you just asked me to prostitute myself! You, Mr. Yardley, need to leave this house."

"So you intend to champion a man like Ashe? You'd side with a declared womanizer? Is it possible you've already fallen victim to—"

"If this is your attempt to win me to your side, Mr. Yardley, you have the skills of a lummox."

He stiffened, the color draining from his face. "You're no chaperone, Miss Townsend."

"No, I am not." Caroline brushed off her skirts and moved toward the open door. "On this one point, you have finally gotten it right."

He stood slowly from the chair. "You should consider your choices very carefully. For while you're not to Ashe's usual tastes, I don't think the truth is relevant. It would be far too easy to drop a few hints to the right people to ensure that every decent door in London is closed to Ashe's American mistress."

"You'd lie? You'd do that?"

"Of course." He smiled as if he'd paid her some great compliment. "London loves scandal, and Ashe has been starving them of late."

"No one in London is starving for tales of Mr. Blackwell. You exaggerate his importance, Mr. Yardley, and flatter the man." She stood beside the doorway. "It's a common mistake."

"Does he know you're being paid to hold his coattails?" Yardley asked sharply.

Caroline gasped in shock and inadvertently gave the man his answer.

"And what would my dear cousin think of you if he were to find out?" he went on relentlessly. "I doubt he'd appreciate how you've come to his defense and instead set you and your baggage on the wrong side of his front door."

"You should go, Mr. Yardley."

He bowed and tugged at his cuffs to rearrange their embroidered edges. "You'll help me whether you intend to or not. I was simply offering to compensate you for your troubles."

He started to leave, but she grabbed his elbow. "Mr. Yardley, you've forgotten something. You'll get nothing when these lies are traced directly back to you. And if you thought I wouldn't send word to Grandfather Walker of this conversation, I'm astonished! You walk into this house, threaten and cajole and think I'll just crumble into tears and beg you to protect my reputation?"

"I . . ." It was clear the man had never considered the elder Blackwell in his plans. "Grandfather Walker?"

"Look to your own reputation, sir. And think quickly, if you can, of the explanation you'll give to defend yourself when asked about this morning's visit—because it seems to me that you've guaranteed Ashe his inheritance by showing your stripes. Even if he pranced down Piccadilly in his birthday suit with thirty known courtesans, I think Grandfather will see him as the better man! But there will be no such scandal and you'll get no satisfaction!" She pulled the door open even wider to hasten his departure. "Good day, Mr. Yardley!"

* * *

Ashe handed over his hat and coat, bone tired but anxious of the reception waiting for him upstairs. The morning had slipped away, and he could only imagine how tense Caroline may have become in the long hours while he was away.

"Is she in her room?" he asked.

"The music room, sir. She retreated there again after Mr. Yardley's social call," Mr. Godwin replied succinctly.

"Yardley?" The world ground to an unpleasant halt. "Yardley was here?"

"He was, indeed, and was handed his hat for his troubles after only a few minutes. Miss Townsend sent him packing, and may I say, sir, she was most vocal in doing so."

Damn! I'd have loved to have heard that conversation!

"Thank you, Godwin. See that we aren't disturbed."

Godwin nodded and retreated without expression, reminding Ashe why he paid the man so well. Ashe took the stairs two at a time to race to the music salon on the first floor to find her sitting forlornly next to the harp, looking a bit like a lost angel in one of her new day dresses.

"Are you all right?"

She looked up, standing with the guilty speed of a child caught at something forbidden. "I'm fine." She held her ground nervously, and Ashe had the new impression that she might bolt for the door if he made any sudden movements. She continued, "How did you find your friend? Mr. Rutherford, wasn't it?"

"Ah, that business . . ." Ashe ran a hand through his hair, wishing he'd sent Michael a ready excuse for his absence instead of disappointing Caroline. "He's an old friend from India and—it doesn't matter. I should have left a word for you before I rushed out. I'm sorry, Caroline."

"No, don't apologize. You're no more tethered now than before, and I'm no harpy to extract explanations, Ashe."

He drew closer, enjoying the change in her coloring as he approached her. "I never used the word harpy, did I?"

"No, not harpy," she supplied, a smile teasing the corner of her lips.

"Did he come to warn you about your guardian's true character?"

"Something like that."

"Any revelations?"

"He knows about the wager, Ashe. Your grandfather must have told him, and now he is circling like a vulture waiting for you to fail. He has threatened to tell everyone . . ."

"Then you'll be the toast of London as the darling novelty of a lamb set out to keep track of a wolf."

"And you'll be humiliated."

He laughed. "Hardly. Though if you'd said as much at the beginning of this venture, I would have agreed with you. But now"—he drew close enough to reach out, sliding his fingertips up her sleeve to send a shiver of heat down her spine—"I cannot think of a reason to care."

"You will care if he learns of us. If he were to—"

"Winston is an idiot, Caroline. I won't waste a single breath on speculation where he's concerned. Frankly, if a weasel like Yardley has the means to trouble me, then I have greater problems."

She captured his fingers in hers, staying the seductive spell of his touch. "A giant can be felled by the smallest adversary, Ashe." She shook her head with a sigh. "I didn't aid your cause by angering the man and practically calling him an ass."

"You called me one when we first met. Perhaps he also found it endearing."

"Mr. Blackwell, perhaps we shouldn't—"

"No retreat," he said softly, lifting her fingers to his mouth to kiss each fingertip.

"Who is retreating?" she whispered.

"I wanted to make it up to you, Caroline. For losing my self-control so completely last night."

"Did you?"

He nodded. "I was going to spend the day demonstrating restraint and ensure that I had your trust."

Her cheeks flooded with a delectable peach color. "There is nothing to . . . I don't want you to demonstrate restraint, Mr. Blackwell."

"You don't?"

She looked at him, her eyes mesmerizing as they conveyed without artifice her hunger. There was something vulnerable about her, and for a moment, it set him back on his heels. She wasn't hiding anything from him or shielding her heart—but his own desire pushed the thought aside.

"Then I won't, Miss Townsend."

He stepped forward to cradle her face in his hands, kissing her like a starving man drawn to the feast. She tasted sweet against his mouth, her tongue darting out to meet his, and immediately the unsteady grip he'd had on his control began to slide. He explored the contours and textures of her lips and tongue, sampling and savoring the heady intimacy of the act. The release she'd given him last night had been so profound, he'd craved her ever since. No other woman, not even the girl he'd once tragically loved and lost, had ever evoked such a reaction.

How the impossible Miss Caroline Townsend had managed such a feat was a mystery he was determined to resolve.

Unfortunately, his silent vow to approach her less savagely in light of her freshly deflowered state was evaporating with each kiss, and when she nipped his lower lip between her teeth, it was forgotten.

Her hands slid upward to smooth over his chest, the long, cool blades of her fingers sending sparks over his skin. One hand continued up until she tangled her fingers into his hair, pressing him closer as his entire body warmed and pulsed in rhythm with her touch.

Hell, who needs restraint?

A molten weight at the base of his spine unfurled, and Ashe's cock dutifully hardened until the pressure of his clothing against it was enough to make him want to roar in frustration.

Speech abandoned him. There was only the throbbing heaviness between his legs and an overwhelming urge to have her, to end his torment and take all that she would yield to him—quickly and without mercy.

She moaned softly, deep in her throat, and Ashe moved into action. His hands caressed the velvet of her day dress, his palms warming to the lush, firm curves of her body beneath the circumspect layers of her clothing. He had seen the vixen beneath her prim exterior, and the memory of her spread out beneath him made his hands shake.

She shifted her weight, and he reached down to catch one of her legs, lifting one thigh to pull her against his stiff cock, her wet, warm core bucking up to meet him.

Lust poured through him and he surrendered to it, his last coherent thought a prayer that his Quaker could forgive him if he overstepped.

He ended the kiss and turned her around to face away from him, sucking on her earlobe as he placed her palms down onto the surface of the piano. She moaned and tipped her head back to give him more access and Ashe almost crowed in triumph. He bent down and, with a sweep of his hands, caught the hem of her skirt and crinoline to draw it up, pulling up the heavy fabric to reveal her bare legs for his touch. She gasped at the swift maneuver, but before she could protest, he ran his hands up the backs of her thighs, his fingers spread wide to frame her delectable, ripe ass for his pleasure.

He cupped each firm, creamy curve with his splayed fingers, savoring the heat of her skin and the tantalizing scent of her arousal. As his hands moved, he had a fleeting fantasy of molding her flesh, like an artist rendering raw desire into the shape of a woman—as if the lust in his own body could flow through his fingertips and bring her to life.

An erotic Pygmalion.

The sight of her, partially bent over the piano, her skirts bunched up at her waist with that delicious derriere offered up like an exotic sacrifice, made his cock ache. She was so beautiful.

Her thighs had naturally parted for his touch, unknowingly treating him to the sweetest glimpse of her ripe, wet sex, pink and glistening, and Ashe worked the buttons of his pants free to release his rampant erection.

Without hesitation, he fisted his cockstand to press it against her clit, working it across the tight little pearl until she began to buck and shudder, coating him with the slick honey from her core.

"Ashe, please!" she begged, rocking her hips back onto him, teasing the swollen tip and guiding him up inside of her where she desired him.

Ashe could wait no longer. He notched himself at the succulent entrance of her core and pistoned into her in one fluid stroke, burying himself to the hilt, the tight inner muscles of her body sheathing him, clenching him in spasms of release that pushed him over the edge.

He slid his hands down her outer thighs, pressing her legs together to add to their pleasure. Now with each thrust of his hips, her body tightened around him and he reveled in the sensation, drawing out each movement so that he could pump into her with all his strength until her feet were literally being lifted from the floor.

"More! Please, more!" she cried out, and Ashe gave into all of it. Civilization fell away and there was nothing in existence but his need to empty himself inside of her and lose this burning hunger that raged inside.

He came in a rush, the sudden pressure of it making him grit his teeth as his release tore from his body and he sagged against her, attempting to be mindful of not crushing or injuring her.

A bit late to worry about the lady now, wouldn't you say? he chided himself silently. *Damn.*

"Caroline," he finally managed. "I'm . . . sure I meant to go slower. . . ."

Her breathing was as ragged as his, and her tone betraying that she was equally astonished by what had just happened between them. "I don't know if I could survive going slowly, Mr. Blackwell."

His cock jumped at her words and he smiled. "Well, that's just something we'll have to see about."

Chapter

15

Winston Yardley rapped the knuckles of the poor tailor attempting to pin his sleeve, his temper making him lash out with a random viciousness that was making the shop-keeper start to tremble. "Watch the seams! I'll not have loose threads and a cobbler's coat to show for my coin!"

The man ducked his head, wisely not arguing that he had yet to see too many of Winston's coins as his credit line was stretched to its limits. But it wasn't uncommon for a gentleman to string along his tradesmen, and Yardley had made it no secret that he expected to be flush beyond his dreams very soon.

Winston turned to see if the bright satin lining of his evening coat would show a bit when he wished and smiled at his reflection in the glass. His meeting with the American had flirted with disaster, but he wasn't the sort of man who dwelt on the details.

He'd allowed his temper to get the better of him and tipped his hand. But the desire to hasten his rival's quick disgrace had been too strong to dictate a delicate approach. No-nonsense American women no doubt respected straightforward conversation, and Winston had been confident that Miss Caroline Townsend would admire his arguments.

Hell! It's not as if I couldn't have done my worst without offering to include her in the reward! I was being generous, but I see the error of my ways now. Puritan or no, that American bitch has decided to turn a blind eye to Ashe's vile nonsense and protect him.

But the plain woman he'd heard described from various sources had gained a bit of polish, and when he'd met her at Worthley's, Winston had almost questioned his plans. And he now conceded that if she followed through on her threat and sent a letter to the elder Blackwell, then he was in a potentially precarious position. But it was difficult to believe that she would do such a thing—especially if she was to act as a disinterested third party in the wager. If she actively took Ashe's side, wouldn't his great-uncle see it as a sign that she'd stumbled from her pedestal?

She won't send a word to "Grandfather Walker"! And I'll just have to see to it that the next news he gets makes anything she might say irrelevant.

Ever since his childhood, Ashe Blackwell had seemed to lead a charmed life just out of Winston's reach. Every grim twist of his own path had been mirrored by a happier bend in Ashe's. He'd learned to hate the golden-haired boy who never behaved but never got caught, while Winston's every transgression had earned him soul-scarring punishments and cemented the rivalry between them. He'd shadowed Ashe for years, and when Blackwell had set out for India, Winston had prayed that some tropical fever would take him or he'd be a jungle cat's dinner. The Sepoy uprising had appeared to be a miracle and Ashe's subsequent disappearance had been a cause for rejoicing, but the celebration had been far too short. After only two years, Ashe

Blackwell had risen from the grave without a word of explanation or apology.

A decent man would have died in some heroic battle against the natives, but my cousin has the nerve to vanish and get a man's hopes up—only to saunter back onto the London streets and then make light of his good fortune by offering to toss it away on a bet!

Fate had been a cruel teacher, but at last, the chance to seize Ashe's life and future for his own had fallen into his lap.

Weak men gambled, in Winston's opinion, and he had no intentions of letting chance play any part of his future. He would sabotage and undermine his nemesis in any way possible and without apology.

He didn't believe for a moment that Ashe would touch a cheerless chit like Caroline Townsend, but he'd been so sure that at the first hint of a threat of a rumor to that effect, she would see the error of her ways. And if not, there had been a vague chance that she'd have even been flattered by the idea of playing the femme fatale and helped him frame Ashe. But she'd turned the tables on him before he could finish making his case.

Has Ashe already managed to seduce her? Is that what has brightened her cheeks and eyes?

Winston chuckled at the ridiculous notion. He had seen too many of the exotic birds his cousin favored in the past to let the idea set. It would be too tawdry and cliché a choice for his adventurous relative and too easy—exactly the reason he'd tossed it out so carelessly as a threat to goad his chaperone into cooperating rather than truly considering it in his grand scheme.

The only whispers around Town about Blackwell's eccentric ward hinted at an admiration for the American's talents for drawing her guardian out into respectable company and the delightful surprise at seeing Ashe behave around this spirited young woman.

Exactly what Winston feared most.

He wanted to kill her, but that wasn't entirely practical.

"The blue! Let me see the blue coat again!" he barked at the tailor loud enough to almost set him on his backside. It pleased him to vent his frustration on the tradesman. *When I'm the master at Bellewood and a known man of means, I'll have every tailor in London jumping to do my bidding. And I will be the master because, unlike my dear cousin, I deserve to be.*

And once again, Winston's confidence in his plans returned. All he had to do was silence Miss Townsend's defense of the worthless Ashe by demonstrating just how immoral the man was. Then nothing she said to the elder Blackwell would make a difference. He would set up a trap too tempting for Ashe to ignore and then see to it that there was press and there would be nowhere for Ashe to turn. The scandal would be irrefutable and take on a life of its own. Then the American could sputter all she wanted, all the way home!

Winston shrugged off his coat to exchange it for the blue silk he'd requested, and a new idea began to form in his mind.

My great-uncle said he'd employed her as a spy and chaperone to keep Ashe in check and that it served Ashe right to finally meet a woman who wouldn't fall in love with him. But if I know my cousin, then her opinion of him is becoming far more important than anyone else's because he loves a challenge.

When I bring him down, I'll make sure that Miss Townsend is at his elbow to see it. It will be a small touch of additional salt in the wound and he'll have no one to blame but himself. Pride goeth before the fall, but oh, cousin! I want you to fall so far that you can't remember what your life was like before you handed it over to me.

And with that thought, Winston Yardley began to laugh.

* * *

Caroline's head was swimming with excitement at the turns in her life. It was hard to catch her breath in the few days since she'd landed in Ashe's bed. Except for her turbulent meeting with Yardley, the hours had been filled with one scorching encounter after another—made all the more tantalizing by his efforts to honor her sensibilities and keep things discreet between them. So far, she'd seen no sign that the servants suspected anything and she'd taken comfort from it.

So long as there's no scandal . . . then this will be my sin to keep safe.

Their social calendar had gone unchanged, adding to the clandestine heat between them. This evening's trip to the theatre had been a unique thrill as she sat with him so publicly in their box with the scent of him still on her skin from an afternoon in his library. It was hard to deny that she was falling more and more in love with him, but she was also more and more aware of what she had sacrificed to have him for so short a time.

There'd been no romantic declarations of any kind, but she didn't expect any. He was Ashe, after all, and even if she desired it, Caroline knew that she was in no position to offer him a match. She couldn't think of the future without pain and so forced herself not to let it cloud the strange lightness of her present situation.

"Are you enjoying the performance, Miss Townsend?" Ashe asked, the polite inquiry belying the heat in his eyes.

She nodded. "It's very . . . lively."

"Well, there's a bit of unreserved praise!" He laughed. "Are all Americans so difficult to impress?"

"I'm not difficult to impress, Mr. Blackwell."

"No?" he teased. "Are you certain?"

"Wasn't Mr. Thorne meeting us tonight for the show?" she tried to change the subject.

Ashe sobered immediately. "I received a note before we left the house with his apologies. Apparently something has come up."

"Is everything all right? Is he unwell?" she asked.

Ashe's demeanor became difficult to decipher. "He's fine. But I'll be sure to convey your keen interest in his well-being when I see him next."

Caroline's jaw dropped in astonishment. "You're jealous!"

"Impossible!"

But his guilty expression deflated the denial and Caroline marveled at the strange twist. "One would think so, considering I have had one singular dance and conversation with the man . . . but nonetheless, there you are."

"Only an idiot would be jealous under such a circumstance, Miss Townsend, and if you value my pride, you'll not argue the obvious." Ashe crossed his arms defensively.

She did her best not to smile as her mind circled back despite his charming distraction. "What detained him?"

"He didn't say." He didn't look at her as he spoke and Caroline recognized the lie.

"Was it some business with the Jaded?"

"Who said Darius was a member of the Jaded?"

"You did when you said he would carve a saying over everyone's doorsteps. It stands to reason the man would know whose houses he was defacing by being one of them!" she said, striving not to laugh.

"Damn it, woman! Is there nothing that escapes you?"

"Language!" she chided without any real bite. His cursing had become almost an endearing habit. "It escapes me why you're brooding over there like a wounded lion."

"Let's credit my irrational mood to that annoying soprano onstage and see about getting you home, shall we?"

Caroline set down her opera glasses with a flourish. "How fortuitous! Just when I was going to complain of a headache and beg you to take me home. How lucky!"

He stood and offered her his arm. "You are a difficult woman, Miss Townsend."

"If you say so, Mr. Blackwell." Caroline struggled not to smile. "If you say so."

* * *

On the carriage ride home, it was easy to pretend that there was nothing beyond the fog outside. "There is simply something about the confines of a carriage. It is . . . liberating," she ventured boldly, taking in the long, lean lines of his body as he sat across from her. In his black evening clothes, he was a dashing figure, and more than one woman had sighed in his wake as they'd left the performance. Her eyes lingered on his hands and long, lean thighs, and Caroline's breath quickened as she realized that his body was responding to her study—the unmistakable outline of his swollen member against his trousers changing the landscape. She felt a surge of triumphant power that she could simply look at him and make his blood run hot.

"How liberating?" he asked, his voice blue velvet in the shadows.

This is power. To know that he wants me. Me, of all the women in the world. For tonight, for this moment, I am what he desires.

"Extremely liberating, Mr. Blackwell. Perhaps it is the knowledge that the entire world is separated from us by only an inch or two of wood and cloth, and yet . . . here we are."

Ashe's look became a study in open desire and Caroline had to steady herself on the cushions. *He wouldn't!*

As if he'd read her mind and interpreted it as a challenge, Ashe wordlessly eased off the seat across from her and knelt in the narrow space between them to gently pull her knees forward until she was balanced on the edge of the velvet upholstery, then he began lifting her skirts to reveal her sex to him.

"Ashe!"

"Lean back, Caroline." It was a quiet command and one she could have easily ignored, but for the roar of her own blood in her ears and the certain knowledge that she wanted whatever lesson he was about to give.

Chapter
16

Outside the steps of the jewelers, Ashe turned up his coat collar against the damp afternoon rain. The rebellious act of arranging for something special for Caroline warmed him as he imagined her reaction to the gift. He'd never wanted to see the stones again after they'd escaped India, but now, he longed to see them on his delectable chaperone.

Not that Rutherford would appreciate the irony, but life is all too brief not to—

"Out shopping, cousin?"

Ashe almost groaned aloud before turning around to reluctantly touch the brim of his hat in greeting. "Winston, what a dreadful coincidence meeting you here."

"Buying some extravagant trinket for one of your whores?"

"Cuff links for my grandfather's birthday," Ashe amended, then rewarded poor Mr. Yardley with an arch look of surprise. "You didn't forget the day, did you, cousin? Especially since you hold the man in such high regard, I cannot imagine such an oversight!"

"I-I naturally didn't!" he sputtered, and Ashe forced himself not to smile in relief as Yardley was diverted.

"No, how could you?" Ashe moved toward his carriage, forcing Winston to follow or end the conversation. "Inheritances at stake, and all that."

"You have no one to blame but yourself, Ashe, for my great-uncle's doubts in your fitness and character," he said smugly. "As for this wager, no one forced you to try it."

"True," Ashe said, waving off his coachman from climbing down to open the carriage door. "But I never could resist a challenge."

"Or a temptation," Winston scoffed. "Careful, cousin! I heard you were seen outside Regent's Park well after dark last week! One simple misstep, one wrong whisper after you've forgotten to refasten your pants, and your challenge will come to its inevitable end."

Ashe said nothing at the blatant lie. Only a fool risked the parks after dark, and the common streetwalkers that plied their trade on the greens had never been to his taste— and never in this cold weather! But he was reminded of how much he hated his toad of a relative for the clumsy attempt at inciting a reaction. Ashe climbed into the carriage and shut the door. "Thank you for the warning, Mr. Yardley. Good day."

He rapped on the front wall, and his coachman pulled away, sparing Ashe from any more parting remarks from his rival.

Unfortunately, it also meant he couldn't see if Yardley had doubled back to go into the jeweler's to make inquiries of his own about Ashe's order.

* * *

When he returned to the house, Ashe found Caroline at her desk, penning notes, the very picture of study and grace. She was such a serious creature with her books and papers that he found it fascinating. There was no sign of the nymph that danced and laughed for him behind closed doors. Here was the no-nonsense American he'd come to respect who had turned his household on its side. He smiled at the realization that she'd caused him to learn the names of every single servant in the house and spend more time in his own home without complaint than he could have ever imagined.

He walked up behind her, intending to surprise her with a kiss on the pale column of her neck, but he caught sight of several line drawings and sketches spread out on the desktop. They looked like architectural designs for some grand project to his untrained eyes.

"What are these?"

"Oh!" She turned in her chair, startled at his sudden appearance. "They're nothing," she said, pushing them into a pile as if to hide them, as if she were guilty in some way.

"They are hardly nothing. I like the look of this one. Are you designing libraries since you've exhausted mine?"

"It's . . . foolish." Caroline tried to seize the paper from his hand, a lovely dark pink tinting her cheeks. "They're just . . ."

"Tell me." He held out the parchment, a peace offering in exchange for her confidences. "Is it something from home? Are you feeling nostalgic? Or have you some aspirations to be a feminine Christopher Wren?"

"No." She barely managed a smile, retrieving her stolen sketch. "No such ambitions, Ashe." Caroline turned the papers over, determined not to risk looking maudlin in front of him by dwelling on the loss. "They are daydreams. I have long envisioned a college for women equal to any for men."

"I take it you are imagining something more formal than a finishing school?"

She stood from the desk to face him, aware that he

was deliberately drawing her into a debate—and enjoying it. "There will be no classes on embroidery or painting teacups."

"I'd forgotten you were a reformer." He gave her a wary look. "You realize Lady Fitzgerald will keel over in her salon if she catches a word of *her* American Quaker preaching of impractical education for young ladies."

"I already shared my ideas with her and she remained steady enough on her feet. And why does the word impractical come up when we are discussing a woman's higher education but not when we speak of a man's?"

He shrugged his shoulders. "I couldn't say. Is it because an educated man would have a practical application for that knowledge whereas a woman wouldn't have that opportunity? It's a cruel waste, Caroline."

"Perhaps women aren't given more opportunities for want of education, Ashe. An education is never wasted."

"And where will this feminine utopia of your dreams be built?"

Caroline winced at the innocent question. "Do you think Boston far enough?"

"Not for the dragons of morality and social order." He sighed, openly teasing her. "But I suspect Mars would not be far enough for their kind."

"It won't be for them."

Ashe feared he'd hurt her feelings somehow, but part of him was reluctant to hear more of this fancy that drew her mind homeward and away from England and from him. Here was the future she'd alluded to, and it was far more potent than any single man. Her college was a rival he wasn't sure how to address. "I think it a fine dream, Caroline. And any venture born from that keen mind of yours is bound to astonish the world."

He drew closer to kiss her, and Caroline inhaled the masculine scent of cloves and sandalwood before he enveloped all her senses with the touch of his lips to hers. She opened her mouth quickly to suckle his tongue and savor the gentle friction that pushed all her fears away. She was instantly hungry for more as Ashe lifted her against him, cupping her bottom in his hands to slowly draw her onto his lap.

I am a wanton woman and a shameless creature. The thought was bittersweet, and Caroline ignored the faint echoes of pain as the papers on the desk were pushed aside to make room for their embrace. *Hurry, Ashe! Make love to me before I begin to cry over castles in the air and childish fancies!*

Footsteps outside the door abruptly ended the kiss, and Ashe released her instantly. Caroline struggled not to gasp for air as she held on to the desk for balance, fighting to regain control while Ashe walked stiffly to the windows to put some distance between them.

At the inevitable knock on the door, Caroline closed her eyes briefly. "Yes?"

Daisy came through the door with an afternoon tea tray, dropping a bobble of a curtsy when she spotted Ashe in the room. "I thought you might wish a bit of nourishment, miss."

"Thank you, Daisy. That's very kind," Caroline said, praying her face wasn't as red as it felt.

Ashe marched past them both, making an obvious and necessary escape, mumbling an inaudible apology.

Daisy watched him go but said nothing. Instead she cheerfully set down the tray and began to prepare a small plate and cup. "I didn't mean to interrupt, Miss Townsend. But I'm pleased to see you getting on a bit better."

"Pardon?"

"Not that I ever eavesdrop, but it seems to have quieted down a bit—I mean, from your first days here." She smiled sweetly as she poured the hot water. "Mrs. Clark said this morning that she was praying for a truce for you so that you could enjoy your visit."

"Y-yes! Well, Mr. Blackwell has been very . . . kind. I am very grateful for Mrs. Clark's interest. Thank you, Daisy." Caroline's nerves made her hands shake and she returned her attention to the desk and its contents, removing the pile of drawings to make room for her afternoon tea. But her nerveless fingers dropped the bundle in a noisy cascade of papers, and Daisy rushed to help her.

"Here, no need for that!" Daisy soothed, retrieving the pages while she knelt on the carpet. "I'll get them—Oh, my! Is it going to be a church?"

"They're for a school, just for women. It's just an idea I had."

"A school for ladies?"

"A true college for any girl or woman who wishes to learn."

Daisy's eyes widened. "Any girl? Truly?"

And the hunger in the young maid's eyes was like a hot coal in her stomach. Here was the reason for her journey, here was the inspiration for her strange arrangement and unreal time herding about a grown man. She was to have maintained control and demonstrated her worth, guided Ashe to more gentlemanly behavior . . . and earned her reward and a legacy that would outlive her and give other women hope when they had none.

Hadn't education been her salvation in so many ways when she was growing up? It had given her a glimpse of what was possible. The physical pain of withholding this part of herself from Ashe was crippling, but she couldn't bring herself to tell him about the money and her poverty. She was sure it would seem too trite, too contrived—as if she were some fortune hunter foisted on him or had seduced him for his money. And her honor wouldn't allow it.

"It doesn't exist, Daisy."

"It will, I expect!" Daisy's faith was unshaken. "And what a thing that will be!"

"I'm not—" Caroline took a deep steadying breath and helped Daisy to her feet. "I don't need help with the tray. I don't . . . That will be all, Daisy."

"As you say, miss." Daisy bobbed a curtsy again, barely masking her disappointment. "As you say."

She left quickly and Caroline gave in to bitter tears.

For untold women, I have cast away the opportunity I was given in a moment of weakness—because I'm lost in the seductive blue storm of a man's eyes.

Chapter
17

Lady Fitzgerald's dinner party was a droll gathering. After the men withdrew for port and cigars, the ladies made good use of their chance to gossip and explore less genteel topics with less discretion.

Caroline did her best to stay out of the game, but Lady Fitzgerald beckoned her over to the settee to ensure her a seat at the center of the room's conversations. The chatter swirled around her, rising and falling, and Caroline ignored most of it until the crisp voice of Mrs. Draper caught her attention.

"I have it from a reliable source that Lord Winters founded the Jaded on a lark in India and that they now have over a hundred secret members!" Mrs. Draper stated with firm authority. "It's to do with an ancient heathen religion."

Caroline's spine stiffened. Ashe had described them as a "group of boring men." "The Jaded?" she asked. "It hardly sounds religious."

"Hardly! Naughty things—so mysterious! Men do love their little clubs and secret meetings, do they not?" Mrs. Draper replied.

"Playing at wicked games, more like!" Miss Woodberry chimed in, her lips pressed into a thin line of malicious pleasure. "My younger brother is sure that they learned some dark and twisted magic in India, and that's what makes their members so impossibly rich—and why they keep to themselves! They practice the occult!"

"And indulge in orgies!" whispered another of the older ladies, only to revel in all the shocked gasps around her.

"Isn't Mr. Blackwell a good friend of Lord Winters? Wasn't he also in India recently during the Troubles?" one of the other women asked with a sly smile.

"Blackwell's a leader of the Jaded, I'll warrant, for if any man could be accused of being impossibly wicked, it would be him!" Mrs. Draper nodded with authority, bringing a hush to the room as everyone awaited Caroline's response.

Caroline wasn't having it. "They are friends, but if every Englishman who has seen India is to be a suspected member of this club, it would be hard to conceal such a mob, wouldn't it?"

Some of the women gasped at her cheekiness, but it was Lady Fitzgerald who came to her rescue with an acerbic retort. "Blackwell's too well-heeled to bother with the Jaded, and even if he were, he would never admit such a thing. It is a good parlor game to try to guess about the Jaded. My dear Quaker has no interest in such nonsense! But if she did, mark my words, Miss Caroline Townsend would have them all sorted out before teatime! American girls are apparently made of sterner stuff."

"So are draft horses, but they don't bother to venture into Town." Mrs. Draper arched her eyebrows in the look of a woman unimpressed with American interlopers.

Before Lady Fitzgerald could rally again, Caroline was

on her feet in outrage. "Why anyone would bother with London if such a shallow—"

The tight grip of Lady Fitzgerald's hand on hers cut her off, and the dowager rose to stand next to her. "Ignore Arabelle, Quaker. Her claws are sharper than her wits and I'll not have the evening spoiled by a jealous show."

"I? Jealous?" Arabelle Draper asked, her face red. "Of your Quaker?"

"Certainly. For while you can only guess at the handsome Mr. Blackwell's associations and resort to silly gossip, our dear Miss Townsend has the upper hand and is giving nothing away!" She unsnapped her fan and gave Caroline a gentle push toward the door. "Now, if you'll excuse us both, I want to show the Quaker my new ridiculously expensive window pulls in my drawing room."

Caroline didn't need any additional persuasion to leave, fury and embarrassment warring inside of her for control. With the elderly woman in her wake, she left the women to their whispers and stories, wishing she could stop her hands from shaking.

It was too preposterous, but Caroline wasn't sure if there was any logical rebuttal to be made to such gossip. Ashe would never! The thought was lost in a tangle of memories—of all his odd claims to not be a man fit for civilized company, his avoidance of "decent" women, the courtesan at the museum, and his mysterious disappearances. His friends seemed to call at the strangest hours, and again and again there was the subtle mention of their ties to India. But even more intimately damning was the wicked magic he wielded over her, making her wonder where any gentleman could learn how to unravel a woman so completely and bend her to his will.

Was it possible? That he was involved in something unspeakable? That it had anything to do with these Jaded?

Lady Fitzgerald clapped her hands dismissively as she guided her into a quiet room off the main foyer. It was a warm room awash in gold and ivory damask, an odd lace-accented sanctuary from the grander drawing room. "I told you that every woman in England would set out against you. Arabelle has always fancied Blackwell, but she's too thick a creature to realize it."

"If she cares for him, she has an odd way of showing it by insulting the man!"

Caroline realized her misstep the instant she spoke and watched the confirmation of her error in Lady Fitzgerald's knowing eyes. "Ah! The girl I met in my home recently would have shrugged and said something about letting the catty hag have her wicked prize and good riddance! But to defend him? There's a change."

"H-he's been very kind. I'd have defended anyone in that situation."

Lady Fitzgerald shook her head slowly, walking over to one of the great windows across the room. "I didn't hear a squeak about poor Lord Winters. . . ." Before Caroline could think of a reply she went on lightly, "But how is my American faring in London? I see you have truly abandoned your plain religion and embraced the finer things. Good for you! Have you had many offers?"

"No," Caroline said quietly.

"None? Not a single one?" Lady Fitzgerald sat by the fireplace. "What a disappointment!"

"I'm not disappointed, your ladyship. As I told you, I didn't expect to compete for offers."

"You didn't expect to compete for Blackwell's affections is, I believe, a more accurate accounting of our first conversation." She waved off any protests. "Yes, yes! You care nothing for him! La! But don't think those sharp-clawed gossips won't conclude that you've received no offers because you harbor some secret wish to get one from your delightful villain of a guardian instead!"

"I have . . . no such hope, your ladyship."

"And why not?" the older woman asked without a shred

of humor or encouragement. "Blackwell's heart would be quite the coup."

"He would never offer it—to anyone. He's been very honest in that regard, and if I pay attention to little else, I do seem to remember what I'm told."

Lady Fitzgerald nodded crisply. "You are a wise girl." She stood from her upholstered seat, like a marshal about to inspect the field. "I'm glad that's settled and without ridiculous hysterics. Come now, let me happily imagine my dearly departed George's reaction while I show you my new costly Italian silk draperies and let us sit and discuss your future!"

* * *

"You're quiet tonight." Ashe pulled her across the carriage to sit snugly against him, the heat of his body warming her in the cold night air. "Don't tell me the dragon turned on you! If so, you mustn't give the dowager a single moment's worry."

"No, I am still . . . full of enough pluck to keep her respect. And she approved of my new wardrobe, so you also have a bit of a reprieve."

"Did she fuss that you've yet to land a husband?" He kissed the slope behind her ear and Caroline's fingers clutched reactively at his arm at the spiral of fire that came to life inside of her. "Did you blame your overprotective guardian?"

"I blamed it on my Colonial manners," she whispered.

"I love your Colonial manners."

She pushed away from him slightly in protest. "I find that hard to believe, Mr. Blackwell."

"It's true, although I miss your stern lectures. They were so"—he paused to nip again at the sensitive juncture behind her ear, deliberately exhaling along the moist path his tongue created down the side of her neck—"arousing."

"Tell me about the Jaded, Ashe."

He was instantly still at the sound of the word *Jaded*, but he didn't abandon his strategy altogether as he continued to kiss her throat. "Why do you ask? Did someone mention them tonight?"

"The ladies seem overly curious, but you did say you knew them. Friends of yours, wasn't it?" Her last question ended with a soft sigh as he circled back upward to nibble on her earlobe.

"Odd conversation for the drawing room . . . I'd just assumed there was lively feminine debate on ribbons and the weather." His teeth grazed the outer shell of her ear and she sagged against him in surrender. "And to think we men wasted our time after dinner talking about Hamilton's fondness for hunting rifles."

"Ashe!" she moaned.

His cock stiffened painfully at the sound of her voice, rough with frustration and wanting. But she pushed against him. "Ashe, I want to have one intact conversation with you, without . . ." Her protest faded.

"Without?"

"Without finding myself at a loss to remember my own name or the location of my stockings!"

"As you wish." He straightened his coat and tried to give his best impression of a man in a drawing room and not in the secluded confines of a winter's carriage ride. "Very well. You were asking about the Jaded?"

"No, I don't think I should. Or rather, it is not the right question to ask."

"And what is the right question, Miss Townsend?"

"What happened in India, Ashe?" She reached out to take his hand. "For clearly something must have. Your grandfather isn't the only one to note that you changed after returning, yet no one seems to have anything else to say on the subject."

"There is nothing worth telling."

"Really? Nothing? How long were you there?"

"Three years."

"And in three years, *nothing* of significance occurred?"

"Significant to whom?" He was being obtuse and he knew it, but this was the last subject he wanted to explore with her. In the shadows, it felt too close, and he felt vulnerable somehow. "Her name was Anjali and I fell in love with her in India. It was . . . I thought only of my own family's potential disapproval and I cavalierly disregarded it. Love blinded me to everything. I never thought of her family or her neighbors or the political and religious consequences of my actions while the world around us was preparing to burst into flames."

"Ashe, I—"

"I loved her and she died as a direct result and I don't wish to talk about this ever again."

A small silence spun out between them, and Ashe focused on the way her fingers wrapped so comfortingly around his. She didn't press him for more, didn't sigh in disappointment, and most strikingly of all, didn't look away. Instead he could see, even in the dim light, those large, beautiful eyes of hers looking at him with steadfast support and concern.

It was too much, and guilt almost swamped him. "Things that change us are rarely pleasant. I am sure it is why I have chosen to find solace in pleasurable things that don't have that power."

"There is power in . . . passion, Ashe."

He shook his head. "Give me your hand."

She held out her hand and he peeled off the soft protective layer of her glove, tucking it into his pocket. "Here is passion, Caroline."

Ashe pressed her hand against the carriage window, the heat from her fingers splayed across the cold surface until it warmed beneath her touch. She gasped at the sensation and he covered her hand with his for a moment, trapping her gently between the two extremes of fire and ice. She shivered and leaned back against him, and Ashe indulged in the soft curve of her neck, trailing hot kisses up toward her ear until she moaned.

He pulled her hand back from the window and the detailed imprint of her own palm and fingers remained like a wintry ghost. "There. You see? You affected the glass and warmed it, but you didn't change its nature. That is passion, dearest. A momentary escape from our world, but it need not leave any scars. It has the power to distract and divert but nothing more."

She said nothing, staring at her handprint, and everything in him regretted his words.

* * *

Caroline contemplated her reflection in her vanity mirror as she brushed out her hair for the night and wondered if there were any truth to Ashe's philosophies. It was as if he meant to ward her off and protect her from becoming too attached to him—as if it were possible.

Too late. It is far too late for me to dictate practicality to my heart now. He can speak of passion changing nothing, but for me, it has changed everything. I don't remember feeling anything before I met Ashe. And now I cannot stop feeling. There is no part of him I don't desire.

But that night he'd only underscored the conversation she'd had with Lady Fitzgerald, driving home the reality that no matter how much he wanted her, there was no future match for an American mud wren and an English falcon.

Chapter
18

Caroline waited until the house was dark and quiet before making her way to his room wearing one of her new night-gowns and matching wrap. The rendezvous had been set without conversation, their nightly clandestine meetings simply understood. She knew it was another subtle sign that he was already an integrated part of her existence.

It's hard to imagine a night without him.

In front of the fireplace, he'd laid out an exotic little picnic of crystal port glasses and small sandwiches on a silver platter, arranged for a sultan on the oriental rug, with pillows strewn about. Ashe reclined on the floor with his legs crossed, his shirt unbuttoned to give her a tanta-lizing glimpse of his muscular body. "In case you were hungry, I thought some late-night repast would please you."

She rolled her eyes as she sat next to him on the floor, tossing her wrap over a chair. "So much for your servants not knowing. . . ."

"I never doubted Godwin's omniscience for a minute, did you?"

Caroline smiled. "No, but I prefer to cling to my last tattered dream of discretion."

"Ah! Speaking of dreams." He gave her a gentle pinch on her arm that made her giggle. "I wanted to make sure you were awake, Miss Townsend."

"How noble of you!"

He laughed. "How is it that you are so easy with me? I have never known anyone who made things so . . . entertaining without the slightest show of effort. I am myself completely when you're near, Caroline. And for once, it doesn't feel disappointing to be me."

She shrugged, taking a sip of port from the tray. "Perhaps it's because we disliked each other so much at the start."

"How would that help?"

"It means neither one of us even bothered to try to win the other over. And so here we are."

"Caroline," he began cautiously, "what I said in the carriage about passion—"

"There are people that live their entire lives without a wisp of passion, Ashe. Not that a quiet life doesn't hold a certain appeal, but if you have no choice . . . then nothing appeals, does it?"

She stood in front of the fire, fully aware of the view she offered him, setting her glass down on the mantel. The thin silk would do nothing to shield her from his eyes, and she warmed at the way his eyes trailed over her body and lingered on her face.

"And what would you choose, Miss Townsend?"

Love, Ashe. I would choose to be loved. The answer clamored in her head, but for once, her pluck failed her and she accepted her cowardice. "I cannot say."

"Can you not?" He reached up to tug at the sheer fabric of her nightgown, pulling it taut across her breasts and making them swell as her nipples puckered in response.

"We . . . Quakers . . . like to keep our secrets, Mr. Blackwell."

He caught her wrist and pulled her down onto the rug to straddle him. "I'd forgotten that I'd promised you riding lessons."

"Did you?" she teased. She wriggled her hips to nestle her sex against his, the barrier of his pants doing little to disguise the firm outline of his aroused flesh. The first shimmer of anticipation flared up from her hips and Caroline reveled in the silent promises his body made to hers. She crossed her arms to lift her nightgown up over her head, a nymph unabashedly revealing herself for his appreciative eyes and hands. "I love the feel of your hands on my body, Ashe."

"Then you must close your eyes and imagine them there the next time you are trapped in the dowager's den and fending off Miss Woodberry's poetry readings." He was quick to oblige her, his hands fanning upward from her waist, encircling her back, and then sweeping up over her breasts, where he pressed his palms lightly against the pebble-hard tips to make her gasp in delight and arch into his touch.

Caroline threw her head back and closed her eyes as his fingers pinched each coral nub, sending jolts of fire down her spine and making the inner muscles of her core begin to ache with need. It was as if he knew every invisible line within her, and she moaned as he played the tight strings that would create her release.

"Ashe!"

He slid one of his hands between her legs, instantly finding what he sought. He loved the wet, soft, silky flesh that met his caress as he worked her clit and one of his fingers slid up inside of her, then two. All the while, his other hand continued to tweak and tug at the coral crests that demanded his attention, and he mirrored his strokes to spur her on, striving to make her lose control.

In the firelight, she was a pagan goddess riding him for her own solitary pleasure, her hair burnished bronze curls that fell across her shoulders and down her back. The play of light and shadows made her lush figure even more stark and beautiful, and he was awed at her complete trust and abandonment. Ashe was sure that as a man he would happily sacrifice himself on this altar if it meant watching her achieve her release. But his own needs protested, his cock throbbing with denied access to her slick sex as she moved over him.

"Come, my clever chaperone. Take charge of me, I beg you."

She was quick to show mercy, rocking her weight back onto her ankles to eye the clear cause of his discomfort as his cock pressed up toward the waist of his trousers. Caroline shamelessly caressed and stroked him through the cloth, testing his endurance and openly enjoying her game. Her nimble fingers made quick work of his buttons, finally freeing him for her intimate appreciation. She dipped one pointed fingertip down to touch his mighty erection's eager tip, collecting a single pearl of translucent crème to ever so slowly suck and sample it from her finger, and Ashe nearly spent himself at the sight of it.

"To be a good rider, I must break in my stallion, sir."

Caroline decided she would use her mouth to bring him to the brink. In the rise and fall of the firelight, it was a thing of true beauty, proud and impressive, as hard as steel but sheathed in velvet soft skin that begged for the touch of her lips.

It still amazed her that her body could accommodate the sheer size of him, but for now, she wished only for possession of it—and the chance to make him beg even more.

Caroline took her time, running her fingers over the satinlike skin, teasing then gripping, stroking him just as he'd shown her, and watching the subtle changes as his cock jumped in her palm. The fiery heat of his flesh was intoxicating, and Ashe groaned as she deliberately fanned the wet head of his cock with every exhale to torture him, until she couldn't stand to wait any longer before tasting him.

She lowered her head down and kissed him, reverently drinking in the salty-sweet first drops of his essence before opening her mouth to pull him in. Her tongue encircled the ripe head of it, then dipped into the sensitive juncture at the tip of his shaft to dance along the ridge of skin until his hips shook beneath her hands.

Caroline gripped him with her fingers, alternating the pressure of her touch with wicked wet kisses and the work of her tongue up and over him, until she was lost in the rhythm and ritual of pure pleasure.

His fingers tangled in her hair, and Ashe stared at the overwhelming sight of his prim and proper chaperone wantonly lapping up his sex and parting him from his control.

Just when he was sure he couldn't hold back, she pulled herself back up over him, spreading her legs to hover there for long seconds, squeezing just the ripe tip of him with the tight entrance to her core, allowing him inside of her body by the merest fraction.

"Damn it, Caroline!"

"Shhh! Such language, Ashe! I am learning about passion."

"You're learning how to kill a man!"

She leaned down, her dark blonde hair becoming a curtain that shielded his eyes from the firelight. "I would never hurt you."

She enveloped him in a single glorious move, rocking back onto his cock and taking all of it, impaling the hot, soaking confines of her body with his and forcing him to grip her hip bones to keep himself from bucking upward and bruising her. It was a mindless ecstasy that shocked him as his entire body fused with hers.

Ashe gave into it and they set off at a gallop until the room echoed with their quiet cries and the primal slapping sound of their flesh meeting in a timeless dance. If she was learning about passion, then Ashe was sure he was every bit her fellow pupil. The entire world fell away and there was only Caroline above him and around him, the taste of her in his mouth, and the scent of her in his nostrils.

I'm drowning in this woman and I want more, he told himself. *Enough!*

He shifted to overtake her and force her to lose her seat without dislodging himself from within her. In the space of a heartbeat, Caroline was on her back, a willing captive beneath him, her fingers digging into his shoulders as she locked her ankles around him, holding on for dear life as every vestige of tenderness fell away from them both. This was blinding hunger that demanded satisfaction, and Caroline tilted her hips upward to draw in each ruthless stroke.

Locked together, they became a living intricate puzzle that made every exhale and the slightest movement impossibly erotic and meaningful.

Caroline's eyes widened as the searing hot coil inside of her imploded in a white-hot shower of sensation. The climax stole the air from her lungs and she was helpless in its wake as wave after wave washed through her frame, echoing every thrust of Ashe's hips. The pleasure grew so intense she began to weep.

She feared he would misunderstand and ducked her face into the curve of his neck only to bite his shoulder as another shiver of fire overtook her.

Ashe gritted his teeth to keep from roaring as he came in a cascade of lightning and fire that seared his soul—her climax spurring him on and on as her muscles milked his cock until he was completely drained.

I'm as weak as a newborn, God help me.

One last arc of molten bliss shot down his spine and Ashe decided that he was past all help—divine or otherwise.

Let's just pray we both survive this.

Chapter
19

🌸

"I have something for you." He held out the black lacquered box, wishing he had more practice at respectable gift-giving. He'd invaded her room to surprise her before they left for a masque ball. She was wearing the silvery blue evening gown that he'd requested and it thrilled him to see that she had done just that—to please him. "Though perhaps you shouldn't say they are from me."

Caroline's hands stayed by her sides. "It isn't appropriate—"

"Never mind! To hell with appropriate, Caroline. Say they're a family heirloom or tell the world that I gave them to you because I wanted more than anything to offer you proof of . . . my feelings." He shifted his weight on his feet, nerves making the box heavy in his hand as he continued to hold it out to her. "Take it, Caroline, if only to spare my pride."

She smiled slowly and reached for the case, opening it with the gentle caution of a woman unused to gifts. Ashe watched her with an echo of surprise. Her grandfather had been as rich as Croesus and she would have a mountain of trinkets to show for it. But her demeanor was so sweet, he was humbled by her acceptance of his present.

"To spare your feelings then, for I wouldn't be accused of stripping a man of his pride," she said. Then her eyes widened as if in shock. "Ashe! It's . . ."

"Sapphires. They are star sapphires and when I first saw you in this ball gown at Worthley's, I couldn't help but think that they belonged with you." He took the necklace from the case to place it around her throat with sensual ease. "These are stones from India. Souvenirs from my travels there and ones I thought never to see the light of day, Caroline. But when I look at you, I think what a tragedy that would be. For they come to life in the light, don't you think?"

Just as you've come to life for me, Caroline. Just as I have . . . with you.

Her fingers trembled as she touched the hazelnut sized stones around her throat, the small diamonds encircling each star sapphire setting off its hidden fire. Each stone matched the silver blue of her dress just as he'd envisioned it. "It's too much."

"Hardly." He suddenly wanted to cover her in jewels; a possessive joy seized him at the notion of claiming her in a shower of glittering stones.

"Why were you hiding them, Ashe?" She turned to face him directly. "They're so beautiful and it seems strange that you would keep them from the light of day."

You're too clever, Caroline. I think it's what I've come to admire most about you. "Natural enough to keep them safe, and what would a gentleman do with them? I could hardly decorate my horse's harness or use them for buttons, could I?"

She laughed at the preposterous notion. "They *would* make impressive buttons!"

"Think of this necklace as your own Kohinoor, though it's hardly the size of that infamous diamond." Ashe loved the way she unconsciously began to preen as the metal warmed against her skin. He guided her toward the gilt mirror on her vanity.

"And does my Kohinoor come with its own magic?"

His eyes met hers in the mirror, and Ashe felt a tight heat in his chest, an ache at the sight of the vulnerable beauty looking back at him, her fearless brown eyes so trusting and sweet. "The woman who wears these stones will never come to harm."

"Never?"

"Never so long as I live."

Oh, God, if ever a man spoke a blood oath over stones and meant it to the last breath.

*   *   *

"You're late, Blackwell!"

"I'm never late, Terrance," Ashe corrected his host, Lord Crawley, with a cavalier smile.

"It's said the prince himself is sporting about in a masque this evening, Blackwell! What do you say to that?" Lord Crawley crowed before his eyes lit on Caroline with a predatory gleam. "But who is this petite goddess?"

"May I introduce my grandfather's ward, Miss Caroline Townsend?"

It was a slightly different title, and Caroline marveled at the subtle shift. The rules in polite society would grace-fully bend if she were out from under his direct protection. A keen flare of hope burned even more brightly inside of her, one almost too painful to voice.

The gift of the sapphires as proof of his feelings, he'd said! And now this . . . Can it be that he truly cares enough to risk such a public declaration?

"Isn't she a delight!" Lord Crawley bowed over her hand. "When you tire of Blackwell's ill manners, you must send word. I am determined to restore your faith in English gentility."

Before she could reply, Ashe stepped forward to say, "What faith? She's American, Lord Crawley, and has no illusions about Englishmen, I can assure you." He gently propelled her from the receiving line as Lord Crawley burst into laughter at the exchange. Then under his breath, Ashe continued, "As if that old goat's manners would improve anything!"

"Be kind!" she chided him without conviction as she struggled not to smile. "We are his guests, Mr. Blackwell."

Ashe retrieved two masques from a basket on a large marble table and offered her one decorated with small silver beads, keeping a black and red silk affair for himself. "You're right, of course. Here, a simple affectation and you are transformed! For the night, Miss Townsend shall be a bejeweled temptress and a woman to be reckoned with."

"I am always a woman to be reckoned with, Mr. Blackwell," she said as she took the long ribbon-wrapped handle attached to the masque. "But what will you become tonight?"

His blue eyes glowed at the amusing prospect of his disguise. "I shall be your faithful servant and make sure that Lord Crawley keeps a respectable distance." Ashe tied his masque on and rewarded her with an elegant bow. "Dance with me, temptress."

She nodded her acceptance, not trusting her voice. It was all so perfect and so precarious. Her despair at the destruction of her future had never taken hold, not in the light of Ashe's searing gaze, and new dreams coalesced and began to dance just beyond her reach as he walked her through the marbled halls of the marquis' great house.

For the first time, she felt a sense of belonging that had nothing to do with her family or her fortunes. It was simply Ashe's hand covering hers on his arm as he protectively guided her toward the ballroom. *I am his, and instead of feeling enslaved, I feel completely free.*

They blended seamlessly into the swirling dancers already on the floor, and Ashe held her so closely she forgot to worry about the steps or even consider where her toes might touch the ground. Caroline forgot everything in the whirlwind of color and movement that became their world for a few magical moments.

The mud wren is gone forever! I am a temptress and a woman in love!

The electricity between them left her breathless and giddy.

"What are you thinking, Caroline?" he asked. The warm heat of his mouth barely brushing against the outer shell of her ear made the span between her hips spasm with moisture.

"I was wondering if I was sleepwalking again."

"I can assure you that you are awake."

"How embarrassing to think of oneself walking and carrying on conversations without any memory of it! I'm still not sure I can trust my senses. Are you sure this isn't a dream?"

He looked down into her eyes. "Trust me. When you sleepwalk, I've not known you to remember to wear clothes." The gentle teasing tone made her want to melt against him completely.

"You make a good point, Blackwell. Thank you for clarifying things."

The woman who wears these stones will never come to harm.

The dance ended far too quickly as far as she was concerned, but the sight of Lord Winters and his lady wife gave her a rush of comfort. Lady Winters took both her hands into her own in a warm greeting and Caroline marveled again at the easy grace and lack of pretension she projected.

"What a pleasure to see you again, Miss Townsend!" Haley said. "And how beautiful you look this evening!"

"I meant to say the same, Lady Winters," Caroline replied. It was not an empty compliment to her new friend in a ruby red gown that set off her coloring to perfection.

"You were to call me Haley, remember?" Lady Winters teased her merrily.

"She remembers," Ashe noted with a wry grin. "Miss Townsend remembers *everything* she has ever heard. Trust me. I've experienced it firsthand."

Caroline blithely ignored him. "Mr. Blackwell didn't mention that we might see you tonight, Haley!"

Galen gave his friend a wary look. "Perhaps because Ashe was hoping to have you all to himself for the evening."

Caroline averted her gaze to make a thorough inspection of her masque, checking it for any loose feathers. *Are we that obvious? Will his friends think less of me for it?*

Galen's wife rewarded him with a quick elbow to his ribs as Ashe replied, "A flawed strategy to take a woman out in public if that were my intention."

"Would you care to get us some refreshments, gentlemen?" Lady Winters interjected, the ploy obvious.

"We are dismissed, Ashe. Come, let's slink away to the punch bowls and recover what dignity we can while the ladies discuss your shortcomings." Galen bowed briefly.

"*My* shortcomings? Brace yourself, Lord Winters. For I am bound to come out ahead in a comparison—shall we?" Ashe winked at Caroline playfully before heading off with his friend into the crowd on their quest for drinks.

"They are like children whenever they are together," Lady Winters remarked. "Teasing each other and competing like fools."

Caroline's eyes followed Ashe's broad shoulders until he vanished into the crush. "He does not like to be called a child," she said quietly.

"What?" Haley prompted, missing her words.

"Nothing," Caroline corrected herself. "I cannot believe they would abandon us so quickly if either one fears a conspiracy."

Haley shook her head with a smile. "It gives Galen a chance to apologize for being too outspoken, and Ashe a chance to deny that he's completely besotted; so I believe it entirely. And don't look at me like that! I know what it is to be swept up in the moment, Miss Townsend. I am . . . familiar with your predicament."

"Oh," Caroline said, wishing she could summon more eloquence after such an admission. It was comforting to think that Lady Winters cared enough to empathize, but she wasn't sure they were discussing the same matter. *Besotted? Here is proof beyond sapphires! Fresh eyes are seeing what I can't, and if that isn't cause to celebrate, I don't know what would be.*

"But what a beautiful necklace, Miss Townsend!" Lady Winters exclaimed. "Those are jewels fit for a queen."

Caroline's cheeks warmed, her fingers tracing the arc of the stones at her throat nervously. "Thank you. They were a gift from—"

The rest of her speech vanished at the sight of a very voluptuous woman wearing a peacock blue green dress approaching. Caroline recognized Miss Stillman instantly despite the pretense of disguise as Margot boldly stepped up to them as if they were all old friends. "Ah! I wondered what lucky creature would be the next to wear those sapphires!"

"I beg your pardon?" Caroline covered her throat, instinctively trying to ward off an attack.

"Those stones! I would know them anywhere. Ashe is so generous! And he has such a way with words, does he not? I wore them only on loan. I was hard-pressed to give them back, but when a man like that wishes to move on to his next conquest, it's impossible to say no." The woman lowered her feathered masque, giving Caroline an assessing look. "Better to leave the door open so that they can return, don't you think?"

Lady Winters snapped her fan closed with a furious grace. "Mind yourself!"

Margot took a theatrical step back, but not without assuring herself more of an audience. "I apologize if I gave offense, Lady Winters. I have clearly overstepped. I'm sorry, Miss Townsend. I knew you were far more than his grandfather's ward—for clearly, you enjoy a different sort of relationship with the delicious Mr. Blackwell. Granted you aren't his usual taste, are you, but perhaps you know a trick or two you'd be willing to share?" There were a few gasps from nearby guests eavesdropping on the exchange, and Caroline was suddenly aware of her exposure in this place.

Caroline's throat constricted and she wasn't sure what to say. Just like that afternoon in the museum, there was no mistaking the implication of her words. *He'd lied. He'd made it seem as if he'd had the necklace made for her and her alone, but this woman . . . Apparently every whore who succumbed to him was rewarded at one time or another with a show of Indian sapphires.*

Lady Winters stepped forward as if to shield her new friend from the other woman's claims. "I don't remember being introduced, and frankly, I'm not interested in that honor. Please return to whatever idiot brought you to this party and let him know that it might be best if he took you home—now!"

The woman curtsied, a wicked Cheshire cat grin on her lovely features, and disappeared into the crush of the crowd in the same direction that the men had gone.

Caroline was frozen in place watching her colorful retreat.

"Ignore her!" Haley touched her arm. "She's just some jealous woman he set aside long before he met you!"

Caroline slowly shook her head, despising the numb

ice that was coating the inside of her stomach. "Is she?" *Some jealous woman. Would Margot claw and spit this hard if she didn't still harbor feelings for Ashe? Wasn't it proof that she might have thought herself more than his last conquest?*

Will I feel the same rage if he sets me aside?

"What a surprise to see you here, Miss Townsend!" Winston Yardley interrupted, his timing unsettling. All in black, he gave the impression of a raven standing out in a sea of tropical birds. "Lady Winters?" he asked, then bowed deeply. "I should have known you anywhere. Miss Townsend continues to be fortunate in her acquaintances!"

An awkward silence followed before Caroline realized that it was her place to formalize an introduction, if only for Haley's sake, but she wasn't sure how to phrase it to disguise her dislike for the man. "Mr. Winston Yardley, may I introduce you to Lady Winters? Mr. Yardley is . . . a cousin of Mr. Blackwell."

"How do you do, Mr. Yardley?" Haley managed a curt nod, her expression betraying her distress at the interruption.

"A distant relative of Ashe's too humble to think of intruding on your lovely evening, Miss Townsend, but I must blame joyous shock alone for making me step forward." He bowed again with a dramatic wave of his arm. "I'd understood you were already setting sail for home."

"W-what?"

"I saw Ashe near Fitzroy Square and he remarked on it. Not that I am any trusted friend of yours, but I was so sure of my information! After all, why would he boast about seeing you off and enjoying his reward for a Season well lived?" Winston shrugged. "I'd assumed that everything was settled."

"What is he talking about?" Hayley asked.

Caroline shook her head. "Nothing of consequence," she whispered.

"Victory goes to my cousin, Miss Townsend. I sent a letter of concession to his grandfather congratulating him on his heir's achievements. Blackwell has proved too wily. For he's had us all, and no one can cry foul. Least of all"—his eyes dropped to the sapphires encircling her throat—"you."

He bowed one last time and moved off, leaving Caroline breathless and pale as Haley gently gripped her elbow. "What was that about? Caroline, I beg you not to take all this to heart and—"

Galen returned with a cup in hand. "I had to fend off dragons, but here is your cup of holiday cheer, my dear." Some of the cheer drained from his face as he realized that something was amiss. "What has happened?"

"Where is Blackwell?" Lady Winters asked.

Galen spared a surprised glance over his shoulder. "Ashe was just behind me. I apologize, Miss Townsend, but he must have run into someone in the crowd. Is something wrong?"

Caroline took a small step back, her masque dropping to her side. "No. If you'll excuse me, I need to find Mr. Blackwell."

"No." Lady Winters tried to stop her. "Let Galen fetch him for you!"

Caroline didn't answer but walked briskly past them both, ignoring all protests, and pushed into the milling wall of guests, heading in the direction that Ashe had gone. She was determined to find him and hear his voice soothe and explain and quiet the demons that were tearing her heart in pieces.

It isn't true. No matter what is said or insinuated, it won't be true until Ashe looks into my eyes and says it is true.

She forced herself to keep a slow, measured pace, fighting the urge to race around the room like a wild caricature of a jealous shrew. But there was no sign of Ashe or the malignant Miss Stillman.

One I desperately want to see and the other I would do anything to avoid.

She left the main room, and just when she was about to give up and return to Lord Winters and ask him to take her back to the brownstone, she heard a woman's laugh from behind a doorway. *That woman's laugh!*

Caroline turned to open the door wide just in time to see Margot, her bodice pulled down, her beautiful breasts exposed, stepping away from Ashe in a secluded corner.

Margot screeched in theatrical horror as her eyes met Caroline's. "Oh, dear! Oh, Ashe! I'm ruined!"

She stood frozen in the doorway for just a fleeting second and then realized after hearing gasps in the hallway that another pair of guests were behind her—also apparently taking in the view. Her humiliation was complete and public. Ashe had his scandal after all, and it wasn't his ward's seduction that had brought him down.

It was his ward's heartbreak.

For the space of a single breath, she took it all in and knew that she was expected to play a very specific role in this penny drama and run away in tears, cementing the scene and providing Lord Crawley's guests with an emotional entertainment they'd not soon forget.

And so instead, Caroline Townsend of Boston, Massachusetts, walked into the room with her head held high as if she'd been invited for tea.

Chapter
20

Ashe was in hell. He turned to give Margot a look of pure loathing. She'd approached him with a quiet threat that they must speak or she'd make a public scene—and like an idiot, he'd complied only to get the conversation over with. He'd come too far to risk a ridiculous row.

What he hadn't expected was Margot's strange behavior.

"You're supposed to tell me how lovely I look, Ashe."

"I don't have time to play, and you look like a painted chicken."

She'd simply laughed. "You are a wicked man! I look too beautiful for words and you simply can't recall the best bit of poetry to suit me."

Then she'd begun telling him how much she'd missed their rendezvous and how cruel he'd been to throw his poor friend into the mix.

"That was weeks ago! Are you daft?"

The hairs on the back of his neck had begun to stiffen in warning and she'd started babbling about how she regretted her actions at the museum and pouted something about wishing to make it up to him. "But after tonight, it won't be possible, Ashe."

"Why? What has happened tonight?"

And she'd smiled and, with surreal speed and grace, pulled down the front of her dress and stepped forward to press herself against him. There'd been no time to think. Ashe was stunned as a part of his mind coldly noted that there were footsteps approaching and voices from the gala muffled through the walls.

He pushed her away as the door opened but also tried to shield her from view, awkwardly losing the battle only to realize that Caroline was standing there, illuminated by lamplight, the crushing agony in her eyes unmistakable— but then her look changed and she transformed before his very eyes into the prim and detached chaperone he'd met weeks ago in his grandfather's library.

"Oh, dear! Oh, Ashe! I'm ruined!"

"Caroline!"

Caroline raised her hand to gracefully silence him as she approached Margot with a smile and spoke loudly enough for the eavesdropping guests to hear each cheerful word. "You poor thing! It's not ruined, though. It just looks as if the sleeve has come untied. Here, let me help you with that." Caroline took charge of her as easily as a schoolteacher retying a child's shoelaces, and Margot's mouth fell open in shock. Before the courtesan could summon her next thought, she was dutifully lifting her arms to help Caroline repair her dress and cover her breasts.

"Mr. Blackwell's buttons are treacherous to snag on your dress like that! Aren't these London fashions challenging?" Caroline shook her head with a gentle sigh of female commiseration. "Your seamstress should be scolded for not sewing on these feathers with more care!"

"But, I . . ." Margot looked over her shoulder and must have realized that already her captive audience was now

watching for an entirely different reason and her opportunity for infamy was fading. It was the amazing grace
and calm of the American that was drawing a crowd now.
"There's no need . . ."

"There, you're restored! It's a good thing I was close
by or Mr. Blackwell would have been forced to send for
smelling salts."

"S-smelling salts?" Margot asked in astonishment.

Caroline reached out to catch one of Margot's hands in
hers. "Mr. Blackwell once told me that beautiful women
of good breeding, such as yourself, were prone to fainting
spells."

"Did he?" Margot actually blushed and Ashe knew he
was watching a miracle unfold in front of him. But he didn't
trust his good fortune. Was it possible that Caroline could
be so forgiving? *No woman is this unflappable. Where is
the screaming? Where are the tears?*

"Would you like some warm cider, Miss Stillman?"
Caroline guided her to a seat on an ornate sofa and then
perched merrily next to her as if they were the dearest of
friends. "Mr. Blackwell was just going to fetch some for
Lady Winters when he left us, but I'm sure he'd be happy to
give you her cup. Wouldn't you, Mr. Blackwell?"

I'd like to fetch her a cup of arsenic. "Yes, yes, of course,
if Miss Stillman requires a refreshment."

A flurry of movement at the door interrupted everything
as a red-faced Winston Yardley made an expectant appearance. "Is there some tr—"

His shocked disappointment at finding the two women
sitting together as Ashe apparently served them cider was
palpable. "I thought I heard . . . someone cry for help?" he
offered lamely, and several guests nearby snickered.

"Not at all," Caroline answered, "but what an odd coincidence to run into you again, Mr. Yardley! But how rude
of me. Should I introduce you to Miss Stillman?"

"No! I mean . . ." Winston looked like a man who'd

been offered a dead mouse for dessert. "Under the circumstances . . ."

"I believe they are already acquainted, Miss Townsend." Ashe did his best to swallow his own fury without choking on it. It was so obvious—all of it—and there was Yardley like an unhappy director as his farce reeled beyond his control.

"Thank goodness!" Caroline answered, so unexpectedly that Ashe had to stare at her again. "I am wretched at introductions and never know when they are appropriate. I was about to offer my new friend a ride home, if she wishes. I can't imagine how you're feeling, Miss Stillman, with all of this fuss for nothing, but I'd come to find Mr. Blackwell to complain of a headache and leave the party myself; so if you'd like to join me . . ."

Ashe froze at the surreal nightmare unfolding before him. There was no way to argue against it as several astonished onlookers took note with whispered exchanges about Blackwell's American Quaker innocently befriending a known harlot and offering the doxie a ride home.

All of their attention is on Caroline! She's literally drawn them off and saved me and all I can do is stand here like an idiot and let her.

Margot stood, and Caroline took her hand to tuck it into the crook of her elbow, a mother duck gathering a wayward duckling. "How generous of you, Miss Townsend," Margot said softly, and then to Ashe so quietly that he alone could hear her, "I'm sorry, Ashe. I never realized . . . It was too good an offer to forego, and after all, it's not as if you ever cared one way or the other."

He didn't answer her, unwilling to waste a single second in debate. And then Caroline walked away with Miss Stillman, never once looking in his direction. The damage to his reputation was minimal, but Caroline was all he cared about.

And this hell was all too familiar.

This is what it feels like to lose the woman you love. My God . . . how could I be this blind?

He began to go after her, but Winston stepped into his path, his eyes wild. "Y-you ruined that poor woman and now you're just going to stroll out of here, untouched! How is that possible?"

"Which woman are you referring to?" The words were like chalk in his mouth.

."M-Miss Stillman . . ." Yardley answered too quickly, then realized the missed opportunity and his expression grew even more demonic. "Everyone saw it!"

Ashe didn't need to look about to gauge that their audience was still small but rapt. He didn't care anymore who was listening or how the scene played out. He leaned in to seize the lapels of Winston's jacket, lifting him off his feet until their noses almost touched. "What did you offer her? What could you possibly have to offer, Yardley? Did you promise to marry Margot after she helped you create this little scandal and you'd stepped into my shoes?"

"I didn't—I had nothing to do with any of this!"

Ashe shook his head. He'd wanted to blame Margot. He'd wanted more than anything to yell every vile degrading insult he could think of to tear her to pieces and grasp at the illusion of righteousness. But he knew better now. He'd toyed with her like so many women and never considered for a moment that their lives were altered for it. He'd paid for the privilege of treating her badly and never thought of the consequences.

And then came Caroline . . .

"Of course you did. Don't worry, Yardley. I hate you, but I hate myself a good deal more."

He released Yardley's jacket and stepped back to allow his cousin to recover, although Winston's nervous hands made a shabby mess of his clothes. "I couldn't allow you to bilk my dear uncle out of his legacy. I couldn't allow you to play at respectability only long enough to reassure him—not when you and I both know that the instant the ink had dried on his will, you'd have gone back to your vile and sinful ways!"

Ashe gave him a chilling look. "You may want to stave off this lecture, Winston, while we're in so public a place."

The irony was lost on Yardley and he reddened with fury. "I? I have nothing to hide!"

"You've conspired with her to try to set me up, and when Miss Townsend offered to introduce her, it was clear you knew who and what she was. So much for hiding the truth."

"The truth? The truth about what?"

"About your arrangement with Margot and your penchant for enjoying my leftovers."

The color drained from Yardley's face.

"You see," Ashe continued relentlessly, "I know Margot is only the latest in a long line of doves you cannot seem to keep your greasy hands off of. I credited it to a strange kind of rivalry. As if you thought to better me somehow— though all it did was make it a bit easier for me to cast them off since the idea of you poking around between their thighs instantly ended any attraction I had for the poor things."

"I never . . ." Winston's protest faltered.

"Your mistake was in attacking Caroline. She is, as you well know, not a soiled dove to clutch at coins and play along, and from what Godwin overheard, she nearly boxed your ears like some errant schoolboy."

"That bitch had no—"

Winston's feet had left the carpet before he could draw another breath, his back meeting the wall as Ashe drove him against it with brutal rib-breaking force. "You're an imbecile! Destroy me, if you want to! Hell, I was never in hiding, was I? I'd have probably helped you pack me off to Hades if you'd been man enough to step up and buy the ticket! But you—you spineless piece of rotting flesh! You hurt Caroline, and for that, I'm afraid, all bets are off!"

"You"—Yardley gasped to catch his breath as Ashe refused to lessen his hold and pressed the smaller-framed man to the wall—"you're mad!"

Ashe let go, grimly enjoying the sight of Winston cowering on the floor where he'd landed. "I'll wager that you're right. But you might have taken that into account before you started this business, Yardley, and went too far."

"You're the one who goes too far! And for what? Some poverty-stricken schoolteacher?"

"What?"

Winston replied without leaving the illusion of safety the wall behind him provided. "I have a good friend in Boston who wrote to me about the Townsends when he heard that she was coming to visit my relatives. Apparently, her aunt made enough of a squall about the matter to draw his attention and he thought I'd enjoy the irony. I received his letter several days after your grandfather included me in on your wager and I was sure it was providence that gave me such timely news."

"You're lying! They're one of the wealthiest families in Boston."

"Undoubtedly. But Caroline's father was a bit of a black sheep, and apparently her great-uncle decided to cut them out of all of it after he inherited. The woman has nothing! She is a charity case on her aunt's doorstep who works as little more than a glorified governess at a boys' college! Why else would she have come to England and accepted such a ridiculous offer from your grandfather to babysit you? He must have promised her some money! So there! You see? I won the wager! You never did give up whores."

Ashe pulled him to his feet in one swift move and then promptly punched him squarely in the face. Yardley's eyes rolled back in his head and he fell to the floor, cold-cocked from a single blow.

He couldn't let it stand another minute.

Ashe walked out, ignoring the wide-eyed stares of the other guests as he tore off his masque and threw it on the floor.

Hades can have them all and be damned! I'm not going to lose you, Caroline. Not without a fight.

*   *   *

"Open this door, woman!" Ashe pounded on her bedroom door, frustration adding to the force of his fist to the wood. He'd chased her all the way home, determined to intercept her before she could slip from his reach. "Damn it, Caroline! I'll break down this door if I have to—but you'll not leave things like this without hearing the truth!"

Ashe took a deep breath and stepped back from the door, eyeing the thick oak with a cold calculation of just how to splinter the barrier without breaking his own body.

But just as he determined that kicking it was probably the best approach, it flew open and she was standing there, pale, her caramel brown eyes full of a wild fire he didn't recognize. She'd taken her hair down but still wore the beautiful gown and sapphires.

"I don't want to hear the truth, Ashe."

"Like hell you don't!"

"Ashe—"

He cut her off, "You'll hear me out, Caroline Townsend!"

She shook her head. "To hear you say what? That nothing happened? That it was a misunderstanding? That she lured you into that room and then threw herself at you?"

Ashe's brow furrowed as his every planned speech suddenly seemed trite and inane. She was fury and fire and he was starting to feel like a man who had failed to bring a weapon to the war. "God damn it! You steal a man's arguments as if that proves anything!"

"It was obviously staged, Ashe. I'm an American. I'm not an idiot."

"Of course you're not! Margot is insane and a meaningless creature to even attempt such a thing!"

"Insane? Meaningless?"

"She mistook a passing interest for more and sought some kind of twisted revenge for her trouble."

"A passing interest—how foolish of her!"

Ashe sensed that he'd missed a critical step, but he wasn't going to retreat. "By all appearances, Yardley paid her to play the part and I never dreamt that she would throw herself into my path like that."

She covered her face with trembling hands. "Oh, God, I'm the world's fool."

He reached for her. "Caroline, please! It was a contrived scene meant to humiliate me and incite your jealousy! It is nothing to us!"

"And my jealousy wouldn't please you?" She avoided his hands, keeping him at arm's length.

"No," he spoke slowly, instinctively aware that he was on thin ice now.

"Why not? I thought you found it acceptable enough when it was you pawing and growling about when your friend Darius came within a carriage's length of my person! So why not relish a bit of jealousy on my part?"

He had no ready answer.

She continued, pain fueling her words. "Is it because it implies possession, Ashe? Well enough for you to possess and guard me but not the reverse?"

Oh, God. She has a horrible point of logic. Ashe ran his fingers through his hair in frustration, wishing he'd paid more attention to his debating skills at the university.

"Once again"—her voice trembled, but she held her ground—"you would dictate the rules, Ashe, but not live by them. And once again, I will tell you that you are not in charge of me!"

Ashe reached for her again, intending to sweep past the

defenses of logic and make her see that his heart was the cause of their tangle. "Caroline, if you would just—"

She pushed away from him, furiously striking out to ward off his touch, landing blows against his chest and shoulders, tears weakening her attack. "No more, Blackwell! No more! I want you out!"

Frustration and passion were a dangerous mix. He endured the onslaught of her anger, almost relieved to be on familiar ground. She was still his. If she had retreated with icy indifference, he would have known she didn't care. Need and desire overrode everything else.

In one fluid movement, he captured her flailing hands and bent his knees to pull her over his shoulder. Standing up, he positioned her better, and her feet left the ground before she could manage a single shocked squawk. Ashe made sure he had a firm grip on his prize before striding from the room and out in the hall toward his own bedchambers.

"Put me down this instant!" She kicked out, pounding on his back as she hung over his shoulder, a storm of feminine anger in his arms. "You have no right!"

"No." He pushed open his bedroom door and kicked it shut behind them. "We can fight later about scandals and rules, arrangements and contracts, chaperones and guardians, and anything else you care to explore. We can even have a lively debate about all the lies that Yardley's been spewing, but not now, Caroline."

He walked over to his bed and dropped her in the middle of the mattress in a beautiful disheveled pile. "Now, I'm going to prove to you that nothing between us need change—that I desire you above all others, Caroline, and that you alone can keep me from despair.

"Love me, Caroline."

She shook her head, her lips parting soundlessly as shock and desire, anger and lust warred within her. "I—"

"Love me, Caroline," he repeated the command and she nodded in miserable surrender.

I already do, Ashe. How can you not see it?

He wasted no time, seizing her to tumble back onto the bed in a rushed and glorious embrace that tangled their bodies together. There was no time to even undress completely as they meshed in a fury of raw hunger and emotion. The seams on her décolletage tore as he tugged at it to free her ample breasts, spilling them out into his eager hands, and he kissed away her protests.

She didn't want him to be gentle. Her pain was too fresh and every bruising, crushing touch of his lips to hers was a strange salve that lessened her agony. For Caroline knew that no matter what else this would be, it would be the last time he touched her.

He tasted her bare breasts, lifting them, blazing a trail with his mouth and tongue over every ripe curve, circling each one until her nipples were so hard she thought she would scream if he didn't suckle them. His hands pressed them upward, and at last, he rewarded each pert tip with the roll of his tongue around the jutting flesh, wetting her, drawing from her as if she were all the sustenance he needed. She writhed and shuddered beneath him, burying her fingers in his hair to drive him on.

She held nothing back, more vulnerable than she had ever been. Caroline was determined to feel everything—even if it broke her. Every word he'd uttered condemning Margot could have applied to her and Caroline knew it now.

Meaningless. A passing interest. Paid to play her part. Threw herself in his path. Oh, God. All misfortunes are earned, isn't that what he said? Well then, I have earned every bittersweet kiss, and heaven help me, I will have my fill.

Even now, a fierce need for him rocked through her, and on the heels of it, a terrible shame. *I am no saint to judge him.*

She'd spent a lifetime pursuing her ideals and secretly feeling superior to her morally bankrupt family, comforting herself with dreams of philanthropic pursuits and sacrifices. But Ashe had forced her to look beyond her dreams and face her hidden desires.

I am merely human, after all. All I really wanted was to be loved, and I made a pathetic mess of it.

Her skirts and crinolines frustrated him and Caroline winced as the lovely garment was torn from her body, damaged just enough to reveal her thighs for him and give him the access he demanded.

And then it was as if his mouth were everywhere, dragging hot kisses across her collarbones and throat only to find her rib cage and lick the soft curves of her stomach and hips. She kept her eyes tightly closed, wanting to give in to every forbidden caress and embed every kiss in her memory. His mouth moved downward, worshipping the hot flesh between her legs. She boldly spread her thighs for him, giving him the access he craved, eager for the release she needed.

I want to forget that this will never happen again. That I will never win your heart.

His lips kissed the soft folds of her sex and Caroline moaned when his tongue danced lightly across her clit, each repetitive feathery touch sending arcs of sensation through her body, up into her breasts, and across her skin, until each stroke of his tongue affected her entire being. The hard little pearl became the center of her existence and he ruled her with the searing sweet flicker of his attentions.

Yours. Always.

She came in a slow explosion more like a sigh of release, shivering and shuddering against his tongue. And then everything slowed. The frantic edge of their desires melted away and his every touch seemed reverent and careful—as if he feared that she might vanish. His fingers replaced his tongue on her clit only to allow him to dip his mouth into the well of her entrance and taste her release as she spent herself against him.

And then he was above her and his rock-hard cock was inside of her, Ashe's languid, luxurious thrusts coasting along the soft echoes of her climax, stretching out her enjoyment but not overwhelming her. He stroked the silk of her hair and whispered sweet nonsense in her ears about never hurting her and never letting her go and Caroline could feel her heart begin to rend itself in two.

His climax answered her own, and she hid her face against his shoulder as her hot tears mingled with the salty-sweet smell of sweat and sex.

Their breathing slowed, and after several minutes, she knew that sleep was just beginning to claim him as she slid from the bed and began to gather her things.

"Caroline?" he asked softly, one hand outstretched to try to retrieve her and pull her back into his arms.

"Sleep, Ashe. I . . . I'm just going to retrieve a change of clothes. I don't want . . . Godwin to see me in my ball gown at the breakfast table," she whispered.

He smiled, his eyes closing. "After we're married, I'm going to make you eat breakfast in your birthday suit." His voice slowed as a contented sleep overtook him. "I'd like to . . . see his face . . . wouldn't you?"

"After we're married," he'd said. Her heart fractured at last and Caroline put a hand over her own mouth to keep from crying out. *I've held on to the tiger's tail for too long and now it will destroy me to let him go. But if I don't, I don't think I can survive it.*

Good-bye, my dear Ashe.

* * *

He awoke alone.

Panic made him grab his robe and race to her room, only to find the door still open. Ashe could hear a woman crying and his knees almost buckled in relief.

She is still here. She's upset but tears dry and I'll just apologize until she tires of hearing it or begs—

It was Daisy, sobbing as she sat at the end of a bed covered in her mistress's beautiful clothes. Again, he felt a twinge of relief.

She couldn't have gone. Her clothes are all still here . . .

But then the truth sunk in. The books were missing from her desk.

"Her trunks?"

"She took only the clothes she brought with her, sir."

"The . . . she took nothing else?" The morning light caught the gleam of blue stars and diamonds lying on top of the coverlet, and he knew defeat. "Did she say where she was going?"

"I think to Bellewood and then home, sir. But, if you . . . stopped her . . ." Daisy sniffed loudly.

Why? Who better to convey the worst of it to my grandfather than my beloved chaperone? And how could I stop her—after last night? What else could I say to hold her?

Daisy blew her noise, an indelicate attempt to compose herself. "She didn't take any of the new things because she didn't want you to think less of her. Miss Townsend was a proud thing, and I mean that in the best way! Poor as she was, she was a true lady!"

Daisy burst into tears again and for Ashe the world came to another unsettling halt. "Poor as she was? What do you mean by that?"

"I never said nothing to her—I mean, a lady is entitled to think she has her secrets, isn't she? But Mrs. Clark and I both saw! And Mrs. Clark had a letter from her aunt at Bellewood that said as much, but Miss Townsend was so sweet that none of us wanted to cause her any harm."

Daisy's speech was gaining momentum and Ashe put a hand on her shoulder to try to calm her into a more intelligible report. "Daisy, easy there. Let's have it."

"It was her clothes that set us off! Not where anyone would really see, but a maid's eyes couldn't miss the signs. Her stockings were darned more than a half dozen times over and shoes patched on the insides. The dresses she came with were new enough . . . but nothing a stitch below. And Mrs. Clark's aunt said she was skin and bones when she first came to Bellewood."

"Sh-she's an heiress."

"No, sir. Not that one. An heiress would have complained long and loud about every draft or darkened crust of bread, but she only said thank you again and again for the simplest courtesies. Didn't even yell when I sat on one of her new hatboxes!"

Ashe shook his head. "A good disposition doesn't disqualify her from wealth. Caroline is—eccentric, but her family's financial worth is at least equal to mine, Daisy."

Daisy was adamant, her cheeks reddening. "Beggin' your pardon, Mr. Blackwell, sir. A woman with a dowry wouldn't fret over missing candlesticks." She curtsied a quick bob and left the room before he could respond, a hand covering her mouth to stifle her sobs.

Missing candlesticks? Granted, Caroline dressed like a governess when I met her but . . . can I be that blind? Everything else Yardley ever said was a lie, but was he right about Caroline? Is it just rumors taking on a weight of their own and the servants mistaking an odd frugality for true poverty?

Unlikely.

And because I was so determined to win her with kisses, I neglected to ask. Hell, I didn't think it was important! But now . . . It's all a wretched tangle, isn't it? Ashe's breath came in long ragged pulls, unable to keep up with the scorching pace of his thoughts. *Caroline. Poor. Poor, not eccentric. The books. The college. Oh, God. My grandfather must have promised her that college! And I, I thought nothing of any of it. The scandal. If I'd succeeded in re-*

*forming, she'd have gotten whatever my grandfather prom-
ised her. But I failed. I failed her, in every way possible.*

The gleam of the stones caught his eye and Ashe went
over to retrieve them, hating the cool weight of the necklace in his hand. "Rich or poor," he said to an empty room,
"you leave me no choice, Miss Caroline Townsend."

Ashe knew if he didn't go, he'd always wonder if there
was one more thing he could have done. He dropped the
necklace into his coat pocket and turned on his heels without looking back.

Chapter
21

🌸

"I'm not entirely surprised to see you here, Miss Townsend. Your letters said nothing of a visit, although that last note . . . I was wondering if something drastic had occurred." Gordon Blackwell readjusted the blanket over his legs as she sat across from him on the settee.

"I thought I should explain before I returned home."

"Our agreed time isn't over, Miss Townsend."

"For me, it is finished."

"What did he do?"

Caroline took a deep breath. She'd practiced her speeches a thousand times in the carriage ride to Belle-wood, sure she was taking the only path open to her to save the last glimmer of integrity she had left. *Something good has to come from all of this.*

"He did nothing. It was me. I fell in love with him."

"And he with you?" he asked hopefully.

"His feelings for me are unchanged. Truthfully they may have worsened in light of . . . recent events." She had to swallow hard to dissolve the lump in her throat, emotion threatening to choke her.

"What recent events?"

"I presented myself to him and put him in an impossible position because of our . . . arrangement. He couldn't dismiss the chaperone you'd assigned him, not without revealing how far things had gone."

The elder Blackwell looked at her, astonished. "Did you really come to love him? My blackguard of a grandson?"

"He is not so unworthy."

"And his oath?"

She hesitated. "Ashe would rather cut off his own hand, I think, than disappoint you."

"Yet you speak of yourself and not Ashe as the source of this great disappointment."

"Ashe did everything he could to protect my reputation. But there is no going back and there is more to life than an avoidance of scandal. That's why I sent the note to you and why I'll beg you again never to tell him about your offer of the money. He would rightly think the worst after my behavior, and I don't think I could live with it."

"But the wager did involve public scandal, and you could have both kept the secret of your affections to yourselves. I'd have been none the wiser."

"You'll hear rumors soon enough. I disgraced myself at a masque, and while the details will be muddled and inaccurate when others recount it, you should know from me that I . . . acted out of jealousy when I saw him talking to an old mistress and . . . There were other guests that saw us, and while I didn't exactly tear her hair out, I wanted to, Grandfather Walker."

She thought to burst into flames at such an intimate conversation, but instead, her skin felt cold—her heartbreak too fresh to allow for shame. "I've come here to ensure that the blame lands squarely on my shoulders alone. The seduction was my doing."

"And Ashe is innocent in all of this? That is what you are saying?"

She simply held his gaze, unflinching, until he nodded in satisfaction.

"The heart is a treacherous thing, my dear."

Caroline's eyes filled with tears. "Please, Grandfather Walker. Don't punish Ashe for my weakness and stupidity. He never lied and made more of his affections than he felt. It was my longing that wished for more than he had to give."

"And will you be all right?"

She nodded her head, the tears starting to fall despite her best efforts to keep her composure. "My aunt will be missing me, I'm sure. My cousins will be eager to hear about the sights of London and regain my company." It was the second most blatant lie she'd uttered, but Caroline clasped her hands tightly in her lap to hide their trembling. *My aunt was glad to be shut of me, despite all her squawking, and I'll be lucky if they open the front door when I return. As for my cousins, they probably didn't realize I was gone.*

"Very well. You'll stay until I can arrange for your passage home, and I won't brook any arguments." He held out his handkerchief, the gruffness in his voice betraying his sympathy. "You aren't the first to fall to his charms, and I should accept my own culpability in putting you in harm's way. I was overly confident, and I'm afraid you've suffered for it."

"I'm fine, sir." Caroline did her best to regain her composure. She didn't want the dear old man to feel any guilt on her behalf. "Once I've set sail, this will all be behind me and quickly forgotten." *By Ashe, but not by me. Oh, God, I think I'll carry these scars with me for the rest of my life.*

"Well, good night then, my dear. Rest well," he said, squeezing her hand as she leaned in to kiss him on the cheek.

"Good night, Grandfather Walker."

She went upstairs, returning to the guest bedroom she'd occupied weeks before, so full of hope and confidence. Now, she threw herself across the bed, sobbing and finally giving in to the wrenching pain that had been gnawing inside of her.

It was finally over.

* * *

Ashe raced back down the stairs and out the doors to his waiting carriage, yelling for James to make haste and get them to Bellewood as if the devil himself were on their heels. He'd lost a day following her to try to tie up a few loose ends in London and lay the groundwork for the trial ahead. The delay in pursuing Caroline had been the most difficult decision of his life, but he could only hope that it would help him to earn her back.

He'd barely set back onto the cushions when the final blow struck and the last of his strength seem to give out.

For there, on the carriage window, was the perfect imprint of her small, beautiful palm and fingers—the cold glass still holding the impression amidst a halo of frost.

"There is passion." Isn't that what I said? That it didn't change anything. But that was a lie, wasn't it, Caroline? I didn't believe it would last. I didn't want to believe it. And now . . .

He'd accepted the consequences of his own vows, but he wasn't about to let Caroline suffer for it. Bellewood had been the next inevitable destination, but now, there was new urgency to his journey.

I'm completely in love with a woman I just carelessly threw away.

Chapter
22

Snow and ice on muddied roads made the journey to Bellewood more grueling and miserable than any he could remember, but Ashe hardly felt it. He'd arrived with his hat in hand to see his grandfather. Not to beg for his inheritance, since by all honorable measurements, the wager was lost.

But he was determined to see if there was anything to be done about Caroline's predicament. He was sure that if he could restore her future, she might be able to forgive him. He wanted to find out what his grandfather had intended to pay her—and then see that she received it from his own accounts.

Back in his grandfather's library, he waited. The room hadn't changed, but it felt even more oppressingly dark and gloomy to him in the early winter afternoon. But this time, his anxiety wasn't the imagined echoes of childhood. This time it was the strange knowledge that he was disowned and disconnected to the only family he'd ever known.

"I was wondering when you would arrive," his grandfather spoke from the doorway. "And in what mood."

"Is she here?"

"You waste no time!" His grandfather made his way slowly to his favorite upholstered chair near the fireplace. "Come, sit with me and let's see if we can unravel some of the mess."

"Thank you." Ashe took the chair across from him, aware as he had never been of how much this old man meant to him. In light of their agreement, this could be the last time he would be in his grandfather's presence for anything resembling a conversation. Grief at the loss threatened to swamp him for a moment, but Ashe pushed the emotion away. "Is she here?" he asked again.

"She is here, my guest yet for a while." The elder Blackwell lifted a newspaper set on the table between them. "A day after the masque and there is just a nasty sentence or two. It is a snickering, black giggle at your expense, Ashe, to gain you more sympathy than you expect. But the report is tawdry enough to ensure your circle has grown slightly smaller. Not that I believe you were enjoying Lady Fitzgerald's company."

"Grandfather, I—"

"Not that I ever did either. The old woman is an intolerable bore, and it was a rotten piece of mischief I couldn't resist to make sure you met her more than once." He set the paper back down. "Nasty business."

"I don't know the extent of your agreement with Miss Townsend, but she cannot be blamed for the inherent flaws in my character. Perhaps you could reveal the amount to my solicitor and I'll make arrangements from my own funds to—"

"I doubt the lady would be pleased to accept money from you, Ashe."

"It would be easy to make the funds appear to have come from you."

"All this fuss over money! It's not very refined, sir. Miss Townsend has a fortune of her own, for I cannot see Matthew not doting entirely on such a girl. Besides, it was Miss Townsend herself who sent word over a fortnight past requesting that no payment be made. And now, of course, I understand why."

He doesn't know. That proud and impossible woman never said a word—even to the old man! It was a revelation that hit him hard. She would walk away with nothing and Ashe felt the weight of the world land on his shoulders.

His grandfather sighed. "What a disappointment my scheme turned out to be! Well, begin your gloating and smirk away at how stupid it all seems now. The prisoner behaved better than his jailers!"

"Better? How was I any better?" Ashe scoffed.

"From Miss Townsend's admission, you were a man of your word in the worst of situations, Ashe. Poor girl! I was ready to blame you, quite naturally, but she made an honest confession and I don't harbor ill will toward her as a result. Nor should you! If you've come to berate her, I won't allow it, Ashe."

Berate her? What the hell has happened that the world has left its axis?

Ashe took a deep breath, forcing himself to stay still and calm. "I have no intention of berating her. But I must know exactly what she told you in her 'honest confession.' "

"As you wish." Gordon reached a gnarled hand inside his waistcoat pocket and retrieved a folded letter. "Winston rattled her, and for that I have already apologized. I thought a bit of competition would keep you focused, but I'd forgotten what a clumsy buffoon Yardley can be. Just like his father, really."

"We are speaking of Miss Townsend, sir." Ashe's patience was too thin to allow his grandfather to ramble.

"I do like the tone of her missives. So direct and somehow still a soft feminine voice. This letter exonerating your character and warning me of Yardley's threats was endearing. She was sure we were both in danger and I was touched at how seriously she urged me to protect myself from Winston's greed." He smiled fondly. "She was very convincing."

He held it out to Ashe. "I had my suspicions that you'd turned her head from her previous letter suddenly changing the terms of our arrangement and refusing payment. And of course, her clear admiration for you in this note only clarified my fears. And then Crawley's!"

"The nail in my coffin," Ashe said, taking the letter but not bothering to glance at it.

"If she hadn't presented her case in person, I'd say you'd be on the wrong side of my will at this moment, my boy."

"But the wager—"

"Appearances are always deceiving and Miss Townsend explained the worst of her actions. My only surprise was that you didn't trust me to write of things yourself! I may be old, Ashe, but I'm not so infirm that I can't comprehend that a man caught between two women like that"—he shook his head, his expression almost nostalgic—"can do nothing."

"For the last time"—Ashe gripped the arms of the chair to keep from leaping up like a madman—"what did she tell you?"

"That she lost her head over you and caused an unspeakable ruckus at Crawley's in an attempt to ensnare you." He shrugged. "I never would have suspected her of such immodest actions, but women are unpredictable! Still, to try such an awkward seduction in such a public place! Perhaps I'll credit it to her youth. And knowing how much you dislike the girl, I can see how miserable this is to have the person in place as a safeguard turn into your downfall."

"My God!" *Why would she lie? Caroline, who never lies—but that isn't entirely true, is it? She'd kept her secrets. But hell, I've certainly kept mine!*

"Don't look so shocked! You were there, Ashe! There's no need to go over every tawdry detail, is there?"

"Yes, I think there is." Ashe released his hold on the chair and looked the older man directly in the eye. "I'm going to tell you what happened, wager be damned."

Chapter
23

❦

"Why, Caroline? Why would you impugn yourself like that?" Ashe finally found her in the upstairs reading room, tucked away on a window seat in a bay of windows overlooking the sweeping lawns of Bellewood.

She closed her book slowly, refusing to look at him and instead gazing out into the garden. "It was easy enough."

"It was unnecessary. Since Yardley paid Margot to . . . make an appearance at the masque, my grandfather would never have accepted the situation. It was too heavy-handed and you were too quick for those fools. I was the one who made a scene after you left and guaranteed myself an uphill battle. But when I came home—we never did talk about the truth of the matter."

"No one cares about the truth." She looked at him, her large brown eyes clear and beautiful. "All London simply wants to relish the story of the rogue and the whore and his stupid ward, and who am I to stand in their way? But when all the storms pass, I just couldn't see you paying for my mistakes, not with your inheritance."

"What mistakes can you possibly be referring to?"

"I mistook a passing interest for more than it was. I forgot my place and I forgot that I was meaningless to you."

"You are not meaningless! You've come to mean more to me than I ever thought possible." The painful truth of it knifed through him. *I'm in love with you, Caroline, and I tried to convince myself that it wasn't possible and that you were just another diversion. And I said as much to you in a dozen ways.* Ashe wasn't sure it was the time for declarations. It was as if everything he'd ever done or said now haunted him.

"It seems I am not cut out to live a life full of passion for passion's sake, Mr. Blackwell. I saw no point in lingering for your eventual dismissal."

"Dismissal? Damn it, Caroline! I never once thought of you that way!"

"Why not? Because I didn't ask for a carriage before I begged you to touch me?" She crossed her arms, holding the book against her chest like a shield. "There would have been a public scandal, thanks to me. I did what I could to undo the damage with your grandfather. Now you can go back to your life, your honor restored and your fortunes intact."

"Damn it! I don't care about any of that!"

"Of course you do! You'd never have bothered with any of it if you didn't, Ashe—you'd never have accepted any of it; not the wager, not the worry, and certainly not a chaperone."

"Caroline—"

"Stop saying my name!" She suddenly threw the book at him, and Ashe instinctively ducked to avoid the blow. "You know nothing of me, Ashe! Nothing! I would give anything to have my parents or my own grandfather back! To feel a part of a loving family again, even if it lies in one man's eyes. And I know you feel the same way about Grandfather Walker. I couldn't bear the idea—that you would be alone in the world."

"I'm not alone. My grandfather admitted that he'd quietly settled everything irrevocably on me months ago! This entire thing was some kind of game for him, Caroline. You didn't need to sacrifice your dreams."

"I'm not a martyr and I didn't sacrifice my dreams!" She bristled and gave him a quelling look and Ashe felt a hint of relief to see it. "I have my own honor to think about! Not everything is about you, Mr. Blackwell."

Ah, a debate! There's the spirit I've come to love!

"So my life is restored as if nothing has happened and you're going to just walk away with your pride?" He retrieved the book she'd thrown and held it out to her. "What kind of man do you think I am?"

"I don't know. I know what I wanted to believe, but honestly, I don't know what kind of man you are."

He dropped the book on the floor and captured her fingers in the warm cage of his. "Then I'll tell you. I'll tell you what kind of man I was, before you forced your way inside my doors."

She nodded solemnly, attentive and quiet.

"Before India, I lived for myself and my own pleasure and I didn't think about anything else really. India was a punishment to send me away to what my grandfather was sure would be a sobering environment. I was to gain perspective." Ashe sighed. "Perspective."

"And have you?"

"Not until recently. I thought I had after I spent over a year in a dungeon in the jungles of Bengal. That's where the Jaded met and that is where our brotherhood came into being. For the others, it was an unwarranted punishment, but a part of me always felt as if I'd earned my place in the dark. It was penance for all the pleasure I'd stolen. For Anjali and that blind, stupid, blissful love that demonstrated once and for all what a selfish bastard I really was. Because I never thought of anything but my own delightful discovery of happiness and true love."

"How can love be selfish and—"

"I never thought of the consequences to her or her family. I was her doom. Oblivious to a climate of growing hatred against all things British, I'd put her in danger. They murdered her when the unrest broke out, and I . . . didn't even know enough to think to protect her. When I found out she was dead, I was sure that I'd died with her. Not out of a romantic notion of attachment, but out of the realization that whatever potential I'd held—I wasn't man enough to deserve it."

"Oh, God, Ashe!"

"I was sure they'd just kill me, too, but it never happened. And for a while, I was fairly angry about that."

"Angry that you hadn't died?"

"It was the Jaded that saved my life."

"I can't believe that this is the truth behind all those rumors about that club," she whispered, pain echoing in her voice.

He nodded. "A very elite club, Miss Townsend, that notoriously isn't looking for new members."

Her expression betrayed her horror, but she said nothing, allowing him time to compose his thoughts and finish the sordid tale.

"When we escaped and made it home, I deliberately decided that there would be no reformation or salvation for me. Let other men who deserved it remake their lives or recover their souls. I simply went back to the emptiest pleasures I could find and waited for the rot to set in."

"I'm so sorry, Ashe. It explains a great deal, but it doesn't change anything. You must have learned by now that your sins aren't weightier than another's and you don't get to decide your fate." She took a deep breath, the caramel brown of her eyes growing even sadder. "But you should tell your grandfather about Anjali and give him the chance to know you better."

"The past is the past. I'm not going to try to excuse the mistakes I've made to him. The old monster and I have a special truce of our own, Caroline. But it's you . . . It's you I've come to win, Caroline."

She freed her hands from his. "You cannot."

"I haven't told you these sad tales to bid for your sympathy, Caroline."

"But you have it all the same." She stood, the drab brown cotton of her gown failing to mute her beauty and grace in his eyes. "I wish you every happiness, Ashe."

He caught her wrist and prevented her escape. "I want to marry you, Caroline."

"No."

Her answer hit him like a rock against his chest, but he refused to flinch. "Tell me why not, Miss Townsend."

"First of all, I have no illusions of being some miraculous salve for your wounds. I was simply one more woman you used to forget your past and to pretend that you don't have a heart. And now you've made peace with your grandfather, and perhaps it seems a good time to appease him with a marriage."

"I hadn't discussed it with him, but once you've agreed—"

"This is no jest. I won't marry you, Ashe Blackwell. You've made it clear that you will marry where you do not love. It's a likely and safe choice for you. You would deliberately choose to keep your heart out of the equation, and for many women, they would accept you at any price. But I can't. As much as I—love you, I cannot compromise and live a half-life at your side."

"I think too highly of you, Caroline, to ask you to compromise."

"How is that possible, Ashe? How can you think more highly of me than any other woman in your acquaintance? I'm not your equal in manners or . . . fortune, despite what you think. And as you've pointed out repeatedly, I have the fashion sense of a mule."

"Everything changed when you turned my life inside out, Caroline, and I'm sure I never compared you to a mule. A hairless cat, once, but even I've forgotten why." He recaptured her hands with his, unable to stop himself from smiling at how beautiful she was even in the midst of stubborn misery. "Give me another reason, Caroline."

"Don't—" Her eyes filled with unshed tears. "Ashe, be careful."

"Marry me." He dropped to one knee, shameless in his petition.

"No! I am always serious, I adore conversation above all other entertainments, and I don't believe we've spent a single day together without some argument. By your own criteria, I am a wretched choice for a wife, Ashe. You don't mean it."

"I do, even as I'm secretly cursing that clever little mind of yours that never forgets a single word I utter in haste."

"Clever or not, you don't know me, Ashe. You couldn't—"

"If I don't know you, Caroline, it's because you've been just as cautious to share yourself with me as I have been guarded with you. We are each of us so careful to disguise and hide our weaknesses . . . But you know mine, and it is my turn to petition you to stop this nonsensical charade because you believe that I will think less of you for it. Why? Because your family has cut you out of a fortune out of sheer greed or stupidity? Because you teach?" He shook his head. "You'll have to dredge up a worse sin, Miss Townsend, to deter me."

"Besides coming to England only because your grandfather promised to pay me for my services? I was no better than a servant and I lied and let you believe that we were equals, Ashe. I never intended to . . ." She took a slow steadying breath before continuing. "I never knew what it was to be wanted. I was seduced by the very idea of somehow standing at the center of your attentions. It was intoxicating."

"Marry me, Caroline, and I'll make you drunk with desire for the rest of your days."

"Passion doesn't hold. You said it over and over, Ashe, and I cannot be the wife who politely shrugs when you tire of me and return to your private pursuits outside of our marriage bed." She straightened her spine and squared her shoulders. "I love you too much to allow it."

He stood slowly, drawing her closer. "You cannot love me too much, Caroline." His fingers reached out to gently trace the wet trails of her tears across her cheek. "Just as I have discovered that I cannot love you too much."

"Do you?"

He smiled, the taste of victory so sweet it took his breath away. "You are an impossible creature, an infuriating and contrary thing that is sure to debate me over every breakfast and never allow me to forget what a distinct mess I've made of your orderly life. And I love you, Miss Caroline Townsend."

He risked another small step in her direction. "Marry me, Caroline."

"No." Her voice was quieter, her demeanor calm again, and Ashe felt the first hint that he might actually fail—that she might actually refuse him. And he knew there was no going back or everything he'd vowed and all his claims to have changed and given up the coward's path would be for nothing.

"Is it the college?" he ventured. "Because I'll fund a dozen of them and live in the wilds of America if that is what you require, Caroline."

"You would say anything. . . . But I can't ask you to fund something you don't believe in." Her eyes filled with tears. "It's the difference between us. You see people in terms of their status, be it their wealth or their family—and women, even more so by those terms, I think."

"Not all women!" he protested. "Not you!"

"Why not me? I am poor, Ashe. Truly poor, and my family has as much to do with me as the man in the moon." She crossed her arms defensively. "I know how vulnerable a woman is in this world and I stole every minute of privilege that I've had in my life by carefully following the rules and making sure that no one noticed me. But I could just as easily be in Margot's shoes, and when I looked at her at Crawley's that night—I knew I couldn't turn my back on her or Daisy or any of them."

"I don't want you to." He put his hands on her upper arms, gently holding her in place as he tried one last time to convince her he'd changed. "And you're right about Margot. I was selfish and cruel to her, and it's why I was a day behind in reaching Bellewood. I didn't want to make the same mistake I'd made in India. I didn't want to be so focused on my own desires and forget about another person's well-being. And most of all, I wanted to be able to prove to you that I'd changed."

"What are you saying?"

"I would have just come after you, and I almost did, but then I remembered the look in Winston's eyes when all his plans came to naught. He wanted to kill me. And I struck him and humiliated him, but it wouldn't end there. I couldn't leave Margot to face him alone."

"You . . . saved her?"

"A simple relocation to keep her out of Yardley's hands. I sent her to Bath for a change in society." He shrugged. "I didn't want another woman's blood on my hands, and I knew that if anything happened to her, I would truly lose you forever."

"You saved her." Caroline was suddenly looking at him as if he'd lit the sky and set the stars in place, just for her— and Ashe reveled in it.

"I'm starting to look forward to paying for this college of yours."

"Not so quickly, Mr. Blackwell. Lady Fitzgerald has already pledged to support my efforts, and in an attempt to torture her departed husband, may insist that we name the school after him." She laughed as he drew her into his arms.

"Say you'll marry me, Caroline, or I'll be forced to use drastic measures."

"Drastic measures?"

"I'll tell my grandfather that I'm madly in love with an impossible American girl who refuses to make an honest man of me."

She put her hands on either side of his face and looked up into his eyes. "Yes, Ashe, I will marry you. Though all your friends will think you were forced into it."

"Then I will make a point of open and inappropriate demonstrations of affection for my beautiful bride whenever and wherever I can, and soon everyone will instead be commenting on how dear you are to put up with your overly attentive and clearly lascivious husband."

"You wouldn't!" she exclaimed, her cheeks flooding with color at the thought.

"I will." He began to kiss the fluttering pulse behind one ear and whispered, "So you see, Miss Townsend, you must marry me, for I clearly require a strong hand and a good deal of supervision at all times.

"Ashe!" She sighed, leaning into his touch and clinging to his shoulders as the heat between them grew. "I think I've lost the lines between dreams and the real world. You make me feel as if I've been sleepwalking all along, and only now am I awake."

"Caroline, my dearest chaperone," he said as he lifted her into his arms. "I intend to misbehave for the rest of my life."

She laughed, transforming into the temptress of his dreams as he spun her around in joyous celebration. "I certainly hope so, Mr. Blackwell!"

Keep reading for an excerpt from
the first Jaded Gentleman novel
by Renee Bernard

Revenge Wears Rubies

Now available from Berkley Sensation!

Chapter
1

London, 1859

Galen Hawke's head pounded in a miserably slow fashion that foreshadowed a long afternoon. He eased out of the large bed, stretching his tall, lean frame with caution to allow his muscles to ignore twinges and small aches after a night of little rest. His arrival in London hadn't helped him outrun the restless dreams that still plagued him, and Galen yielded up a long, ragged sigh at the very thought of a lifetime meted out by haunting images of dark holes and suffocating tropical heat.

"You had a nightmare, sir."

Galen winced at the woman's unsympathetic tone and his own lapse in forgetting that he hadn't retired alone. The courtesan stood by the window in a transparent shift, positioned to no doubt let the morning rays highlight the ample curves of her figure and inspire him to lust. Instead, the bright light was making his eyes water, and Galen was in no mood to indulge her. "I never dream. Perhaps it was your snoring that kept me up."

She sniffed in protest, her brass-tinted curls bouncing as she turned mercifully away from the window to sit down in a graceless move at a side table already laden with a morning repast and the day's paper. One glance at the tray told him that his faithful manservant had come and gone while he'd slept. *Damn. I'll be getting that look from Bradley again. And I'll deserve it since I swear to God, I've forgotten this chit's name . . .*

His guest picked up the paper and fanned herself. "Suit yourself, then. Mind you, from any other man you'd hear otherwise, but since you acquitted yourself so wonderfully last night, I'll let it go."

She'd seemed prettier to him the night before, but Galen wasn't fool enough to express his disappointment openly. "How generous of you." He ran his fingers back through his rebellious black curls before reaching for his robe. "Why don't you have something to eat before you go?"

Galen regretted the words the instant he uttered them. It was a clumsy dismissal, but the need for solitude had temporarily overridden the required pleasantries when trying to get rid of an unwanted breakfast guest. He tried to soften the impact by taking the chair across from her. "Shall I ring for tea?"

She snapped the newspaper open in front of her face, effectively ignoring him. Galen waited for a few moments, oddly grateful for the reprieve from conversation. His headache had just started to ease, so he poured himself a glass of barley water.

It wasn't that he'd had too much to drink the night before. Truthfully, he'd always envied men who could merrily throw caution to the winds when it came to distilled spirits, but his own body had never tolerated more than a sip. Ever since his first taste of liquor at sixteen and the disastrous and nearly fatal illness that had followed, Galen had been forced to accept that drinking was one masculine pursuit he would have to abandon. No, this headache was from hours spent in smoke-filled rooms playing cards and a lack of sleep. Last night, he'd hoped a bit of bed-play would drain him physically enough to allow for the dreamless sleep he craved, but once again, he'd met with failure.

"Aren't you friends with Hastings?" she asked, interrupting his peaceful recovery.

"Why?" Galen set his glass down, instantly wary. *What the hell has Josiah done now?*

"Some little odd reference of him here. See?" She waved the paper toward him. "What's this about a secret club?"

He made no move to take the pages from her. "I'm sure it's nothing."

"Truly?" Her smile took on a mischievous flavor. "Talk and rumor of a clandestine gentlemen's club, and it's nothing? Lady Barrow is said to defend 'the Jaded' here, and she is not a woman to be amused by phantoms."

"I do not know the lady well enough to contradict you, but I pay no attention to rumor. And if there is talk, then it's hardly clandestine." Galen shifted back in his seat, confident that the matter was closed.

Her pout was practiced, but not without appeal. "Come, Mr. Hawke. Why not give me a tip? It sounds wicked, this club. Do they exist or is it something your friend made up to keep some blue-nosed beak out of his social calendar?"

I'm going to wring Josiah's neck the next time I see him.

"What makes you think I could answer that question?" he asked, looking across the table with icy regard.

"Because," she answered, squaring her shoulders, "I've heard the Jaded described as a sullen group of impossible men too handsome for their own good, and you—while you are a delectable specimen, you are the dreariest man I've ever met." With another shake of her head, she stood, tossing the paper on top of the tray. "If you aren't one of them, Mr. Hawke, you should be!"

He watched her hastily gather up her clothes and pull

them on with unladylike grunts and snarls, amazed at the speed with which she managed the feat on her own. It occurred to him that he might have offered to help or rung for a maid, but Galen was sure that this time a safe distance was the better part of valor.

She snatched up her shoes with one last angry sniff, and carrying them in her hand, she sailed toward the door. Galen kept a subtle eye on her as she did, just in case her temper got the better of her and she realized what lovely weapons those heels could be and decided to launch one at his head.

She threw the door open and disappeared from view, and he closed his eyes in relief. *Well, there's my day off to a lovely start . . .*

He idly picked up the paper, scanning for the article she'd mentioned. "I'm not that damn dreary."

"Of course you are!" Josiah Hastings replied from the still open doorway, leaning against the ornate wood with his arms crossed. "Bradley let me in and said you wouldn't mind the company." He glanced over his shoulder as if to appreciate the retreating figure of Galen's guest, and then looked back at his friend. "Ever since we made it back to England, you've spent months hiding in that dreary country retreat of yours."

"I was ill." A partial truth, though he couldn't really describe the dark depression that had seized him after their return. Instead of the euphoric homecoming he'd anticipated, nothing had felt substantial to him. The memories were like demons holding him captive, and Galen had lost himself for a while.

"Now, I talk you back into Town, thinking it will cheer you, and yet here you are . . . driving away a perfectly luscious guest!"

"I wasn't going to invite her to take up residence," Galen said dryly. "But I'm sure you can still catch the dove if you think she's to your taste."

Josiah straightened from the doorframe and came into the room. "Another time," he said without enthusiasm.

Galen held up the paper. "The Jaded?"

His friend shrugged and moved to occupy the newly vacated seat across from Galen with an eye on the breakfast tray. "I like the name. It suits us. Not that I'm going to emboss it on my calling cards, mind."

"Talking to the press are we?" Galen wasn't willing to drop the subject too lightly.

"No, we are not," Josiah answered firmly, beginning to set into the plate of pastries and eggs. "And don't start squealing and moaning to me about the impropriety of rumors, Galen. I've had enough lectures from Michael to satisfy a lifetime."

"How did it happen?" Galen asked, his tone more level, as a natural sympathy arose for any man who had survived one of Michael Rutherford's well-aimed speeches. Rutherford was another of the newly dubbed "Jaded" and largely responsible for their survival and escape from India. A fierce friend, Michael hadn't yet entirely relinquished his role of protector of the remaining five men who had shared imprisonment with him.

"Hell, I think I was ambushed! Some informant must have overheard the conversation at Clives, and I can assure you, I said nothing of note. But"—he sighed—"perhaps it was a sin of omission. He who is silent is said to consent, Galen."

Galen smiled. "You are a wiser man, today."

Josiah shrugged. "It may not be such a terrible thing. One small mention, sixteen words, and I'll bet ten sterling we'll have young bucks applying for membership before the week is out."

Galen's smile drained away. "Not if they knew what the entry fee had been for its founders."

"You underestimate the appeal of a good mystery, my friend."

"Are we seeking to appeal?"

Josiah's expression sobered, a dark storm in his eyes mirroring Galen's. "We are seeking to get on with our lives—whatever it takes." He made a dramatic cut of one of the pastries and took a hearty bite. "I don't give a fig what anyone calls us. A rose by any other name smells as sweet, wasn't that what dear William had to say?"

"I don't think Shakespeare had us in mind, but perhaps you're right. Still, we have good reason to keep as far downwind of attention as we can manage." Galen's gaze shifted down to the paper, wondering at the subtle turn of a dinner conversation and its power to nudge at the illusion that they were somehow separate from the world around them. But it underlined the unique position they were all in—souls marked and scarred from their hellish experiences in India, each man fragile in his own way but also inexplicably stronger. And none of them had returned to the society that they had remembered and longed for. It seemed that no matter how much the Jaded had changed, the world had temporarily outpaced them.

Or we've outgrown tea parties and insipid exchanges over cocktails about foreign policies and the price of cotton for— Galen's breath caught in his throat and all thought halted as if he'd been struck by lightning.

A name leapt off the page in his hands, innocuous text suddenly yielding a pattern that made his surroundings shrink and then fall away from notice.

Miss Haley Moreland.

A hundred memories, none of them welcome, flooded through him, and it was as if he could hear John Everly at his elbow—his voice low so the guards wouldn't hear, his stories of home hypnotic for all of them, but for Galen, he had always saved the sweetest bits, about the woman John had loved all his life, about the woman who was a shy angel, about the woman John was going to marry as soon as they escaped . . . about Miss Haley Moreland.

Miss Haley Moreland, newly engaged to . . .

Galen struggled to focus, disbelief and fury warring behind his eyes. It couldn't be the same woman that John had spoken of! She would be in mourning! She would be some distraught, pale version of a girl bemoaning a life without her one true love, not—

Miss Haley Moreland, newly engaged to the Honorable Mr. Herbert Trumble, is enjoying her first Season and has already caught the eye of many notables for her surprising promise and potential as a leading beauty amidst London's social circles. Mrs. Trumble-to-be is destined to make a respectable mark despite . . .

"—right, Hawke? Are you unwell?" Josiah's firm hand on his shoulder finally registered.

"Forgive me." Galen stood abruptly, stepping away from his friend's reach. "I am . . ." He gripped the paper, as if he could squeeze away the revelations that hammered inside his chest.

"Galen?" Josiah's voice was tight with concern.

"I'm fine." He tightened the sash at his waist and turned back to face Hastings. "I recalled an appointment. I'm loath to be rude, but I need to dress and tend to some business. If you can show yourself back out, I would be grateful."

The words sounded stilted and false in his ears, but he knew that Josiah, of all people, would respond to the urgency and not to the obviously fabricated details. They'd been through too much together to nitpick at the little lies a man needed to tell sometimes—and above all, he knew that they'd long ago sworn to support each other without question, no matter what the future might bring.

Josiah bowed in a gallant theatrical gesture, bending his tall frame but keeping his eyes on Galen. "I shouldn't have interrupted your morning without notice, friend. I'll take my leave and await word if you . . . need anything."

The unspoken understanding held, and Galen nodded his head, dismissing his friend. At last, he was alone.

Miss Haley Moreland.

John's angel had apparently fallen. They'd been back with the news of John's fate for less than eight months. He'd made inquiries and located her family to send word of John's loss, but hadn't worked up the courage to face her in person—his own grief too raw. The agent he'd sent had confirmed from some of the locals that John and Haley had been sweethearts since childhood, but now it appeared that Miss Moreland was already reengaged and merrily celebrating her upcoming nuptials with a glorious social Season in Town. Galen grimaced as he imagined this heartless creature laughing, carefree at parties, balls, and soirees.

Faithless witch! Galen began to dress himself, his hands shaking with quiet fury. He couldn't recall ever experiencing a rage so white-hot and blinding. John Everly had been a friend unlike any other. He'd been the wit that had made them smile in the worst hours during their imprisonment. John's stories had kept them all going, and the loss of his blithe humor had almost undone them.

Because they'd been so close to freedom when he'd died. Three more days of running, and they'd reached an outpost. *Damn it, I'd have carried him all the way to Bombay if I could. . . .*

And the memory overtook him again, like a fitful dream he couldn't elude.

It was raining, so hard and cold that it was like nettles against his skin. They'd been trying to keep moving, but John couldn't keep up. Carrying him was difficult, they were each so weak—but Galen had refused to give up.

Finally they'd stopped to catch their breath, hiding in the reeds along some filthy ditch. And when he'd looked into John's eyes, he'd known John was dying. Dying, right there, in muck and mud and icy rain, and there was nothing to be done, except crouch over him to try to keep the rain out of his face—and pretend it wasn't happening.

And John smiled up at him. That wry, devil-may-care grin that defied even a monsoon. "Promise me, Galen."

"We're not doing this, John. You're going to outrun all of us when you get a whiff of some mutton pasties and catch a glimpse of the Union Jack."

But the heat in John's eyes began to retreat, and he'd reached up to grip the rags at Galen's throat to pull him closer. "Swear to me, you'll see to her. You'll tell Haley . . . how much I . . . wished for her happiness. That I love her. Swear it, Hawke."

None of the others could hear the exchange. And Galen didn't want them to. It was too intimate and heartbreaking. And the vow, so easy to make. "I'll see to her, John. I swear it to my last . . ."

He was going to say "breath." But John's ragged exhale had silenced Galen, as he'd demonstrated just what a last breath meant and Galen was left staring down into an empty shell. And he'd stood up, numb and clumsy in the mud, and Rowan had steadied him as he was forced to step over the body. Not one of the six of them had dared a word of memorial or farewell.

Galen pulled on his morning jacket, marveling that he recognized his own reflection in the gilt mirror in the corner of the bedroom. Three years in India had altered his appearance, but not enough, he thought. A man should be more changed after . . . everything that had happened.

Miss Haley Moreland.

He hadn't forgotten the promise. He'd meant to seek her out personally and ensure that she knew of John's last words, knew that his last thoughts had been of her. But he'd put it off for too long, guilt and shame holding him prisoner.

I'll see to her, John.

Oh, he would "see to her." The words took on an ominous note that foretold of a world of pain for a certain English miss. Months of lethargy vanished, and Galen felt a new power and force of will take shape inside of him. All his instincts to be cautious vanished in the space of a single breath.

Oh, Miss Moreland. I believe you are going to get exactly the Season you deserve. I'll see to you. I'll see that you learn the cost of cruelty, firsthand. You think to trade one fiancé for another without regard? I'll see that you end up without one. You think to play with a man's affections and cast him off without a care? I'll have your heart and return it to you in a thousand pieces. I'm going to laugh, Miss Haley Moreland, when you cry at my feet, for you owe John Everly a river of tears, and this is a debt I'm going to collect for him.

I'll have you and then I'll have you.

* * *

"You can at least let the man buy you a hat!" Aunt Alice protested, holding up the lovely bonnet again as if to show off its ribbons and win her arguments.

"I cannot!" Haley's frustration gave way to her lively humor as she stepped forward to pat her aunt's arm consolingly. "It's not as if I need a new bonnet, and even if I did, it's hardly proper to ask Mr. Trumble to pay for such a trifle. But if you'd like, I can ask him to buy *you* one."

"Pish!" Aunt Alice pouted and set the beribboned creation back on the counter, before her own good nature asserted itself again. "I'd look like a gray carriage horse in that thing! And it's my job to fuss about what propriety dictates, Haley. See that you leave your elderly relatives a few things to do, won't you?"

Haley nodded obediently, making no effort to hide her smile. "I will endeavor to be as much trouble as I can."

"Ah! Just what a chaperone longs to hear!" She took Haley's arm as they left the milliner's and made their way down the busy and fashionable shopping street back toward their hired carriage. "Truly, dearest, it's nothing to see a man provide for his future wife's trousseau—not that you aren't lovely in the gowns you already have, mind! But if you play the frugal woman now, he may think to keep his wife with very little expenditure, and when you want to indulge yourself later, he'll remind himself how well you did with nothing."

"It's not . . ." Haley let the argument fall away, unwilling to reveal just how unhappy she felt at the moment. "I'm sure you're right."

Aunt Alice had used the excuse of needing a new set of buttons for her favorite coat to lure Haley into something resembling a shopping trip. But her aunt knew far too well that Haley had spent too many years economizing and stretching any farthing she could harbor to open up her purse strings without good cause.

And Aunt Alice was right in that Mr. Trumble had continuously urged her to use his good credit to buy her heart's desires.

But her heart desired nothing in London's best stores and, secretly, nothing that Herbert possessed. And while she was in no position to ultimately refuse him, it gave her a small amount of comfort to retain the last illusions of independence she could. In a few months, she would be his to dress and dictate to, in all things. As Mrs. Herbert Trumble, the wife of a successful industrialist, she would be his property to manage and care for. And while the thought chilled her to the bone, her aunt had repeatedly assured her that true affection would follow as a natural result of this masculine care.

"You should enjoy this more, Haley. You're young, and a London Season . . . it's what I always wanted for you. And if only my brother, Alfred, had—"

Haley looked away, gently but effectively cutting off her aunt's speech. Haley didn't want to hear another round of wishful thinking or a hurtful and useless condemnation of her beloved father's character flaws.

We are just as we are, and wishing for the moon doesn't bring it any closer.

Her father, Lord Moreland, would have disagreed and then given her a dozen examples of how often he'd once had the world in his pockets (ignoring their current state of emptiness). She'd abandoned the painful pretense of daydreams, and where her father seemed to do little else, Haley had deliberately grounded herself in the practicalities of life.

Nothing about Lord Moreland spoke of restraint. He'd loved Haley's mother beyond measure and wasted his fortune on frippery and foolishness to please her. From all accounts, her mother hadn't had the heart to refuse any gift or extravagance since it gave her husband so much joy to buy her things—and they'd neither one of them seen beyond the moment to the possibility of a grim future when the money ran out.

So when Lady Moreland had died of a sudden illness, her father had plunged into mourning with a tenacity that made most of their country friends shake their heads in wonder. He didn't wish to see a world without her, and so he'd drowned his sorrows with distilled spirits and escaped drab reality whenever possible.

As a child, she'd always known her father had been generous with her mother, but it was only after the funeral on Haley's fifteenth birthday that the full impact of it had struck home. She'd sorted through a mountain of trunks full of dresses she'd never seen her mother wear, laces and notions, ribbons and buttons, bolts of sumptuous fabric all reverently set aside. There'd been countless boxes of stockings and gloves in every hue, enough to outfit an army of ladies. She'd found duplicate gowns in four different shades of red, as if her father had been unable to decide which one best suited his beloved Margaret and so he'd ordered them all.

The sheer audacious waste of it! She'd adored her mother,

but once she was gone, Haley had discovered how precarious their existence had become, and the blind, selfish indulgences of her parents had staggered her. Where Lady Moreland had been unwilling or unable to take charge, it was Haley who was ultimately forced behind the scenes to maintain some semblance of sanity. Responsibilities beyond her years had crushed any remnants of her childhood, but Haley had squared her shoulders and taken charge.

She'd sold the carriages and cleared the stables first, learning quickly when her father was deep enough into his cups to cooperate but not so far gone that he couldn't provide a signature on a bill of sale to keep them fed. With the housekeeper, Mrs. Copley, as her ally, she'd cut back on the household staff and released anyone not critical to their upkeep. She'd even gained their land manager's blessings and ridden out to the tenants and the village regularly enough that their people had begun to call her the "Little Mistress" out of affection and loyalty.

But affection and loyalty weren't currency to keep the larders full and the servants paid.

There'd been no money for a debut and little hope for a rescue—at least until Mr. Trumble had rented nearby Frostbrook Manor for the hunting season. Haley hadn't needed anyone to remind her of the practical miracle of a wealthy man in need of a wife who didn't seem to mind a lack of dowry. When he'd asked her to marry him, it had felt like the worst kind of dream because of the suffocating weight of the inevitability of it all. She remembered trying to smile and then crying, and Mr. Trumble had assumed she'd been overcome with joy and he'd run to tell her father the happy news.

What other answer could she have given him? Was it conceivable to refuse him and see her father ousted from his ancestral home and end up begging for shelter and support from her mother's indifferent and disapproving relatives? No daughter who cared a fraction less for her father would have done differently than accept the man even if he'd had three heads. Not that Mr. Trumble had more than the requisite number of limbs and appendages! He was ultimately the most ordinary of men, regular in all his habits and very courteous.

All she could do was pray that her Aunt Alice was right to believe that her heart would inevitably come around to agree with her desperate decision to marry a man prone to drifting off the instant the conversation abandoned breeding dogs and gun collections.

"There are worse fates than a courteous husband," she intoned softly.

"What was that, dearest?"

"Nothing. A stray thought about how fortunate I am, indeed. And Mr. Trumble has been very generous. Surely you can understand my desire to respect that generosity and not overtax him? He has paid for our accommodations and provided carriages and servants for our stay. It seems petty to bother him for trifles when he's already done so much for us."

They'd reached the carriage and the footman moved forward quickly to assist them inside its interior. Aunt Alice sighed as she settled onto the cushioned seat. "I understand more than you think, my dearest."

Haley took the seat across from her, pushing the window open wider to lessen the sense of being confined. She hated small spaces and avoided them whenever she could. It was an irrational fear she'd never overcome, and one she'd never told another soul about, since it was hard for her to admit that her imagination could overpower her intellect so easily. If a lady's character was measured by her amount of self-control and discipline, it was a crippling flaw to lose both in any circumstance—especially in public.

Aunt Alice went on with another theatrical sigh. "Still, fortunate or not, I'd say a bonnet or two wouldn't tip the scales, Haley! You must learn to spoil yourself."

"Are you sure this is what chaperones often dictate? Cause more trouble and spoil yourself?" she teased gently.

"Absolutely! Chaperones with *you* for a charge, undoubtedly!" Aunt Alice laughed. "I can consult a few reference books, but I don't think there's a wise grand dame within thirty miles that would disagree with me."

"Ah! There's a conference I'd love to see!"

"Pish! We'd put ourselves to sleep now that I think on it, and what a mess of tea trolleys and cucumber sandwiches!" Aunt Alice made a playful gesture of dismissal. "You'll just have to rely on my judgment and there's an end to it."

The lively exchange continued and made the ride seem to go very quickly despite the afternoon traffic. Arriving at the brownstone, Aunt Alice excused herself to rest before their evening outing, and Haley took a few moments to enjoy the quiet. She headed up to the first-floor sitting room, eager to get back to the novel she'd left on the window cushions that morning.

Her steps slowed at the doorway when she realized her father was already occupying the window seat in question.

"Your mother used to read a great deal." He held up the leather-bound novel she'd been seeking, his eyes watery despite his smile. "I was so jealous of those hours with her pretty nose pressed against those pages."

Haley shook her head and walked forward to gently retrieve her book. "She pressed her pretty nose against your cheek often enough, if I remember rightly, Father."

"She did, didn't she?" He leaned back and Haley noted that his waistcoat buttons were mismatched, a clear sign that he had already had a bit too much to drink before lunch.

"Papa, let's see to this." Haley sat next to him and began to refasten the ivory buttons, patiently setting him to rights. "Martin would be horrified to think you'd left your rooms with your clothes askew."

"Best valet in the known world, my dear."

"Yes, and you should tell Martin so more often. Poor man!" She smiled, too charmed by her father to really fuss at him. "We'll have you looking the dandy in no time."

"Where are all your boxes, Haley? Didn't you go out shopping this morning?" His focus on the present suddenly fell back into place, and Haley was grateful for the distraction of the buttons. She missed these fleeting moments when he truly looked at her and was once again the father she'd long adored.

"I did. And nothing suited." She finished her task and shifted back onto the cushions, doing her best to look him directly in the eye. "Aunt Alice was more disappointed than I was, I think."

"Alice wouldn't hide it, if that is true. Which makes the lack of boxes even more remarkable, I'd say." He put his hands over hers. "Empty the stores, dearest. Our troubles are behind us."

She pulled her hands away and stood. "Almost behind us, Papa."

"You're too practical!" He pouted, standing unsteadily.

"If I were a son, you'd not say so." She reached out to touch his arm to help him gain his balance. "Now, why don't we ring for something to eat to fortify ourselves before tonight's party?"

His gaze drifted past hers to the side table and the decanted wine in a cut crystal pitcher. "I'm not hungry. Go rest and change, Haley, and I'll . . . see you off with Alice later."

"Father, please come with us. Don't you wish to—"

"I wish to be obeyed and left alone!" He retreated past her to the tray and poured himself a glass of the deep ruby, ending any debate.

Haley collected her novel and began to leave without another word. But her father spoke again and delayed her escape, his tone far more contrite and gentle. "I'm . . . feeling a bit under the weather. You'll make my apologies, won't you, then?"

She forced herself to smile. "Of course."

"Wear the red, Haley. You look like your mother when you wear that dress." His eyes became glasslike with unshed tears, and Haley averted her gaze.

"Yes, Father." She hurried from the room without slowing her steps or looking back. *There are worse fates than a courteous husband. Would I be my mother and love so blindly that I leave devastation in my wake?* She shook her head as she climbed the stairs to the second floor. *Wishing for the moon doesn't bring it any closer, but God help me, why do I keep looking at it?*

Enter the rich world of historical romance with Berkley Books.

Lynn Kurland

Patricia Potter

Betina Krahn

Jodi Thomas

Anne Gracie

Love is timeless.

penguin.com

Penguin Group (USA) Online

What will you be reading tomorrow?

Patricia Cornwell, Nora Roberts, Catherine Coulter,
Ken Follett, John Sandford, Clive Cussler,
Tom Clancy, Laurell K. Hamilton, Charlaine Harris,
J. R. Ward, W.E.B. Griffin, William Gibson,
Robin Cook, Brian Jacques, Stephen King,
Dean Koontz, Eric Jerome Dickey, Terry McMillan,
Sue Monk Kidd, Amy Tan, Jayne Ann Krentz,
Daniel Silva, Kate Jacobs...

You'll find them all at
penguin.com

*Read excerpts and newsletters,
find tour schedules and reading group guides,
and enter contests.*

Subscribe to Penguin Group (USA) newsletters
and get an exclusive inside look
at exciting new titles and the authors you love
long before everyone else does.

PENGUIN GROUP (USA)
penguin.com

M224G0909